the promise of love

the promise of love

LORI FOSTER

ERIN McCARTHY

SYLVIA DAY

JAMIE DENTON

KATE DOUGLAS

KATHY LOVE

BERKLEY SENSATION, NEW YORK

THE BERKLEY PUBLISHING GROUP
Published by the Penguin Group
Penguin Group (USA) Inc.
375 Hudson Street, New York, New York 10014, USA
Penguin Group (Canada), 90 Eglinton Avenue East, Suite 700, Toronto, Ontario M4P 2Y3, Canada
(a division of Pearson Penguin Canada Inc.)
Penguin Books Ltd., 80 Strand, London WC2R 0RL, England
Penguin Group Ireland, 25 St. Stephen's Green, Dublin 2, Ireland (a division of Penguin Books Ltd.)
Penguin Group (Australia), 250 Camberwell Road, Camberwell, Victoria 3124, Australia
(a division of Pearson Australia Group Pty. Ltd.)
Penguin Books India Pvt. Ltd., 11 Community Centre, Panchsheel Park, New Delhi—110 017, India
Penguin Group (NZ), 67 Apollo Drive, Rosedale, Auckland 0632, New Zealand
(a division of Pearson New Zealand Ltd.)
Penguin Books (South Africa) (Pty.) Ltd., 24 Sturdee Avenue, Rosebank, Johannesburg 2196,
South Africa

Penguin Books Ltd., Registered Offices: 80 Strand, London WC2R 0RL, England

This book is an original publication of The Berkley Publishing Group.

These stories are works of fiction. Names, characters, places, and incidents either are the product of the authors' imagination or are used fictitiously, and any resemblance to actual persons, living or dead, business establishments, events, or locales is entirely coincidental. The publisher does not have any control over and does not assume any responsibility for authors or third-party websites or their content.

PRINTING HISTORY
Berkley Sensation trade paperback edition / June 2011

Library of Congress Cataloging-in-Publication Data

The promise of love / Lori Foster . . . [et al.].—Berkley Sensation trade pbk. ed.
    p.   cm.
  ISBN 978-0-425-24107-3 (trade pbk.)
  1. Love stories, American.   I. Foster, Lori, 1958–
PS648.L6P76   2011
813'.08508—dc22   2011005548

PRINTED IN THE UNITED STATES OF AMERICA

10   9   8   7   6   5   4   3   2   1

Contents

shelter from the storm

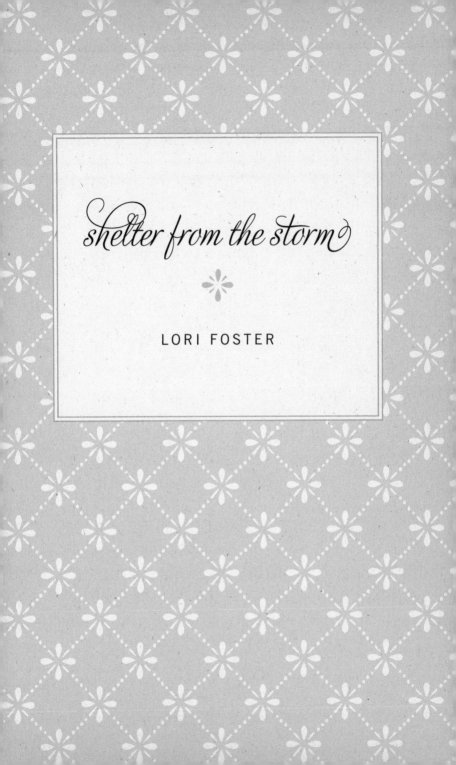

LORI FOSTER

one

✣

When the storms woke him, his first thought was of Sabrina. As lightning shattered the darkness of midnight and the growl of thunder set everything trembling, Roy Pilar bolted upright. She'd be ashamed but terrified, thanks to a history of violence so sinister it still gnawed on him, making him want to resurrect the dead just so he could exact some personal vengeance.

Throwing back the sheet and climbing to his feet, Roy felt around on the chair for his boxers. Hopping on one foot and then the other, he pulled them on with haste. He was on his way to the front door when the frantic knock sounded.

His guts clenched and his eyes burned. As he hurried to the living room, he called out, "Be right there." On another series of panicked raps, he opened the door and Sabrina Downey launched into his arms.

Against his naked chest she felt so soft and warm and so damn right.

Heart breaking for her, he cradled her close a moment. "Shh. It's all right. I've got you now."

"S-sorry."

"Don't." It wasn't her fault that raging storms always brought out memories too harsh to deal with on her own. Abuse. Death. Displaced in the system.

Roy lifted her into his arms and, after kicking the door shut, went to sit on his couch.

When he started to reach for a light, she tightened around him and whispered, "Please leave it dark."

So she could hide. But she didn't need to hide from him. He'd been there that night, and he understood her reaction because he still suffered reactions of his own. She had no reason for shame, none at all. But that was something he could explain to her later. "All right, kiddo. Whatever you want."

At twenty-five, Sabrina was extremely independent. It was a testament to her spirit and intelligence that she'd accomplished so much, that she acknowledged her past by working with abused children. Only someone special, someone with an innate empathy for victims, could deal so gently with the things she saw on a daily basis.

She lived alone, worked in an emotionally draining field, and when necessary, she fought for the rights of others with fierce intensity. She despised injustice of any kind and opened her heart to one and all.

It was only when Mother Nature raged, breathing life into old nightmares that Sabrina needed to borrow his strength.

Tucked in close to his chest, her fingers digging into his shoulders, Sabrina felt small and frail and very much his.

But she wasn't, not yet.

She accepted their close friendship. She'd even rented the

apartment across from his as soon as it became available. But anything more? He didn't know how she'd feel about that.

She didn't know that he'd loved her forever. Even before his parents got guardianship of her, he'd been drawn to the young girl who moved in next door. At first he'd felt protective of her, seeing her loneliness and her sadness, suspecting her abuse. He'd befriended the girl with hair like liquid moonlight, her eyes big and blue and hungry for understanding.

Later, when she'd been only seventeen and he twenty-one, he'd accepted that he felt more.

A lot more.

But for years her circumstances and her age kept him from going down that path. They hindered him still because Sabrina saw him as a friend, or maybe even a pseudo–big brother.

In the dark and quiet of his living room, Roy held her secure and settled back into the corner of his deep couch. Drowning in protective instincts, he pressed a soft kiss to the top of her head and stretched out his long legs, propping his feet on the coffee table.

Her silence worried him, so he asked, "Comfortable?"

She nodded without allowing a single inch of space between them. A loud crack of thunder sent her pressing closer.

He soothed her with easy strokes over her back. As if he hadn't noticed her violent reaction to the storm, he asked, "Not cold?"

Experience told him that her shivers could be the remembrance of a long-ago night still churning through her.

"No." He felt her mouth against his chest. Voice small, she asked, "Are you?"

Hardly. Resting his hands on safe ground, one on her waist, the other on her shoulder, Roy said, "I'm good." At least, as good as a man could be while holding the woman he loved, he in his boxers, she in a short nightgown, in the middle of the dark night—while she clung to him with bone deep terror.

Time ticked by and neither of them moved. Emotion kept his thoughts churning; love for her kept him keenly aware of her bare legs over his, her breath on his skin, the scent of her hair.

Eventually the storm began to fade. Flashes of lightning still illuminated the room with a lazy strobe effect, but the accompanying thunder offered only a distant grumble, barely perceptible. The wind died down so the rain became a simple, almost soothing patter against the patio door.

Sabrina's breathing was so light that if he didn't know better he might have thought she'd fallen asleep. It satisfied something deep inside him to know his nearness helped to calm her, that when she needed someone, she came to him.

He wanted much, but settled for brushing another kiss over her forehead. Looking across the room at the clock on the wall, he saw it was nearing 3 A.M. He had a lot to get done at the shelter tomorrow, but for right now, for this moment in time, nothing mattered but Sabrina.

As if she'd read his thoughts, she burrowed her face closer to his neck. "You have to be up in a few hours."

"Yeah."

Her small body clenched. Agonized, she said, "I'm so damn sorry."

"Hey." Roy tipped up her chin. Even in the darkness he could see the paleness of her blue eyes. And her mouth. God, she had the most beautiful, sensual mouth he'd ever seen. "I'm where I want to be."

She gave a short laugh devoid of humor. "Right."

With the storm abated, she sat up on his lap. His eyes had adjusted enough that he could see her, the pale yellow gown with little flowers, her naked knees, her cleavage.

Pushing hair from her face, she looked around as if she'd never seen his apartment before. Truth was, it was identical to her own across the hall.

Roy just waited to see what she'd do, what she'd say—if she'd acknowledge the growing rise beneath her bottom, a reaction he couldn't help now that she wasn't mired in panic.

"I guess every guy enjoys getting woken up in the middle of the night by a clinging, hysterical woman who falls apart over the weather."

"Maybe not every guy and definitely not every woman." He opened his hand over her narrow back. "Just you, Sabrina."

She cast him a quick, uncertain look.

Her face was so sweet and vulnerable and it made him feel ten times more a man. "I understand why you react the way you do. I hate seeing you upset, but I like holding you. A lot."

As usual, she took his comments all wrong. Giving in to a self-conscious laugh, she said, "Roy Pilar, you have always been the most uniquely kind guy I've ever known." She slipped her arms around his neck and gave him a hug of gratitude. "Thank you."

When she started to lean away, he held on. "You're okay now, Sabrina?"

Close to his mouth, she smiled and whispered, "Yes, thanks to you."

So tempting. But not yet. "You want to talk about it?"

"God no." She squeezed him again, then forced space between them. "I should get back to my place."

"Why the rush?" He fingered a hank of silky hair draped over her shoulder. Naturally curly and very pale, her hair had always fascinated him. "We both need to be up in a few more hours. And there's no guarantee the storm won't return."

With that, her expressive face stilled with worry. "I hate this, you know?"

"Yeah, I know."

"If I could help it . . . If I could *stop it*, I would." Frustration curled her hands into fists. "Storms during the day, or when I'm in crowds don't faze me, not like this. But at night . . ."

"When you're alone. I know." And he was so glad that she'd moved close to him. The idea of her going to any other person, any other *man*, would be unbearable. "If you hadn't come to me, I would have been knocking on your door."

"Thank you."

"No thanks necessary." He scooped his arms around her and came to his feet with her held against his chest. She was so petite, so damn female, that his every nerve ending sparked with awareness. "I'm glad you live right next door so that I can be here when you need me."

"Uh . . . Roy? Where are we going?"

"To my bedroom." He maneuvered through the darkness, around tables and a chair.

She went still and alert. "What?"

He kept going. "To my bed."

"Oh, uh . . ." Her fingers curled against his shoulders, not for a secure hold but out of reaction. She breathed a little faster, a little deeper. "I . . . um, need to use your bathroom first."

Why that threw him, Roy couldn't say. Maybe because he'd expected outright objections, not a simple delay.

But she hadn't objected, and that had him smiling. "All right." Stopping outside the bathroom door, he slowly let her slide down his body—and tortured himself in the bargain. Standing, her head barely reached his shoulder. He brushed a thumb over her downy cheek. "You okay by yourself now?"

"Definitely."

She did seem steadier. "All right. I'll wait on you here."

Her eyes went wide in the dim shadows. "You don't have to."

He turned her, gave her a light swat on her rounded tush, and said, "I'm waiting."

She shook her head as she went in and closed the door.

Dropping back against the wall, Roy let out a pent-up breath. At twenty-nine he wasn't a saint, but he wanted Sabrina more than he'd ever wanted any woman. Mixed with the familiar lust was the all too unfamiliar affection, so sharp that it sometimes took his breath away.

But she didn't see him that way, so he didn't want to push her. Much.

But tonight . . . well, he'd waited for her to mature, to come into her own. She now lived alone, although across the hall from him. She had a rewarding job she loved that utilized her unique ability and empathy for others in need. She'd dated a few times, but it never amounted to anything serious.

He'd given her plenty of opportunity to experience life on her own terms, and now he wanted to pursue her.

Really pursue her.

Tonight he could start building on what they had, and maybe, soon, he'd be able to get to where he wanted to be.

Even as he made that decision, he thought of the past. He could still remember Sabrina as a scrawny fifteen-year-old when she came to live with them. He'd been in his first year of college. Squeezing his eyes shut, Roy thought of the times his parents had fretted over her, how they'd hear the noise next door, the unexplained bruising they'd seen on her.

Calling Children's Services hadn't gotten the desired results. It had only earned the enmity of their druggie neighbor, Will. Sabrina's father hadn't liked their interference, and he'd threatened all kinds of retribution if his "nosy neighbors" didn't mind their own business.

Of course, that hadn't fazed his parents. If anything, it made them more determined to get to know Sabrina better and to find out the truth. Little by little, when Will wasn't around or when he was passed out, Sabrina came to visit.

In the process, she stole his parents' hearts. And when push came to shove, they fought for her—and won.

Within a minute Roy heard the toilet flush and water running in the sink. Looking especially shy and very sweet, Sabrina opened the door again.

She stood there before him, shifting her feet and toying with the end of a blond curl. Like a long sleeveless T-shirt, her nightgown hung to her knees. She was about the sexiest thing he'd ever seen.

"You know. . . . Roy . . ."

He scooped her up again and started down the hall. "We'll be more comfortable in the bed." Turning sideways to get her through the doorway, he carried her into his room. The bed was still disheveled from his hasty retreat. He set her on the side of the mattress and straightened the covers, then held them back. "In you go."

She puffed out her cheeks, then released her breath. "You're *sure* you want to do this?"

Oh yeah, real sure.

She rushed on, saying, "I mean, you have to be at the shelter early. And taking care of all those animals isn't exactly easy work."

"Sabrina." Her nervous chatter bothered him; he couldn't bear the idea of scaring her. "You trust me, don't you?"

Without hesitation, she answered, "More than anyone."

"Good." Never would he abuse that trust, but he had to let her know how he felt about her. "Then stay. Please."

She softened, relaxed. "All right." After crawling into the bed, she rested back on one of his pillows, clasped her hands together, and looked at him with expectation.

Seeing her in his bed gave Roy incredible satisfaction.

She lowered one eyebrow in suspicion. "Why are you grinning?"

He shrugged. "You look good there, that's all." Lying down next to her and pulling her into his side amplified everything tenfold. This wouldn't be easy, but then nothing with Sabrina ever had been.

He released a tense breath and felt her do the same.

Nestled up along his side, her head on his shoulder, her arm around his waist, she whispered, "Roy?"

Talking wasn't easy, not with a semi-boner. "Hmm?"

"Did you know that I wanted to stay?"

"You did?"

Her silky hair teased his skin with her nod of assent. "Knowing how I react to storms makes me anticipate it. You know what I mean?"

Of course he did. "You fear that you'll panic, so when it starts to rain, you start worrying."

"And that just makes it all worse."

"I know, because I do the same." Whenever dark clouds rolled in, his concern for her came alive to the point that he couldn't think of anything else. "You can always come to me, Sabrina, you know that."

She was quiet a moment before saying, "That's why I moved next door to you. But then, you knew that already." Her fingers moved over his chest, brushing his chest hair, inadvertently skimming his left nipple.

"I figured as much. And I'm glad." He closed his hand over hers to keep it still. He was already on the ragged edge, but given her earlier upset and the lateness of the hour, sex was out of the question.

He wasn't that selfish.

"It's bad enough for you to see me like this."

"Hey." He could tell her that she looked soft and sexy and he wanted her. But that might not be what she wanted to hear.

"I wouldn't want to advertise it to everyone else."

On that, they agreed. "And I wouldn't want you to go to anyone else, so it works for us." Roy lifted her hand and kissed her knuckles. "Besides, having you here makes me feel better, too."

"Yeah, right." Frowning, her mouth pursed in doubt, she looked up at him.

Sabrina always made the most adorable faces that would look comical on anyone else.

Roy couldn't take it. Slowly leaning down, giving her time to lean away, he took her mouth in the gentlest of kisses.

Surprise grabbed her, and like a deer caught in headlights, she froze—her breathing, her movements. Rather than rush things, Roy left the kiss simple and rested back on the pillow.

After a long silent minute, she relaxed again, too. "Do you think I'll ever get past this?"

Huh. So she planned to ignore the kiss?

He'd let her get away with that—for now. Especially given the seriousness of her question. "When I think about that night, about what your father planned and all that happened to you, I still break out in a sweat. And I was just your neighbor, observing it all." *And dying inside for her.* "For you to have lived through it . . ." Fury choked him. "I don't think it's something that will fade away very easily."

"You were only nineteen then." Her busy fingers teased over his ribs. "Home from college for a weekend visit."

"Full of testosterone and independence, thinking myself invincible." He'd had so much, and she'd had so little. Unlike other college guys his age, he'd had no interest in weekend parties or sports. He'd even skipped dating to come home so he could check up on her.

God knew Sabrina had few enough people who cared about her. Her own mother had left years earlier only to be killed in a car accident. When her estranged maternal grandmother passed, she had no one to leave the house to except Will. The day he and Sabrina moved in, anyone could see that he had a drug problem.

Things were bad enough during the week, but on the weekends he'd party and get so stoned that he sometimes forgot he had a daughter. That's when Sabrina would sneak out to Roy's house. With his parents, *with him*, she could let down her guard.

When Will couldn't find work, his drug use escalated while the once tidy house went into disrepair. His facade as a father, or even as a decent human being, quickly deteriorated.

Knowing the situation, Roy made it home as often as he could, as much for his parents as for Sabrina.

On that final, significant night, he'd only been home a few hours when the storm broke—both figuratively and literally.

They heard Sabrina's frantic crying first. And then, as they all rushed out to the covered porch, they saw the guy trying to take her from the house. At the time, no one realized who the man was leading her away, only that she didn't want to go. It wasn't until later, after everything had settled down, that they learned the awful truth.

Wishing he could somehow go back and remove all the ugliness from her life, Roy clenched her closer to him.

"You're thinking about that night, too, aren't you?"

"Can't help it." The ugliness would forever be burned in his memory. For once her father had remembered that he had a daughter—and he'd chosen to trade her for a fix. "I think that's the only time I've ever seen my dad so violent."

She swallowed hard. "If it hadn't been for you and your parents . . ."

"Don't say it." He couldn't bear to think what would have happened to her, how she would have been used by that drug-peddling scum. Crushing her closer still, Roy recalled how his mother had put in a panicked call to the police while his normally passive, quiet dad had charged across the yards in the pounding rain. Before Roy could join him, his dad had freed Sabrina and beat down the dealer without mercy.

Roy had wanted his own turn at violence, but Sabrina had rushed to him through the pouring rain. He'd still been holding her close, lightning cracking around them, thunder shaking the earth, when the police showed up.

As usual, whenever he thought of that night, emotion threatened to overwhelm him.

"I was scared when they took me away," Sabrina whispered to him. "But I was glad that I didn't ever have to see my dad again."

Memories rushed through his mind, the flashing police lights, the fury of that storm, Sabrina's face ravaged with tears and fear and heartache over a father who couldn't love her, a father who, after handing over his daughter to a vile fate, had overdosed.

The police found him dead on the floor in a puddle of his own vomit, a needle still in his arm.

His parents never said it, but Roy knew they were relieved, because he was relieved, too. Sabrina would never have to face that bastard again. His time for hurting her was over.

The drug dealer was arrested on numerous charges, not the least of which was murder.

And though his mother had begged to keep her, a representative from Children's Services had insisted on taking Sabrina away that night.

Protocol had to be followed, and that left Roy and his parents on the sidelines as helpless spectators.

God, he'd wanted to push past the cops, to snatch Sabrina away from the well-meaning strangers and protect her while also annihilating her no-good father, who was already dead, and the pusher who was already handcuffed and in the back of a cruiser . . .

"You were a comfort to me that night."

Tangling a hand in her hair, Roy rubbed her scalp. "I didn't do a damn thing. There wasn't anything I *could* do, and it made me nuts." Still made him nuts whenever he thought of it.

"You were there, Roy. The whole time. Even as the car drove away with me, I saw you standing there in the storm, drenched to the skin, watching until I was out of sight."

"None of us wanted to let you go." His parents had moved heaven and earth to become her guardians.

She leaned over him. "You can never really know what that meant to me. When your mother came for me, when they told me that she wanted me to live with all of you, I couldn't believe it."

Seeing her like this fired his blood. "Mom and Dad were both relieved when they got you back." They had a welcome-home party for her, and she'd been so shy, so withdrawn, and so unsure of herself. They'd all worked overtime to put her at ease and to make her feel comfortable with them.

Now she was so comfortable with him that even being in his bed didn't seem to throw her.

"No one had ever wanted me around like that." She touched his chest, her eyes downcast, avoiding his gaze. "No one had ever . . . defended me like that."

Roy framed her face in his hands. Though years had passed, Sabrina still lived with the fact that her mother had run out on her, her father mistreated her, and her grandmother hadn't cared enough to get involved. "My parents love you."

"I love them, too." She looked at his mouth. "And you."

His heart started pounding, especially when she leaned down and kissed him, a butterfly brush of her lips on his.

Before Roy could assimilate the importance of that, she nestled back down on his chest and yawned. "The storm has passed, and I'm exhausted. Let's try to get some sleep, okay?"

Roy stared at the ceiling, torn between lust and so much more. Obviously Sabrina thought the kiss was just another gesture of affection.

He'd made strides tonight, and now that they were on the right track, the rest would come.

Even if it tortured him, he *would* be patient.

He closed his eyes, and to his surprise, her nearness didn't frustrate him sexually as much as it fed something hungry in his soul. Her warmth and her scent surrounded him, and within minutes, he dozed off.

LONG after Roy's breathing evened into sleep, Sabrina lay awake, aware of his big muscular body, the heat of him, and his strength, both physically and emotionally. For as long as she had known him, he'd always given her whatever she needed. Comfort, security, protection, friendship . . .

What would he do if he found out she needed more from him? If he discovered that she wanted . . . everything?

Taking advantage of his sleep, she put her nose to his skin and inhaled deeply. Overriding the lingering turmoil from her storm-induced panic was the burning need to touch him, taste him, everywhere.

Of course she resisted that.

Her feelings for him had started years ago as a child's infatuation and they'd expanded into a woman's deeper desires—for the emotional and the physical.

She wanted him, but knowing that he saw her as a needy victim kept her quiet. She'd brought enough drama to his life. Even now, as a woman grown, she asked him to fight her demons for her, with her.

Her face burned.

Long before that monumental night brought a turning point to her life, she'd sought refuge at his home, with his parents.

With him.

The entire Pilar family had opened their arms to her, and she would forever be in their debt. They were all such big-hearted, caring people that she never doubted their love. Amy and Doug Pilar had been better role models, better parents, than her own parents had ever hoped to be.

And Roy . . . he'd been everything to her.

She couldn't ask for even more from him. But neither could she get serious about any man other than him.

He'd kissed her, but he'd also called her "kiddo," his pet name for her—the name he used for that sad, scared kid she'd once been.

So much to think about.

She touched her lips with her fingertips. Tonight he had kissed her, and though it hadn't felt platonic to her, it wasn't exactly a passionate kiss, either.

Maybe . . . maybe she'd take him off guard tomorrow and kiss him the way she wanted to kiss him. She'd gauge his reaction and go from there. If he seemed appalled, she could laugh it off, act like she'd been teasing.

And if he kissed her back? Then what?

Sabrina closed her eyes and instead of sleeping, she just enjoyed being in his arms and in his bed, where she really wanted to be.

Two

✤

Continued rainfall brought a gray, dreary dawn. There was no bright sunshine to make waking easier. On her stomach beside Roy, her chin propped on her hands, Sabrina watched him stretch and struggle to get his eyes open. Even this early, with beard shadow on his face, he looked amazing to her. And even while sleeping, he'd kept an arm around her, his hand open and lax on her body.

Suddenly he went still, and then his hand on her hip moved, sort of caressing, exploring. He frowned—and his eyes shot open.

Chocolate brown, filled with awareness and more, Sabrina *loved* his eyes, always had. They glittered when he laughed, went soft when he hugged his mom, and often heated with anger when he talked about the abused and abandoned animals he sheltered.

As director and founder of the nonprofit organization, he championed animal rights just as she championed children. On more than one occasion, their professional paths had crossed so that they could work together.

He blinked lazily when his gaze met hers. His lashes were long and thick, shades darker than the light brown hair on his head and the hair on his body.

Sabrina watched him intently. "Good morning."

His gaze went all over her; his hand contracted. He lifted up to an elbow. "How long have you been awake?"

Unwilling to tell him that she'd never gone back to sleep, she shrugged. "Your alarm is due to go off any minute."

He looked at it, then at the window.

As he reached over to turn off the alarm, the sheet dropped down to his waist. Now, even with the day overcast, she could clearly see him.

Her mouth went dry and her body temperature spiked. Roy had an incredible athlete's body, strong and fit, large boned, and very capable. He took his strength for granted, but she never had.

After rubbing his jaw, he said, "Still raining."

"A nice soft rain." It suited her mood this morning. "I don't mind it."

"Good." He collapsed back on the bed and, with both hands now on her waist, urged her closer. The touch was familiar, as if he'd awakened with her a dozen times. He looked at her mouth. "About last night . . ."

His rumpled hair drew her hand. She threaded her fingers through the cool thickness of it, smoothing it down.

A little hopefully, she asked, "What about it?"

He started to speak—and his cell phone rang. Brows coming together, he said, "Just a second," and reached over to the night-stand to snag his phone.

Sabrina listened to his side of the conversation, and she knew something was wrong, especially when, while still talking, he threw back the covers and left the bed.

He wore only snug-fitting black boxers.

And he had . . . well, a morning erection.

Her jaw loosened and her eyes went wide.

As if she weren't there, he strode down the hall and into the bathroom.

She stayed motionless in the bed, unsure what to do.

When he returned, he had closed the phone and he wore that thundercloud expression reserved for news concerning animal abuse or neglect.

He spared her only a quick glance. "Sorry, kiddo, but I have to head to the shelter."

Kiddo again. The nickname proved a great reminder that she wasn't a romantic possibility.

Now she knew what to do. Sabrina sat up on the bed and swung her legs over the side. "What's wrong?"

He stepped into jeans. "That was Chad. He just got to the shelter."

Chad often opened up the place. He was one of the few actual employees; most who worked at the shelter were volunteers. "He's okay?"

"Chad's fine. But someone left a dog on the front steps during the night. There's no telling how long she's been there."

Sabrina rushed to her feet. "In that awful storm?"

He paused, maybe hesitant to stir up memories.

At the moment, her only concern was for the dog. "Is she injured?"

"She gave birth."

Oh God. Sabrina stumbled back to sit on the bed again. The horror of such a thing nearly flattened her. "How many puppies?"

"Eight." Roy rubbed the back of his neck. "They're all drenched, and Chad says the momma seems pretty weak."

All too familiar with that level of abandonment, Sabrina pictured everything in vivid detail. Determined to help, she left the bed again and faced Roy. "That storm had to be terrifying to her, especially while giving birth."

"At the very least, she'll need some TLC. But other than bringing the box into the shelter, Chad doesn't want to do too much until I get there. He's not trained, so he can't tell if the mess is from the birthing or an injury."

She and the puppies would have been pummeled by rain. And the noise, that god-awful thunder . . .

Roy watched her, his distress obvious. "Chad said a couple of the puppies aren't moving much."

Sympathy for the animals choked her. "I don't need to be at work until the afternoon. I'll go with you to help out." Sabrina started out of the room. "Give me two minutes to get dressed. I'll meet you at your truck."

"Hey." Before she'd cleared the doorframe, Roy caught the back of her nightgown, bringing her to a halt. "You had a rough night yourself. Maybe you ought to just . . . I don't know. Hang out and relax until you go into work."

It was her fault that he thought her so fragile. She took his hand. "I *want* to go with you. Besides, I'm fine now—thanks to you." Better than fine, in fact, since the weather had calmed, it wasn't night, and she wasn't alone.

He chewed his upper lip, undecided. "It could be rough, honey. I don't know what I'm going to find."

"So we should hurry."

"You don't have to do this."

Of course she did. Any good, caring person would want to help, and despite her parents, or maybe because of them, she cared. A lot. "Two minutes, Roy. I promise."

His thumb rubbed the inside of her wrist. "Make it five. It'll take me that long anyway."

"All right." She started to leave, then remembered her resolve of the night before. After a second of hesitation, she went on her tiptoes to kiss him.

She meant it to be a quick kiss—a test of sorts—but Roy caught the back of her neck and he didn't let her retreat.

This kiss was far from platonic. He tasted warm and musky, and his beard shadow abraded her chin and cheek.

She loved it. Every second of it.

But what the heck did it mean?

He reluctantly released her. "You and I have a lot to talk about."

Sabrina nodded. Boy, hey, he wasn't kidding. "Okay. But right now, we're needed at the shelter."

"Soon." He kissed her again, hard and fast, and then he turned away and headed to his dresser.

And this time when she raced out, he didn't stop her. He was too busy getting ready himself.

ROY couldn't keep his eyes off Sabrina. She had the gentlest touch and an air of caring that encompassed every living thing, including animals.

The puppies were in better shape than the poor momma. The births had been hard on her and being exposed to the weather had compounded the problems. She was weak, panicked, and in discomfort, but luckily there were no serious injuries.

Sabrina worked her unique magic, helping the dog relax as Roy put in an IV to get her fluids back up.

All his life, he'd had a knack with animals. Becoming a vet

didn't quite cover all he wanted to do for and with animals, so with his dad's help, he'd opened the shelter a few years back. Splitting his time between the clinic and the shelter, he used one to help fund the other. The work kept him too busy for anything resembling an active social life. His "dates" were few and far between.

But then, he didn't want anyone other than Sabrina, anyway.

"I don't think there's any permanent damage." When Sabrina stayed quiet, he glanced up and saw the fat tears clinging to her lashes. It didn't sound in her voice or show up in her touch, but he knew that seeing abuse of any kind left her devastated. "Sabrina."

She sniffled and turned her face away.

"It's going to be okay."

"I know you'll make it so." Her chin firmed. "I'm just so . . . furious."

Ah. So her tears were from anger, not upset. He should have realized. Many times over the years he'd seen Sabrina get red-eyed and tearful when enraged.

He preferred her anger any day.

Hell, he was angry, too. If he found out who had left the poor dog in front of the shelter, in the storm, instead of following the procedure to get her admitted, he'd use every legal venue to see them prosecuted. As a no-kill shelter, they rarely turned down the admittance of any animal. It was cowardly and unconscionable to just abandon the dog, especially in her condition.

The IV fluids helped alleviate the dog's discomfort as Roy finished his exam. He cleaned her up with Sabrina's assistance and then put her in a crate lined with warm, soft blankets and a dish of high-calorie puppy food. Even weak, she seemed hungry and quickly finished off the food.

"Good girl," Roy praised gently.

With her most immediate needs met, the dog watched him, and her little furry face pinched with worry. Roy took one look at those soulful brown eyes and knew what she wanted.

"Let's get her puppies back to her."

He and Sabrina made quick work of moving the wiggling little fur-balls into the crate. After two grateful thumps of her tail, the momma lifted her head to lick each pup, then settled back and let them nurse while she rested.

"Little gluttons," Roy said with a smile. He trailed a fingertip down the back of each pup and then stroked the momma again.

"She enjoys your touch." Sabrina watched the animals intently. "But I'm not surprised."

"No?"

She didn't look at him, but she sounded wistful when she said, "I think you could gentle a bull."

Was she thinking of the times he'd gentled her through raging storms? He watched her profile, his heart full. "Touch is important."

"Yes." She settled her hand around the momma's head, so gentle and easy. The dog sighed. "Especially now when she needs to learn to trust again."

Sometimes it drove Roy crazy trying to figure out Sabrina's thoughts. He didn't ever want to do or say anything that brought up bad memories for her. Yet because of the vocations they'd each chosen, they would forever be reminded of human cruelty.

"I think they were mostly just miserably cold and wet before." Now that each little pup was dried and comfortable, they took right to feeding. He pulled back and closed the crate.

Sabrina slipped her hand into his. "She's a good little momma, isn't she?"

Because he knew Sabrina so well, there was no mistaking the

comparisons she made. Even in the worst of circumstances, most mothers had the instinct to care for their young.

But Sabrina's mother hadn't cared, and neither had her father. She knew that wasn't the norm, but knowing it and living with it were two different things.

"When she gets a little stronger, I can bring her and the puppies over for the kids to see."

She squeezed his hand and nodded. "They would enjoy that so much."

Many times he and Sabrina had coordinated to bring a birthing cat or dog to the children's residential home where she worked. Seeing what love should be, what Mother Nature intended, helped to heal the most wounded spirits.

It had helped Sabrina back when he'd first opened the shelter. He'd grown up with a menagerie of family pets, but Sabrina never had. Roy could still recall the way she'd watched the first birthing with wonder and how she'd been so emotionally moved. Seeing the process had given her a new perspective on things, and for days on end she'd hung out at the shelter whenever she could just to be near the new mother and her babies.

Without animal therapy, some kids never understood what should be, because they were so damaged by what had been. They grew afraid to touch or be touched. But animals gave unconditional love, and in caring for them, interacting with them, kids were able to learn to trust again, and hopefully they healed.

As Sabrina watched the puppies nursing, Roy watched her. Her expression was so tender, so filled with pleasure that it left him edgy with desire.

He released her hand to put his arm around her shoulders. "You look exhausted," he said against her hair as much to remind himself of the previous night as to comfort her.

She slanted him a silly, self-conscious grin. "I look a mess. It's a wonder the dogs aren't all howling in fright."

"No way." He liked being with her like this, so casual, motivated by the same things. Ruffling her mussed hair, he said, "You look very earthy."

That made her laugh.

"Seriously, it's a good look for you—even though I don't see you like this very often. You're usually such a girly girl, refusing to answer your door if you don't have your hair brushed."

She poked him in the ribs and laughed again. "I didn't want to take the time for sprucing up this morning."

"I know, and I appreciate it. Besides, you really don't need makeup."

She snorted.

"You honestly don't know how pretty you are, do you?" Pretty—and sexy, too. He looked her over, head to toes. Now that the animals were okay and settled, his mind moved on to other things. "Beautiful even."

"You're obviously in need of more sleep, Roy, but thank you, anyway." She leaned her head against his shoulder in a show of camaraderie. "And thank you for letting me help today, too. I've always loved seeing what you do and how you do it."

Did she love him?

Roy shook his head. He would *not* rush her.

"I should be thanking you. I'm always a little short-staffed this early in the morning." Most of his volunteers worked regular jobs or had college classes. They started trickling in after noon, but crack of dawn? Not so much. Chad was the only one he could get to come in that early, and that's because Chad was paid on the clock.

As if she hadn't heard him, Sabrina said, "You make such a difference."

"As do you." Probably in more ways than she realized.

Very matter of fact, she admitted, "Some days it feels pretty hopeless."

"We do what we can, honey, but no one can eradicate cruelty. It's always going to be a part of our society. Against animals and kids. Against anyone who can't fight back." He tipped up her chin. "But you do make a difference. The kids at the home love you."

"I know." She looped her arms around his waist and held on to him. Nothing more, but it was enough. They stayed like that until Abner, one of the bigger dogs that wandered freely in the shelter, came and leaned against them. Since Abner weighed around 175 pounds, he almost knocked them over.

Laughing, Sabrina went to her knees to hug the massive dog. She came away with black fur clinging to her T-shirt. No matter how much they brushed Abner, he shed. But despite her fastidious manner with her appearance, Sabrina never seemed to mind the messes made by loving animals or kids.

Abner had been with them for a year now, and although enormous, he was one of the gentlest dogs they'd ever had. When his owner died of old age, Abner mourned him. But thanks to Sabrina and all the attention she lavished on him, as well as his regular visits to the Children's Home, Abner now flourished.

He had the same type of empathy as Sabrina; he might be an old man himself, but Abner loved to mother all the other animals. Sometimes he'd lie on the floor and a dozen kittens would crawl all over him. Abner would wince at the sting of small sharp claws, but he never disrupted them.

When Abner rolled onto his back in doggy bliss, Sabrina scratched his belly. In record time, he'd become one of her favorites. Abner adored her and vice versa.

"One day I'll get a house with a yard, and then I'll fill it with animals and children."

Picturing that, Roy said, "Sounds like the perfect plan to me."

She looked up in surprise, and their gazes locked.

Did she understand that he wanted those things—*with her?*

Just then the front door rattled and Jenna, one of the college girls who volunteered between classes, tried to get in. She pressed her face close to the glass and frowned when she saw Roy there with Sabrina.

"I forgot it was still locked," Roy said. Chad was now out back cleaning up debris from the storm. He'd use the rear door, not the front.

Roy strode over while digging out the keys from his pocket. With an umbrella over her head, Jenna waited impatiently.

The second he got the door open, she sailed in, dripping rain from her jacket and full of energy and enthusiasm. Probably because she knew Sabrina was watching, Jenna dropped her umbrella beside the door, shrugged off her outerwear, and threw herself against Roy for a giant hug.

"Whoa." Jenna had been clear in her desire to "hook up," but she wasn't usually so physical with him. To ensure that Sabrina knew the embrace wasn't a common occurrence, he asked, "What brought that on?"

"I missed you, that's all."

Feeling helpless, Roy tried not to look at Sabrina. "You were here yesterday."

Jenna laughed. "I know, and I'm back today. I have a few hours before my classes and figured I could do some of that leftover paperwork for you."

Jenna wasn't much for direct contact with the animals. She

was not a girl who liked doggie kisses or mucking out kennels. And no way in hell would she have gotten involved in cleaning up after newborn puppies. But she was a whiz with mailing out flyers, and he appreciated her help.

Determined to take control of the situation, Roy set her an arm's length away. "That'd be great. Thanks."

Her hand to his chest, she said, "My pleasure. And since I'm here . . ."

Uh-oh. Roy braced himself.

"If you're not busy tonight, I have an extra concert ticket." Her fingertips stroked him. "What do you say?"

Sometimes her pursuit wore on him. "Tempting, but I can't make it." He took her wrist and moved her hand away from him.

"Why not?" She looked at Sabrina.

Roy glanced back, too, and he saw Sabrina's stiff expression. Jealousy? Or just discomfort at being an audience of one for Jenna's blatant flirting?

"I have a lot of work to do."

"Oh, come on." Jenna stepped close again, her air suggestive, her tone more so. "Play a little."

He planned to—with Sabrina. "Why don't you invite Chad? I bet he'd love to go."

Disgruntled by the suggestion, Jenna flipped her long dark hair over her shoulder. "Maybe." She slanted her pretty green cat eyes toward Sabrina. Smile cutting, she nodded at Sabrina. "Am I interrupting?"

Using that as an opening, Sabrina said, "Nope," and after giving Abner one last pet, she came to her feet. "I was just leaving."

Like hell!

As she started past, Roy took her hand. She tried to subtly free herself, but he held on and kept her at his side.

He'd driven, so she couldn't go anywhere without him, anyway.

He understood Jenna. She was young and temperamental, and she liked to flirt with him just for the sake of flirting. That he would never return the favor didn't dent Jenna's pride one iota. Eventually she'd give up and move on to some other guy.

"Sabrina was helping with new puppies." Roy briefly explained to Jenna what had happened.

Jenna eyed Sabrina with resentful aversion. "You're like a regular Florence Nightingale, aren't you?"

Ignoring the snide tone, Roy answered for Sabrina. "You have no idea." He kissed Sabrina's knuckles. "But I'm glad you're here, Jenna."

She smiled.

"I need to drive Sabrina back to her place."

Jenna's smile fell. "How long will that take? I've only got a couple of hours."

"Less than half that time." He held on to Sabrina's hand when she again tried to pull away. "Chad's out back cleaning up if you need him. You have my number if anything comes up, but I won't be long at all." And then to Sabrina, "Ready?"

Stony-faced, she said a polite good-bye to Jenna and let Roy lead her out the door.

Once outside, Sabrina stopped him and propped her hands on her hips. "I don't need you to drive me, Roy. I can catch the bus at the corner."

He shook his head at that idea. "No way."

"Jenna came to see you."

"She can see me when I get back."

Her spine stiffened. "Really?"

The acerbic tone surprised a grin out of him. "You know I have no interest in her."

"Yeah, well . . ." The dark sky drew her attention and she said absently, "That doesn't stop her from having an interest in you."

"You shouldn't take Jenna too seriously. I don't."

"Looks like it might rain all day."

The switch in topic suited Roy just fine. "All the more reason why you shouldn't be standing outside, waiting for the bus."

"I won't melt, you know."

He smiled. "I know." And now that the night had passed and the streets were busy, any reoccurring storms wouldn't affect her so strongly. "But I wanted to talk to you, anyway." Talk, touch, taste . . . He opened the passenger's door to his truck and waited for her to get in.

Sabrina waffled, undecided for only a moment before she relented. "All right."

She'd barely gotten in before the rain started in earnest. Roy ran around to the driver's side. He had to turn on the defroster to see out the windshield. The whooshing of the wipers offered a nice backdrop.

They rode in companionable silence for several minutes. Roy waited until after they were on the main road to ask, "Will you have dinner with me tonight?"

She tucked in her chin. "That's what you wanted to talk about?"

"In part." A very small part. "Most of what I want to say can be discussed over dinner." Some place private—like his apartment.

Or maybe even his bed if he could get her there again.

She didn't look like she believed him. "I wish I could, but we have a local guy donating several computers. I need to go pick them up at the end of the day."

"So how about I go with you?" They both relied heavily on private donations. "If it's more than one computer, you could probably use the help loading it all up, and afterward we'll grab a bite to eat."

"It could end up being late."

"So?" He turned on the street to the apartment complex. Even though he already knew the answer, he asked, "Did you have any plans afterward?"

Shaking her head, she said, "No, but—"

"But what?" Sabrina's social life was more barren than his. She visited his parents regularly, and she had girlfriends that she liked to shop with. But dates? Few and far between—thank God. "You have to eat, right?"

"Of course." She gave an exaggerated huff of breath. "But you certainly have better things to do than keeping me company."

"No, I don't."

"Yes." She frowned at him. "You do."

Ah. When he caught on to her meaning, he grinned. "We're back to Jenna."

Sabrina turned to stare out the window. "I don't want to tie up any more of your time, that's all."

Silly woman. "I'd rather wait out a storm with you or clean up a fresh litter of puppies than suffer through a concert with Jenna, believe me."

That confession left her speechless for a few seconds. "Really?"

"Absolutely."

She searched his face, and finally nodded. "All right, if you're sure."

"Great. We can use my truck." He pulled into the apartment parking lot.

When he started to turn off the engine, she held up a hand. "There's no reason for you to get soaked again."

"I have an umbrella."

She shook her head. "It's all right. I was going to take a nice long shower, anyway."

Roy pictured that, and his body tightened. He had to clear his throat to speak. "What time did you want me to pick you up?"

As she opened her seat belt and turned to face him, she said, "I finish up around five."

Luckily he had a lot to do to keep him busy between now and then. "Why don't I pick you up here at the apartment around five thirty, then? That way your car will already be here. We'll get the computers moved, and when we're done, we'll come back to my place." Knowing it was her favorite, he said, "I'll grill steaks."

For the longest time she watched him, and something soft and warm showed in her blue eyes. Finally she nodded. "Sounds delicious."

Yeah, it did. In more ways than she realized.

He wanted to give her time, to ease her into the idea of a sexual relationship, but every hour with her made waiting more impossible.

He needed her. Soon.

For now, just a taste would have to do. It'd help him to get through the long hours of the day.

Leaning across the seat, Roy took her mouth with his. It pleased him that she no longer seemed so startled by the intimacy.

The rain left the car windows opaque and sealed them in a cocoon of warmth scented by her dampened skin. Because she'd rushed to leave with him today, her hair was the same as when he'd awakened—tumbled, soft, and sexy. The lack of makeup emphasized her natural beauty.

Her naked mouth could tempt a saint.

Because he wasn't in any way saintly, Roy couldn't help but touch his tongue to that delectable mouth, not slipping past her teeth but prodding gently, exploring her bottom lip.

Her breath shuddered in, parting her lips enough for a brief taste. And just that, such a simple kiss, ignited his lust.

Resisting a deeper kiss was one of the hardest things he'd ever done. "Damn, you taste good."

"Roy?" She sounded confused and uncertain. Her eyes were heavy, her skin flushed, and it made him nuts.

He forced himself to move away. "I'll see you tonight, kiddo."

She blinked fast, drew back, and frowned. "I don't understand you."

"I know." He tucked her hair behind her ear. "But I promise to make everything clear over dinner tonight." Or if things worked out right, maybe even before dinner.

Giving him another dubious look, Sabrina sighed. "Fine. Be cryptic. I just hope you know what you're doing."

He grinned as she opened her door. "Count on it."

three

The kids had been giving her funny looks all day, and no wonder, Sabrina, thought. Knowing she'd see Roy right after work, she'd taken extra care in her preparations for the day. To make up for her bedraggled appearance that morning, she'd taken an extra long shower where she'd used a loofah to buff her skin, shampooed and conditioned her hair, shaved her legs, and slathered on lotion everywhere.

After polishing her fingernails and toenails, she blow-dried her naturally curly hair until it was smooth and shiny.

For her eyes, she'd really gone all out with her favorite shades of eye shadow and extra mascara to show off her lashes. And since Roy suddenly seemed so preoccupied with her mouth, she'd dressed it up with shiny pink gloss.

The kids were used to seeing her in a ponytail with minimal makeup that, while enhancing, still looked natural. Contrary to what Roy had said, she didn't spend a lot of time in front of the mirror. Yes, she liked to look her best but within reason.

For work, her clothes were usually casual and comfortable. But today, she'd dressed up a little more. Instead of the usual shirt and slacks, she wore a khaki skirt and button-up ruffled blouse with strappy white sandals.

Now, as the workday came to a close, the skirt proved to be a bit of a problem. Chandra, a ten-year-old girl who was leaving them later that day, had set up a tea party on the floor. She wanted Sabrina to join her.

Maneuvering in the short skirt wouldn't be easy, but no way would Sabrina disappoint Chandra.

"Oh goodie," she said with enthusiasm. "Time for tea. May I join you?"

Chandra nodded and gave her a shy smile. "There's cookies, too." She held up an empty plastic dish that didn't quite match the cups she'd set out.

"My favorite kind!" Sabrina went down to her knees. "Thank you."

Chandra pretended to serve her. "You look real pretty today, Ms. Downey."

Sabrina reached across the table and smoothed her hair. Not that long ago, Chandra would have flinched away. But now she reveled in the attention. She still had her moments of uncertainty, but thanks to a distant aunt who would be taking her in, Chandra had a chance at a happy life.

Sabrina would miss her terribly, as she did all the kids. She'd worry about her, too. But she thanked God that Chandra had a caring relative who wanted to make her a part of their family.

"Thank you, Chandra. Coming from someone as pretty as you, that means a lot."

The little girl blinked at her. "I'm not pretty."

"Are you kidding me? You're beautiful."

Her mouth flattened and she stubbornly shook her head. "Not like you."

"Way better than me." Remembering the tea party, Sabrina pretended to sip. "Do you remember what your aunt said?"

Slowly, Chandra grinned and ducked her face. "She said I was the cutest thing she'd ever seen."

"And she meant it—because you, Chandra, are a super-cutie." To Sabrina, all the children were adorable, despite their own various image issues and sometimes flagging confidence.

Chandra smoothed her shirt. "It's cuz of the clothes you guys gave me."

"I'm glad you like the clothes, but it's *you* who make *them* look good."

Around them, the children played, some with more enthusiasm than others. While another assistant praised the artwork of those coloring, the director went to her office to answer a phone call. She dealt with the never-ending business and sometimes insane politics involved in running a home for abused and abandoned children.

Suddenly Chandra blurted, "You're so perfect."

Taken aback, Sabrina laughed. "Me? Oh, honey, no. I am far, far from perfect."

"You always know what to say and do."

Sabrina reached for her hands. "Actually, Chandra, I rarely know what to say or do. But you know what? I found out that it's okay. You try your best, and you hope it's right, but if it's not you try again." She lifted her shoulders. "That's what we all do."

Chandra chewed her bottom lip. "What if my aunt decides she doesn't like me, after all?"

Sabrina wanted to tell her that such a thing would never happen. But sadly, it sometimes did. The kids came with a lot of baggage, sometimes major issues, and they required extensive understanding and attention. Not everyone was cut out to handle the demands of a child recovering from abuse.

"Give her a chance, okay?" She gave a gentle squeeze to Chandra's hands for encouragement. "But know that I will always be here for you."

The young girl drew a breath. "What if you're not?" Fear sounded in her tone. "What if when I come back, you're gone?"

Sabrina fought off tears because Chandra was so sure that she would be coming back. "I don't plan to go anywhere, honey, but even if I did, the others here would know how to reach me. I promise."

Five-year-old Dion sidled over, his expression hopeful. Sabrina said to Chandra, "Would you like to invite Dion to join us?"

She swallowed, then nodded. "Okay."

Dion rushed to his place on the floor, and when he realized they didn't have real cookies, his face fell.

Sabrina reached over to rub his shoulder. She was about to explain about tea parties when suddenly Abner came loping through the doorway.

Surprised, she turned and found Roy right behind him. He leaned in the doorway, his expression intent as he watched Sabrina, a small smile on his mouth.

How long had he been there?

Sabrina was trying to think of something to say when the director came out to greet him. Abner made a beeline for Sabrina and the kids, and they all rushed forward in excitement.

Like a magnet, Abner drew them. They loved him and he loved them.

After speaking quietly to the director for a moment, Roy came and sat down across from Sabrina. "May I?"

She closed her mouth. "What are you doing here?"

"Chandra's leaving today, and Abner wanted to say good-bye."

"Oh."

His smile widened. "The director invited us. She knows how much Chandra loves that dog."

Together, they turned and saw Chandra was the center of attention as Abner tried to sit on her. The kids laughed aloud, and that made Sabrina grin. "A proper send-off."

Chandra succumbed to Abner's nuzzling kisses and licks, and again Sabrina had to fight off tears.

"You're going to miss her," Roy said.

She nodded. "Her aunt seems wonderful. She's not married, and she doesn't have any other kids, but she has a cat and a mixed-breed dog."

"Chandra will love that."

"Later this week, after Chandra gets settled, they're going shopping to decorate Chandra's new room."

"Something for her to look forward to."

Sabrina drew a breath. "I can't help but worry anytime one of them leaves."

"Of course you do."

Wearing a beatific smile, Chandra rejoined them at the table. Her cheeks were flushed and her eyes were alight with happiness. She plopped down beside Roy. "Abner slobbered all over me."

Roy picked up a napkin and handed it to her. "He slobbers on everyone he loves."

"I know." After a cursory swipe of her face, Chandra said, "My aunt has a dog and a cat."

"I heard." He lifted the plastic teapot. "May I?"

Giggling, Chandra nodded.

As Roy pretended to pour, he said, "They're going to love

you, too, I bet. Just remember that animals have to get to know you. Show them that you care, and I bet you'll get lots of animal kisses."

For the next half hour they continued their tea party while Chandra asked numerous questions about animals and Abner gave love and affection to each child. It both impressed and amazed Sabrina that Roy was so at ease in all situations, even with scared little girls.

But then, he'd always been that way with her, too.

Sometimes when she thought back on their history, she felt stung with humiliation. For such a long time, Roy had been protective of her, seeing her as needy, as emotionally wounded.

Because of their special relationship, what he thought of her mattered most. With all others, she didn't think about perceptions; she was confident enough that she didn't care about opinions. But with Roy . . . she wanted, *needed*, him to see her as a strong, independent person.

As an equal.

But how could he when she continued to run to him in terror over a stupid storm?

And yet they were having dinner together tonight. Nothing too unusual in that, but what did he want to talk about? And that last kiss . . .

Knowing Roy watched her, Sabrina shook off the distraction and forced a carefree smile. His gaze dipped over her with appreciation before another child drew his attention.

As the recess rolled to a close, the director gathered the kids together, and Sabrina began picking up.

So that Abner wouldn't interfere with the director's routine, Roy leashed him and kept him at his side. The big dog flopped down to stretch out on his side and let out a lusty sigh.

"He looks exhausted." Sabrina smiled at him. "I can sympathize. Sometimes the kids are extra energetic."

Roy looked around at all the displaced toys and papers. "I'd offer to stay and help out, but I have some adoptions in half an hour."

"That's great news." Sabrina stacked papers into a pile. "Dogs or cats?"

"One of each." He hesitated, then stepped closer to her. "You did great with Chandra."

Scoffing, she asked, "How long were you there?"

All too serious, he said, "Long enough to know she adores you."

"The feeling is mutual." A little embarrassed, Sabrina shook her head and laughed. "She thinks I'm perfect."

Roy didn't join in her humor. "You're wonderfully flawed, Sabrina. And I'm glad. Perfection would be so boring."

"You're far from boring."

"Because I'm not perfect, either." He gave a light tug to the leash to get Abner back on his feet. "You want to tell him good-bye?"

"Yes." She bent down and hugged the dog. "Thank you, Abner."

His tail drummed the floor.

Voice low, Roy asked, "Do you want to tell me good-bye, too?"

Belatedly, Sabrina realized they were alone. But then, they were often alone.

So why did it feel so different now?

One look at Roy and she knew why. It had a lot to do with how he watched her, the heat in his eyes and the expectation in the air.

Nervously, Sabrina licked her lips. "Thanks for bringing Abner over."

"You're welcome." And he waited.

God, she felt clumsy, and there was really no reason. In many ways, Roy knew her better than she knew herself. In a rush, she put her arms around him and gave him a tight but brief hug. "Bye."

He searched her face. "I'll see you in a few hours."

"Okay."

"Do me a favor and don't change clothes. I like the skirt. A lot." His gaze dipped, and one eyebrow went up. "Very convenient."

Sabrina felt her face go hot, but Roy was already on his way out the door. Luckily she had an hour before she had to directly interact with the kids again.

After the hot way Roy had looked at her, she'd need every minute to recover her aplomb.

THE drizzling rain finally let up and the sun crawled out, sending a steamy haze into the summer air. Sabrina was waiting outside when he pulled up to the apartment complex.

She still wore the skirt—and a look of uncertainty.

As she came to the truck, he got out to open her door for her. Nervously chatty, she asked, "How'd the adoptions go?"

"No problems. They seemed like good families." He waited until she got buckled in and then closed her door and went around to the driver's side. "Chandra?"

"Gone with her aunt." With a wistful smile, she added, "They both looked very happy."

Roy briefly took her hand. He wondered if Chandra's leaving—

even as a happy occurrence—would dominate her emotions. He wanted her, and waiting even a day more would be damned tough, but he knew Sabrina got very involved with each child at the home. "You going to be okay?"

"Yeah." She released his hand, exhaled a deep breath, and said again, "Yeah. I'm good."

Her strength, always tempered with compassion, was one of the things he most admired about her. In many ways she seemed like an angel on earth, giving so much of herself to help those in need but never letting it destroy her optimism. "You're something else, Sabrina Downey. Something very special."

To keep her from refuting that, Roy asked for the address of where they needed to go, and from there they talked about computers and other donations, dogs and cats, the weather and the wonderfulness of air-conditioning. She relaxed and they fell into the same easy, comfortable companionship they'd always shared.

No matter what happened, Roy didn't want to lose that.

They reached the location and had the computers loaded within an hour. Roy had parked his truck in an alleyway between shops. The normally congested business area felt lazy this time of day. In contrast to the dismal and dreary afternoon, the early-evening sun shone brightly, sending a colorful rainbow across the sky. Everything seemed to have slowed, with less traffic, less noise.

Standing outside the truck bed, a hand shielding her eyes, Sabrina took in the surrounding area of telephone poles, streetlamps, brick buildings, and bus stops. "It's a peaceful evening."

"Hot." He swiped the hem of his T-shirt over his face—and caught Sabrina staring at his abs. Nice. He hoped she found him as physically appealing as he did her. "Let me grab a couple of colas from the cooler."

Behind his seat, he dragged out a small personal cooler and

retrieved two Cokes. When he stepped back out again, he didn't see Sabrina. He slammed his door and walked around the truck—and found her on her knees looking under the bed.

She had her rump in the air, tempting him. He crouched down beside her. "What are you looking for?"

With her knees on the dirty concrete road, she said, "Shh."

Roy bent to look, too, and saw a scraggly little black cat. Young but not a kitten. Fearful and gaunt with hunger. One ear was injured, and there was a bend in the tail.

Softly, so as not to scare the cat, he said, "Shit."

Sabrina held out a hand, and the cat watched her with big yellow eyes.

"Don't touch it, Sabrina. It could be sick. Back out."

She didn't question the direction, but once she'd moved away, she asked, "What are you going to do?"

He retrieved his wallet and pulled out a five to hand to her. "There's a little mom-and-pop store at the next corner. See if they have anything that'll appeal to a cat."

"All right." She backed slowly away from the truck and then hurried down the sidewalk.

Hoping his evening wouldn't be ruined but unable to resist an animal in need, Roy considered the cat. "You don't like the alley life, do you, baby?"

The skinny cat twisted against the back tire, petting herself, wanting to come close but staying out of reach. A smile tugged at his mouth. "I wouldn't like it, either. Stay put while I find something to contain you."

Like Sabrina, he moved slowly to keep from startling the cat. Luckily he had a soft carrier tucked under his seat. He got it opened and ready and then waited for Sabrina.

She was back within five minutes with a can of tuna.

"Perfect." Roy pulled the tab and opened the can. Before he'd even gotten it inside the carrier, the cat smelled it. She poked her head out from under the truck and started an almost panicked meowing. "Back up, honey. You never know how a feral cat might act, but you can be certain she won't like it when I close the lid on her."

Sabrina moved well out of reach.

He put the carrier on its side and set the can of tuna in it. He'd barely taken two steps away when the cat rushed in. He hated to startle the poor thing before it got to eat, so he waited a minute, and when the can was almost empty he crept in and shoved down the lid.

The cat went nuts, screeching and circling furiously. Holding the lid shut, Roy said, "Get me a bungee."

"Where?"

"Toolbox, behind the rearview window."

"Oh." Scrambling, Sabrina climbed up into the truck bed. Under other circumstances he would have enjoyed the view, especially in that short sexy skirt, but not with a frightened cat trying to escape.

As she opened the large truck toolbox, Sabrina asked, "What's a bungee?"

"A stretchy cord. I need it to secure the carrier. It's not meant to hold a pissed-off cat bent on clawing her way out."

"This?" She held up a multicolored cord.

"That's it."

She rushed back to him and then, with his instruction, wrapped it around the carrier and hooked the ends together.

Once they had the cat secured, Roy had to laugh. Sabrina was wide-eyed and breathing hard. Stupefied, she met his gaze, and he laughed harder.

"Good God." Her mouth twitched as she swatted at him. "I've never seen a cat carry on like that."

"It's mostly feral," he explained. Still chuckling, relieved that they'd gotten the cat contained, Roy carried it to the truck cab. "You okay with it being on the floor by your feet? I don't want to leave it in the bed."

"It can't get out?"

"No. And she's already settling down, I think."

"Then I don't mind." As he got the carrier stowed, Sabrina said, "You're sure it's a girl?"

He shrugged. "Sounded like a girl when she was screeching at that high pitch."

Sabrina swatted him again. "After all that, she's probably covered in tuna."

"Hungry as she looked, I doubt she'll mind that much." On impulse, he pulled her into his arms, right there on the public sidewalk, and gave her a firm, quick smooch. "Ready to go, kiddo?"

Looking a little dazed, Sabrina said, "Uh . . ."

"Come on." Clasping her waist, he lifted her up and into her seat, and then, against her mouth, he whispered, "I'm getting hungrier by the minute."

He closed her door with her still mute.

She stayed that way until they were almost to the Children's Home. With the carrier taking up much of the floor, she had her legs bent, her knees turned toward him.

A cute and provocative pose.

When Sabrina realized where they were, she said, "Shouldn't we take the cat to the shelter first?"

"Nope. She's quiet now so I'd just as soon let her rest until we're done." He glanced at her, but she wouldn't quite meet his gaze. "That is, if you don't mind having her by your feet a little longer."

"I don't mind." She stared at the carrier. "Luckily, it won't take us long to unload the computers. We're putting them in the storage barn for now."

Roy pulled around back behind the home. "When we get to the shelter, you can prep a crate for her while I check that wounded ear." Even as he said it, Roy realized that they made a good team. Whenever they'd worked together, it was as smooth as clockwork. "By the way, I appreciate it that you didn't question me earlier."

"About what?"

"When I asked you to stay away from the cat or to get the tuna."

She flapped a hand at him. "You know what you're doing, and I didn't want to get in the way."

Roy knew she didn't mean that to sound so grave, but he frowned, anyway. As he put the truck in park, he said, "You will never be in my way, Sabrina."

She went still for a second, absorbing the words. After flashing him a smile, she nodded and got out of the truck to unlock the storage door.

The home was quiet, all the kids inside, but they often stayed busy out back. They had a flower and vegetable garden, a variety of playground equipment, and a volleyball court. It wasn't an ideal environment for growing up, but it was far better than the abusive homes they came from.

Sabrina directed him on where to stack the computers and within a few minutes they were on the road again.

Since the shelter was close, they made it there just as the sun turned a blazing red and began sinking from the sky.

This time of night, the animals were mostly quiet. They'd all been walked, given fresh water and bedding, and now they slept. But at the sound of the front door opening, a cacophony of outrage echoed around the interior. The mingled barking and meow-ing proved deafening.

Roy took a moment to go quiet them all. Once they saw him, the noise turned from alarm to joy.

Sabrina had the crate all ready when he returned. Donning long protective gloves, he withdrew the cat. She was more fear-ful than enraged, and she used her claws on the gloves, clinging tightly.

She was skittish but not as feral as he'd initially thought. Her injuries were old and healing, and right now, all the cat needed was peace and quiet to adjust to her new circumstances.

He put her in the large crate, isolated from the others until she could be checked for disease and parasites. The petite cat hun-kered down in a corner and watched them. "Good night, little girl. I'll see you in the morning."

Sabrina stood there waiting for him, her expression soft, her eyes warm.

He took in that look and smiled. "What?"

"I like how you talk to the animals. I think it comforts them."

"I hope so." He took her hand and headed out the door, anx-ious to get her home.

In the truck, she watched him still, her scrutiny intense. "The way you talk always comforts me, too."

"Yeah?" He drove out into the traffic. Now that they were fi-nally heading home, his blood thrummed and his heartbeat ac-celerated. "You don't need comfort all that often." These days, she only needed it during loud thunderstorms.

As if he hadn't spoken, she said, "I like a lot of things about you, Roy."

He gave her a quick look. "That's good, since I like an awful lot of things about you, too."

"Did you notice that storm clouds are rolling in again?"

He hadn't, but then he'd been focused on other things. He leaned forward and looked at the sky through the windshield. "Hope we don't lose power at the shelter."

"I was thinking . . ." She reached out and touched his upper arm, her fingers curling around his biceps. "Maybe I could stay with you. Tonight, I mean."

That threw him. He'd expected to have to work to get her to stay over again. "In case the storms return?"

She rolled one shoulder, and her mouth tipped in a small, secret smile. "I guess."

She guessed? What did that mean? Even as he pulled into the apartment parking lot, a low rumble of distant thunder sounded. He hoped it didn't get bad, because he wanted her with him every step of the way, not frozen in terror over bad memories.

"Crazy summer weather in Ohio," he groused. "Rain, clear skies, and rain again."

"Roy?"

He parked and turned toward her. There was something else in her tone, something he hadn't heard before. "What is it, kiddo?"

Her finger smashed up against his mouth. "Shh."

He lifted a brow, and waited.

She looked at his mouth, and her fingers moved to his jaw, then down to his shoulder. "I know what you want to talk about."

Enjoying her touch, Roy asked, "You do, huh?"

She bit her bottom lip. "But the thing is, I think it'd be better if we talked about it . . . after."

God, he hoped they were talking about the same things. "Hold that thought." He rushed out of the truck and around to her side. She didn't wait for him to open the door but was already out when he reached her.

Grabbing his hand, she started a long-legged stride toward the building entrance.

Roy wasn't quite sure what to think. "In a hurry?"

She stopped and turned to face him. "You've been teasing me all day, so *yes*."

"Sabrina." Holding her shoulders, he drew her up to her tiptoes. "Do you understand what I want?"

She nodded slowly. "I hope you want me. Because I want you. A lot."

That sweet admission nearly pushed him over the edge. He crushed her close for only a second, and then they were again racing for his apartment, through his apartment, and thankfully, to his bed.

four

✤

A deafening crack of thunder startled Sabrina just as Roy lowered her to his mattress. The lights went out and the air-conditioning stopped, filling the room with an ominous silence.

She inhaled sharply—and then his mouth was on hers, hungry and hot. Taking advantage of her parted lips, his tongue sank in, exploring and wickedly sexy while his hands roamed over her shoulders, lower . . .

She forgot about the storm, caught up in the pleasure of feeling Roy's hand on her breast, cuddling, caressing. His thumb moved over her nipple and her back bowed. He kissed her throat, sucking at a sensitive spot that made her toes curl and her breath catch. Before she realized it, her blouse was unbuttoned and he had her bra pulled down.

Now as his thumb stroked her, the sensation was so intense she groaned.

"Damn." He bent, and then it was her nipple he sucked at.

Sabrina held on to him, shoving up his shirt so she could stroke the bare hot skin of his back, his shoulders.

In a rush, he sat up. Lightning sent shadows flickering as Roy reached back and grabbed a fistful of shirt, yanking it off over his head and tossing it away.

She reached for him, but he pressed her hands down to her sides so he could finish stripping away her blouse and then her bra. This time when he lowered himself over her, she relished the feel of skin on skin.

Taking her mouth again, Roy slid a hand up her thigh, over her bottom, and then around to the front to cup over her. Gently, his fingers slid over the satiny crotch of her panties, teasing unbearably.

She groaned, but the sound was lost beneath their heavy breathing and his consuming kiss.

Against her mouth, he said, "I need you naked."

The room illuminated with another lightning strike, and Sabrina saw his face, the heat in his dark eyes, the possessive way he looked at her. His hair fell over his brow, and his jaw was set.

So sexy—and for the moment, all hers.

Thunder chased the lightning, but it competed with the loud thundering of her heartbeat.

She touched his jaw. "You first."

The smile showed in his eyes before his mouth tipped crookedly. "Whatever you want, honey."

As he stood at the side of the bed, Sabrina lifted up onto her elbows. The sky had grown so dark that seeing wasn't easy, but she could make out the width of his shoulders, the narrowness of his hips, his long thighs.

He toed off his shoes and then his big hands were at the snap to his jeans. The quiet hissing of his zipper affected her like a well-placed touch.

He bent, and when he straightened again he was fully naked. Where was that darned lightning when she needed it?

Voice low and rough, Roy murmured, "Your turn." Watching her, he wrapped a hand around her right ankle and tugged her sandal free.

It was a unique thing for Sabrina, feeling like this, turned on and sexy and so very much in love.

"Hurry," she told him. If he didn't stop teasing, she'd implode. She'd been waiting long enough already.

He had her other sandal off in seconds, and as he leaned over her, Sabrina went flat in the bed so she could run her hands over his chest, feeling his crisp chest hair and solid muscles.

He kissed her while he tackled the zipper on her skirt. Freeing her mouth, he said, "Lift up, baby."

She did, and he whisked away her skirt. She started to reach for the waistband of her panties, but went still when Roy kissed her ribs, her navel, a hip bone.

Her hands knotted in the quilt beneath her.

As he kissed a path down her body, he naturally fit between her legs. His hands on her inner thighs opened her more, and she felt his hot breath. She closed her eyes and, trying to urge him to haste, lifted up against him.

His mouth opened over her panties, and it was so intense that she cried out. The press of his tongue was indescribable, and the hungry, openmouthed kisses left her panties damp on the outside—and the inside.

While Roy prepared her, the storm intensified with rain lash-ing the windows and thunder crashing. Bold lightning split the dark sky and the wind howled.

But all Sabrina's senses were focused on Roy.

He got her so close that every muscle rippled and her skin burned.

Before she could catch her breath, he stood and stripped away her panties. The seconds it took him to roll on a condom felt like an hour.

As he came back to her, he hooked her sprawled legs in the crook of his elbows. "Hold on to me, Sabrina."

Sabrina wrapped her arms his neck—and then he was rocking against her, slick and hot.

"So wet," he groaned. "God, I've waited forever for this, for *you*."

She didn't know what that meant, and she couldn't think enough to sort it out. Especially when he entered her, just a little, being so patient that she thought she'd scream.

"*Roy*," she demanded.

With one long, solid thrust, he filled her.

Gasping, she arched her back, driving him deeper, and for a single suspended moment, they both froze, Roy rigid above her, Sabrina shuddering in reaction.

She couldn't stay still, not while being filled with him, surrounded by him. She kissed his shoulder, his neck, and her fingertips dug into his shoulders.

Though he felt a little too big inside her, stretching her and making her burn, it didn't matter. She loved his scent, the strength of his body, and the way he strained over her, struggling so hard to remain gentle.

She looked up at him, their gazes locking, electric. This time when she said his name, it came out a soft, breathless plea. "Roy."

Groaning, he pulled back only to sink in again, and again. The tantalizing friction built as he stroked harder and deeper, *faster*.

Within minutes they were both lost.

A wave of sensation swept up from her thighs, down from her breasts, and pooled between her legs. She tightened around him, needing the climax, reaching for it.

He kissed her and she came.

Unable to control herself, she groaned harshly, moved against him, with him, until the feelings faded and her body went lax.

As she drew a shuddering breath, she watched Roy take his own pleasure. She felt awed by the force of his release.

When he freed her legs and moved to the side of her, she automatically turned into him. He gathered her close, his arms enclosing her, his mouth against her temple.

Never had she felt so relaxed, so empty of tension. That is, until Roy said, "Time for us to talk."

ROY listened to her yawn and wondered if she was falling asleep. Amazing, given that the weather had turned more than a little nasty. Not that she'd seemed to notice.

God willing, she'd have new memories for her storms now.

With her head on his shoulder, her slender thigh over his, she whispered, "It can't wait until the morning?"

He smoothed her hair back behind her ears. "No."

She twisted up to rest against his chest. Fingers shaking, she touched his mouth before looking into his eyes. "Everything has changed, hasn't it?"

"Yes." Her makeup was smudged, her hair tumbled, and her lips puffy. She was the most beautiful thing he'd ever seen. "Indefinitely changed."

Her face warmed with pleasure. "We'll do this often?"

"Bet on it." He hadn't even come close to all he wanted from her and with her. He wasn't sure a lifetime would be enough.

"Good." She snuggled down against him again. "Next time I want the lights on so I can see you."

He wanted the same, but since the "next time" would probably be within the hour, it was a toss-up whether the electricity would be working or not. "You said you knew what I wanted."

"I think so." Still snuggled close, she smiled up at him. "You want us to be friends with benefits, right?"

Roy went rigid. He half sat up and turned her onto her back. "No, not even close."

Her face went blank, then pinched with worry. "But . . . we've been friends forever."

And now he needed her to understand that they were more. "Our relationship has always been beyond friendship."

Uncertainty had her chewing her bottom lip.

"Sabrina." He smoothed her lip with his thumb. "Tell me what you're thinking."

She drew in a shuddering breath. "To me, you're . . . everything. My best friend, my confidant, my closest relative." She swallowed. "You're the one I always go to when I get . . ."

Scared. She didn't have to say it. "Do you love me, Sabrina?"

"Yes."

He started to relax, but he needed her to clarify. "I don't mean as a pseudo-relative."

"I love you in every way possible."

A weight lifted from his chest—until he realized that she wouldn't meet his gaze. "But?"

"But . . . you've always had responsibility for me. Even now, with me a grown woman, you have to deal with me falling apart over a stupid storm."

He brought her face back up to his. "It's storming now, and you didn't even notice."

She froze. "It is?"

"The electricity went out awhile ago." Just in case it bothered her, he stayed very close, his arm over her waist, his leg over hers. "Listen to the thunder."

Blinking in surprise, she whispered, "I sort of realized it. I mean . . . I was able to see you better when the lightning flashed."

Roy had to kiss her. "You know you're the only woman I've wanted for a while now, right?"

Looking a little shell shocked, she said, "But . . . you still call me kiddo."

"So?"

She scowled as if he should already understand. "It's like . . . I don't know. A reminder of that sad, scared kid I used to be."

"No. It's just a pet name for the woman I love."

Visible from a bright flash of lightning, her eyes widened and she stared at him.

He pressed another kiss to her soft mouth. "I do love you, Sabrina."

Her lips trembled. "You really do?"

"God yes."

"Just because the storm didn't bother me this time—"

"I love every part of you, honey, fears and all. In fact, the last twenty-four hours, even with furious storms, abandoned dogs, and rescued cats, has been one of the best days I've had in a long time—because I spent it with you." He held her face between his hands. "If you'll marry me, every day will be the best."

She searched his face, then nodded. Slowly, her smile came. "So . . . we could get a house?"

"Hell of an idea."

"And we can adopt Abner?"

Knowing she loved animals as much as he did, Roy said, "For starters."

She laughed out loud. "Wonderful!" Pushing against Roy's shoulders until he went to his back, Sabrina crawled up over him. "Now let's wrap up this talk so we can move on to"—she kissed his chin—"other things. Okay?"

Her breasts were against his bare chest, her soft belly over his groin, but he wouldn't let himself get distracted just yet. "Tell me that you'll marry me."

"I love you, Roy, so much." She hugged him tight. "Of course I'll marry you."

Roy turned her beneath him.

Outside, the wind whistled through trees and rain lashed the landscape. Thunder rumbled and lightning fractured the blackened skies.

But inside, in love and together, neither one of them noticed.

take me home

*

ERIN McCARTHY

one

❀

Sara Parker stared at the check Evan Monroe had just handed her for ten thousand dollars and swallowed hard, the numbers on the paper blurring. "I can't take this," she said, shoving it back at him.

"What? Why not? You'll need it for your expenses until the baby is born."

God, he was being so nice and she wasn't being totally honest with him. Sara, in all her years in foster care and even during her brief stint out on the streets, had never felt this lost, this filled with self-loathing.

Nor had she ever strode so far from home and the values her last foster mother had instilled in her before she had died. Sara stared at the Formica table in Waffle House, unable to look at the man in front of her. He had made millions of dollars during his career as a stock car driver. She knew ten grand wasn't really that much to him. Yet she had told him this baby was most definitely his, and the truth was, she didn't know that.

It was possible Evan was the father.

It was just as likely it was the bartender at the Sly Fox who Sara had spent another boozy night with just before she had done the same with Evan.

Her hand slid down to her firm belly to rest over her daughter. This was a wake-up call. The chance to shift the direction she had been going in. Starting with the truth.

"Evan, you've been really good to me. Here you are just married and everything and you don't really know me, and you're being really sweet and kind." Sara took a deep breath and blew it out, ruffling her bangs that had gotten unruly. "But the truth is, I did sleep with someone else around the same time. I don't know for certain this baby is yours."

She figured he'd probably rip the check up and call her a slut, but she'd feel better knowing the truth was out there. Evan deserved that much, and she needed to be honest with herself and him.

Evan did stare at her for a minute, before asking, "But it could be mine?"

"Yes." She felt her cheeks burn a little. It hadn't seemed like such a big deal at the time when she'd been slinging back vodka, but now she was ashamed of herself and her behavior. Casual sex was one thing, but she'd gone too far.

He shrugged. "All right, then. Who is the other guy, does he know you're pregnant?"

Sara shook her head. "I don't have any way to contact him." She didn't even remember his last name, and when she'd gone back to the bar, she'd been told he'd quit. She could have pursued it further, but the truth was, she hadn't wanted to. It was too humiliating. Like this conversation.

"Take the money, then, Sara. If the baby is mine, great. We'll work out raising our daughter together. If it's not, finish school, make a life for yourself. I have more money than I know what to do with, and you clearly need some help."

Her lip started to tremble. "I can't take your money if it's not yours. That isn't right."

"I want you to." He tried to push the check back to her.

Sara felt the tears falling and she stood up in humiliation. "I'll be in touch, Evan. I have to go."

Rushing out of Waffle House, Sara let the tears take over as she dug in her purse for her car keys.

She knew what she needed to do. It was time to go home to Kentucky, to the one person who could always make her feel better.

She needed her best friend, Travis Fenway, and the hug he would offer.

TRAVIS was washing the dust off his truck, his Labrador, Sadie, frolicking around at his feet, when the small sedan pulled into his driveway. Curious to know who was visiting him on a Tuesday without a phone call, he squinted against the sun as he tried to see into the car.

The door opened and a familiar blond head popped up. Travis broke into a grin, turning off the hose. It was Sara. He hadn't seen her in over two years, since she'd headed east determined to get herself a fancy education and marry a rich man, not necessarily in that order. He'd heard from her from time to time but never enough for his liking.

Heading toward her, Sadie barking in excitement, Travis was prepared to scoop her up and squeeze her in a giant hug. Until her belly rounded the corner of the car door and he saw she was pregnant.

His heart sank. He should be happy for her if Sara had found herself a man she loved, but he couldn't squelch the keen jab of disappointment. He had always wanted Sara for himself, even when he'd known how foolish that was, and seeing her carrying another man's child just drove his stupidity home.

"Well, look what the cat dragged in," he said, still damn happy to see her as he crammed his feelings down. He'd take whatever scraps of attention from her he could, just like he always had. And he was still getting a hug.

His arms were reaching for her when he realized that Sara's eyes were watering, her cheeks stained with dried tears, her nose sniffling as she tried to keep it together.

"Baby, what's wrong?" he asked her, reaching out and wrapping his arms around her.

She sank against him and burst into tears. "I've made a mess of everything, Travis, I'm such an idiot . . . God, what am I going to do?"

Holding her tight, Travis rubbed a hand gently on her back, taking in her scent, letting his eyes drift closed for a just a split second. "Hey, shh, it's okay. Nothing we can't fix."

Her shoulders were shaking with her sobs. Pulling back slightly, she lifted red-rimmed eyes to him. "I can't fix this! I'm pregnant, did you notice that?"

He had definitely noticed. Holding her close to him, that round belly was pressing against his own abdomen, a noticeable difference. Sara had always been tiny and this was an odd and amazing transformation. "Of course I noticed." Using his thumbs, Travis wiped her tears off her cheeks. "Want to tell me about it?"

"I've really screwed up this time." Her brown eyes were filled with tears and worry, her nose swollen.

"Come onto the porch and sit down and we'll sort it all out. Did you drive all the way from Charlotte alone?"

She nodded. When she made no move toward the porch, Travis took her hand and pulled her, just like he had countless times when they were kids. Sara had always been terrified as a girl, her wide eyes watching the other kids in the group home with a naked longing to fit in. Travis had always pulled her along, taking Sara everywhere with him.

He had a million and one questions for her, all starting and ending with that baby growing inside her, but he was going to let her tell him everything all on her own time. Travis deposited her on a rocker. Sadie wagged her tail and inserted herself between Sara's knees.

"Hey, Sadie," Sara cooed, still sniffling as she leaned down and took the dog's face between her hands. "I missed you."

Travis settled into the chair next to her, wishing he weren't so pathetic that he wished she'd say the same to him.

"You'll always love me, won't you, puppy? No matter how dumb I am." Sara kissed Sadie's head.

Biting his tongue, he looked out across as his yard, his truck half washed in the drive. "So, you want something to drink?"

"I can't drink, I'm pregnant."

Travis frowned. "I meant a lemonade or an iced tea or something. I wasn't offering you liquor."

"Oh." She gave a small laugh. "Guess I've been hanging around the wrong people." Then she sighed. "Actually, that's not fair. My friend Nikki has been good to me. I'm the one who found myself going out way too often."

Travis leaned forward in his rocker and wondered the right way to circle around to the real question here. "So, are you still in nursing school?"

"Yeah. I'm going to have to take a semester off, but I'll be able to go back if . . ." She trailed off and her cheeks stained pink.

"If what? You know you can tell me anything. I'm here for you." He always had been, always would be. Hell, if he could lay his head in her lap like his dog was doing, he would.

"If Evan is the father. If he's not, then I'm shit out of luck." The blush on her cheeks deepened as she struggled to meet his eye. "Won't know for sure until the baby is born."

Ah. So that was the rub. Travis struggled to control his own emotions. He was angry at both himself, for letting her go off to Charlotte in the first place, and at Sara, for giving herself away so easily to men who didn't give a damn about her. Unlike him.

Then again, maybe he was wrong. "Is Evan your boyfriend?"

Sara forced herself to shake her head, so embarrassed that she wanted to crawl under Travis's front steps and die. That he could sit there so calmly on his tidy, freshly painted porch, while she told him she was a bad talk-show episode, just made her feel even more ashamed, if that were possible. To her, Travis had always been the person whose opinion of her mattered the most.

"No. It was a onetime thing on a camping trip . . . but I told him about the baby and he's being really cool about it, all things considered. He's a stock car driver and he offered me ten thousand dollars."

"To do what?" Travis's voice had taken on a steely tone of outrage.

"No, I don't mean that." Sara reached over and touched his jeans covering his knee. "For me to live on, get through school. But I refused it because I just don't know for sure if he is the father."

Travis's jaw worked, like he was debating what to say.

"There's only one other possibility," she said. "I'm not that big of a slut."

"I didn't say anything. And you're not a slut, that's not what I was thinking. I don't want to hear you talking like that."

It made her feel even more awful knowing exactly how Travis felt about casual sex. Being dumped at the orphanage by his prostitute mother had left Travis with a resolve to never use women the way his mother had been used. He respected the women he was involved with, and he didn't approve of sex for sex's sake. Sara had been the recipient of that respectful attitude since the day she'd met him, and she was beyond grateful for his friendship. She wasn't sure what she would do if she lost his approval.

"I don't even know who I am anymore, Trav. I left Kentucky thinking I was meant for bigger and better things, never wanting to see this place again. Why did I hate it so bad here anyway?"

Travis had a cute bungalow with a wide front porch and a green plot of land surrounding it. He was clearly about to plant a substantial garden, the earth freshly tilled behind the fence designed to keep out critters. Travis was a teacher and a football coach here in Boone County where they'd grown up and he seemed happy. Why had she thought chasing after labels and married men had mattered? She couldn't even wrap her head around why it had driven her to take off two years earlier.

"You didn't have a fabulous childhood, Sara. It's natural you'd want to go off and see a little of the world."

He was calm, unruffled, like he always was. He just rocked in his chair, his T-shirt pulling across the muscles of his chest and biceps. His hair was longer than it had been the last time she'd seen him, and the wind ruffled it a little. The air smelled sweet, like the spring flowers blooming in front of his porch, and a longing rose up in her, desperate and fierce. She wanted to have her act together like Travis did, she wanted to be a good mother and be able to provide her baby with a home.

The home she'd never had.

His eyes widened in alarm. "What? Why are you crying again? I didn't mean to . . ."

Sara pressed her eyes, trying to get a grip on herself. "No, it's not you. I just . . . I don't know what to do. I really don't."

"Let me get you a cookie." Travis stood up, his rocker banging the wall behind him as he hurried to placate her.

Giving a watery laugh, Sara swatted at his leg as he moved past her. "You still think a cookie fixes everything, huh?" That had always been his solution when she had gotten upset. He'd find a way to pilfer a cookie for her, knowing how much Sara loved sweets.

When a bully had knocked her into the dirt at age nine, Travis had found her a cookie. When her mother had finally overdosed and the social workers broke the news to her, Travis had scored Fudge Stripes for her. And when Billy Pratt had broken her heart at sixteen, Travis, who was a grown man by then and off at college on a scholarship, had shown up with three boxes of Girl Scouts Thin Mints.

"Hey, it always made you feel better, didn't it?"

"Yeah. Yeah, it did."

Actually, what had made her feel better was knowing that Travis would always be there for her.

Two

＊

Travis watched Sara dunk her chocolate chip in the glass of milk he'd given her and raise the soaked cookie to her lips. Her eyes were still puffy and she looked like she needed a good night's sleep, but she looked less fragile, less on the verge of tears.

"See, told you you'd feel better."

She gave him a smile, sitting next to him at his rickety kitchen table. Glancing around, she licked the dripping milk from her cookie. "You've done a nice job with this house, Trav. It feels like a real home."

Pride swelled in him. "Thanks. It's been hard work but worth it. It's not much, but this is all mine."

It had been a yearning he'd had his whole life as he had bounced from sofa to sofa when he was still living with his mother, to his aunt's for a while, then finally into the orphanage at twelve, to have a home. A place to set down roots, to create a life for himself that no one could take away.

Sara had wanted to run away from the past, from their difficult childhood, but Travis hadn't felt the same call to leave. He had wanted to stay here in Rabbit Hash, Kentucky, and prove to himself and everyone around him that he was more than his mother's son. That he was a good man, who had built a life for himself. He craved stability more than anything, life's simple pleasures. His world only lacked a woman to share it with. He did date a high school classmate of Sara's, but he could never bring himself to take it to the next level because, unfortunately, he had spent half his life casting Sara in that role in his mind, something she had never wanted, and never would.

This simplicity didn't appeal to her.

Or it hadn't, anyway.

Seeing her at his table, contently munching cookies, made him wonder if somehow that had changed.

"It's a lot more than you give yourself credit for," Sara told him passionately. "This—" Her arm swung around. "This is the kind of house you stay in forever."

It suddenly occurred to Travis to wonder why she had driven all those miles alone. "So what are you doing here? I'm really glad to see you, but it seems like a helluva drive for a drop-in visit."

She just shrugged apologetically. "Tell you the truth, I don't know . . . I was staring at that check that Evan gave me, knowing I hadn't been completely honest with him and I felt sick. So I told him that I didn't know if he was the father or not, and he was really kind about it, and I just stood there wondering, what am I doing? I didn't know, and so I just knew I had to come home. To you. Knew that you would help me."

His chest tightened. That meant the world to him, that she had reached out to him, over anyone else, when she was scared.

It was almost a little bit like love. "Of course I'll help you. You can stay here as long as you like, now and after the baby is born."

She looked pleased, but skeptical. "You don't know what you're offering. Babies cry."

Travis rolled his eyes, swiping one of her cookies. "Like I don't know that? Of course they cry. In case you hadn't noticed, a few tears don't scare me off."

Sara gave a small laugh. "I guess that's true. But I don't have any money, how can I just mooch off you?"

"It's not mooching if I offer. You can cook dinner for me. I hate to cook. And beyond that, I don't give a damn, Sara. I just want you and that baby to be healthy and happy, do you understand me?" He couldn't stand the thought of her going back to Charlotte where no one could take care of her the way he could.

"You'd really do that for me?"

"Yes." Why was that so hard for her to comprehend? "That's what big brothers do."

"Is that how you think of me?" She looked wistful, her eyes glassy, cheeks bright, fingers turning her cookie over and over. "As a sister?"

No, that wasn't how he thought of her. Travis thought of her as his everything, as the girl he'd cherished and protected, as the woman he wanted more than anything to be his lover, his wife, his future. But he couldn't tell her that. Not knowing she didn't feel the same way. He couldn't risk damaging their friendship. "Yes. Isn't that how you think of me?"

"I've always thought of you as my best friend."

He'd take it. "So you're saying you wouldn't let a friend help you out? You wouldn't stay with a friend?"

"Are you sure you don't mind?"

"Don't be dumb. You can stay here as long as you need to in my spare room. We'll even go buy a crib and a car seat and all that other baby stuff."

"Neither one of us knows a darn thing about babies."

He shrugged with a nonchalance he didn't necessarily feel. "I'm sure there are manuals. We'll figure it out."

"Thank you." She licked the tip of her finger where some chocolate had melted from the cookie. "I guess maybe that's what I wanted you to say . . . maybe that's why I drove all the way here. So you could help me. I'm sorry, that's selfish of me."

Travis reached over and took her small hand in his. "Hey. You're my family. Do you understand that?"

He meant that from the depths of his heart.

Sara burst into tears again. She couldn't help it. Travis was being so sweet. She didn't deserve his kindness, not when she'd turned her back on him and Rabbit Hash, and had been so selfish. That he thought of her as family sent a surge of both relief and love through her. She wasn't sure she could manage without knowing that Travis was still a part of her life.

"All right, now, it's okay." He rubbed her back gently.

"If you try to shove a cookie in my mouth, I'm going to be very upset."

"Nah. But I will get you a tissue for that snotty nose of yours."

As he walked out of the kitchen to the bathroom, Sara wondered why his use of the word *brother* had bothered her. It was a great thing for him to say, an indication he felt an incredibly strong bond with her, and it should have made her feel wonderful. Yet it had hit her ears wrong and she wasn't sure why. Nor was she sure why she suddenly felt self-conscious about the mucus trailing out of her nose.

It wasn't like he hadn't seen her at her worst before.

When he came back with the box of tissues, she dabbed at her nose instead of giving a healthy blow. Then picking at her stretchy top, she sighed. She was a sweaty, snotty mess.

"What?"

"It's hot in here."

"No AC, sorry. But I have a pool out back. Want to go swimming?"

"It's only the middle of May. Isn't it too cold to go swimming?"

"You're hot, you're cold . . . there's just no pleasing you," he teased. "It's damn near eighty out and you're hot, so why not? I bet it would feel good, take some pressure off your back."

"How did you know my back's bothering me?"

"You've been kneading it the whole time you've been here." He tapped his head. "No genius here."

Floating weightless did seem appealing. "I don't have a bathing suit."

"Just wear your T-shirt and panties. Or I'll give you some boxers. Don't make it complicated, girl."

She stuck her tongue out at him. "Fine. I'll take the boxers." The thought of being just in her panties weirded her out, and she wasn't sure why. "Are you going swimming, too, or will it just be me bobbing around in there looking like I swallowed a beach ball?"

"I'm going, too. I didn't fill the thing with water to watch other people use it."

Ten minutes later Sara gingerly sat down on the deck of Travis's aboveground pool, using a hand to lower herself. She couldn't believe she was actually going to get bigger than this. She already felt like she was waddling off balance all the time. As soon as her feet dipped into the chilly water, the baby gave a good healthy kick.

She dropped her hand to her stomach, amazed at she always was at the sensation of a life growing inside her.

Travis dropped beside her, glancing at her stomach. "Is the baby moving?"

"Yeah. You want to feel her?" Sara hadn't let anyone else touch her stomach. Not that anyone had asked, besides kindly old ladies in grocery stores. But she wanted someone else to experience the awe she felt, someone like Travis, who mattered.

"Sure." His big man hand hovered uncertainly over her belly, covered with one of his old T-shirts.

Sara pulled the fabric tighter so there were no lumps and took his hand and put it on the lower left side of her belly, where the baby was kicking or punching straight out. Travis's hand jerked when he felt the movement.

"Holy crap, it moved."

Laughing, Sara, put his hand back. "It is a she. And she moves all the time."

Travis moved his hand around, the astonishment she frequently felt reflected on his face. "That's amazing, Sara. There's a little girl inside you. She's going to be as beautiful as her mama."

She shrugged. She wasn't feeling very beautiful these days, inside or out.

"How far along are you?"

"Twenty-four weeks. I'm due September thirteenth."

"So we have some time to get all the gear we need."

Trust a man to call baby items "gear." "Little bit of time. Long enough for me to be scared." She gave a shaky laugh. "What if I can't do it?"

"You're going to be a wonderful mother. I don't doubt that for a minute. You have a lot of love to give."

With his hand still resting on her she voiced her fears for the first time out loud. "I don't know how to be a parent. I didn't have parents in the truest sense."

"Me neither. But your heart will tell you what to do." His fingers caressed back and forth on the cotton of his shirt she was wearing. "What are you going to name her?"

She took a deep breath, not sure how he would react. "I was thinking of naming her Casey. Casey Anne. If that's okay with you." Casey was Travis's middle name. Anne was the name of the foster mother she'd had at seventeen, the only woman Sara felt had really cared about her in any way. Anne had done her best to undo some of the damage of her childhood, and Sara missed her terribly still. She could use Anne's help right now.

But at least she had Travis.

He nodded. "I think that's a fine name. And I'm honored."

"Thanks." Sara edged forward a little, letting her legs go deeper in the water. She was hot in the sun, and her forehead and upper lip were getting sweaty.

"Parker?"

"Huh?"

"You're giving her your last name?"

"Yeah, I think so." She didn't know the bartender's last name. If Evan Monroe was the father, well, she still couldn't see using his name. This was her baby, her responsibility.

She tried to move forward again, wanting to get in the pool, but afraid if she launched herself off the deck, she'd drop like a ton of bricks in the water.

"You need some help?" Travis slipped into the water and moved in front of her, reaching toward her with his hands.

Feeling frustrated, Sara shook her head. "I'm fine."

"Don't be stupid," he told her. "Your cheeks are red from the heat and you keep wiggling around, like you're trying to figure out how to get in, but you're afraid to jump."

Trust him to always know what she was thinking or feeling. "Fine. I feel like a whale. I don't know how to move with this big body."

"If I hear you talking fat one more time I will take you over my knee." With a firm grip, he put his hands on her waist and lifted her gently into the water.

Sara laughed as the cool water lapped over her. "You wouldn't spank a lady with a baby."

"No, I guess I wouldn't."

Her laughter died out as she realized Travis hadn't let go of her and there was a look in his eyes, something deep and intense that she didn't understand. He was holding her like she weighed nothing as she bobbed a little in his old T-shirt and navy blue boxer shorts.

This was what Travis was to her—solid, strong, always there for her.

But there was something else, something she didn't quite understand.

"So do you have feelings for this Evan guy? If the baby's his do you think you two might work something out?"

Holding on to his shoulders, Sara shook her head. "No. He just reunited with an old girlfriend and they up and married."

Which Sara should be more upset about, honestly, but here, back home, it didn't seem to matter so much.

Travis searched Sara's face for signs of a broken heart, but she didn't look overly upset. In fact, she looked like she was finally relaxing a little and losing some of the tension that had been on her face from the minute she'd stepped out of that car. "I'm sorry."

"It is what it is. I've made some poor choices."

"And the other guy?" He shouldn't ask, it was none of his damn business, but he couldn't help it. He was worried about her, and he'd admit it, jealous.

"Not even worth mentioning." Sara let go of his shoulders and kicked off, going onto her back. "Ahh, this feels good."

It was odd to see her body looking so different, her belly jutting out of the water. Sara had always been too thin, with dark circles under her eyes. She had been the kind of kid who looked like she'd flinch if you reached for her. It had brought out every protective instinct Travis had had. Now she looked rounder, softer, healthier. She had lost some of the artificial tan she'd been sporting the last time he'd seen her, and she looked oddly more peaceful, despite her current worries. Travis still wanted to protect her like he had all those years ago, but he also appreciated the woman she'd become.

Sara was much scrappier than she'd ever given herself credit for.

"I'm glad you're here," he told her.

"Me, too."

She had closed her eyes as she floated, the receding sun reflecting off the water onto her.

"You should stay here," he told her, blurting out what had been rolling around in his head before he lost the nerve to say something. "Even after the baby's born. No matter what the DNA tests say. There are nursing schools here. Cost of living is so much cheaper here, and you can stay with me." Feeling agitated, Travis pumped his fists in the water, making arches of liquid shoot up with a squirting sound. "It's practical."

Which was true. But practicality certainly wasn't the only motivation behind his suggestion. He couldn't stand the thought of Sara going back to North Carolina all alone, struggling to make ends meet and raising a baby by herself. Getting up at 2 A.M. with no one to help you night after night sounded really damn hard, and Travis didn't want that for her. Plus he selfishly wanted her company. He wanted to see her smiling at him every day, and he wanted to hold her hand when she needed it.

"I definitely want to stay here until the baby's born. After that, we'll see. I have a few months to decide. It's a big decision. I don't know if I should take the baby away from Evan if he is the father."

Travis hated the guy and he'd never even met him, just for the simple fact that he had slept with Sara and hadn't wanted to date her. How could any guy have a crack at her and not want to slap a ring on her finger and make her his forever? Travis just didn't get it.

"I understand." Movement out of the corner of his eyes made Travis jerk forward in the water. "Sadie, no!"

His lab was poised on the edge of the deck ready to jump and as Sara's eyes flew open, the dog launched herself into the air and crashed down into the water an inch from Sara.

"Holy crap, are you okay?" Travis jogged through the water as best as he could, hoping the mutt hadn't actually landed on Sara.

She was sputtering and laughing, face soaked, hair soaked, T-shirt soaked. "I'm fine. And cool now." Reaching over, she rubbed the dog's head, who was paddling beside her. "Thanks, Sadie."

Sara gave him a smile. "And thanks, Trav. It's good to be home."

If he had anything to say about it, she'd never be leaving again.

three

Sara looked around for a ladder to climb out of the pool and didn't see one. "Uh . . . where is the ladder?" She wasn't exactly known for her upper-body strength in the best of times and she was tired from the long drive.

But she was relaxed. It was amazing what two hours in Rabbit Hash or, more specifically, in Travis's house, had done for her stress levels. She felt calm, like she could tackle her life. And she felt safe.

That didn't mean that she could get herself out of this pool, though.

"There isn't one. They're overpriced." Travis gave her a sheepish shrug. "I just, you know, jump out."

"Well, maybe you and Sadie can do that, but I can't." That was not going to happen.

"Don't worry, I'll get you out."

Sara put her hands on the deck and tried to pull herself up, but all she did was bump her belly against the wall.

"Wait for me." Travis hopped out, water dripping down his face and over his muscular chest.

His very manly, attractive chest.

So shocked at the unexpected thought, Sara fell back into the water.

It must be the hormones and the lack of sex, because Travis had said he considered himself like a brother. If she was thinking any part of him was hot, then she was just a pervert. When he bent over to help her, she looked to the right, well aware how close her face was to his crotch in those soaking wet swim trunks. She did not want to see anything she shouldn't.

He smelled like chlorine and his hands were cold when he reached down and gripped her under the shoulders. "Just relax and let me haul you up."

Relax. She'd been doing such a good job of that.

Until his naked man chest with water droplets racing down its hard contours had suddenly leapt out of nowhere and smacked her sexual consciousness.

"Okay." Sara closed her eyes as Travis lifted her out of the pool and set her down. She wobbled a little but was on solid decking.

"Sara Parker, is that you?" a woman's voice called from her left.

Sara almost fell back into the water, but she managed to hold on to her balance with Travis's help. She stood on the deck, peering past him. It was Amber Wynstock, a classmate from high school, and one of the few people who had actually been reasonably kind to Sara growing up.

"Hey, Amber, how are you?"

"I'm great." Amber beamed up at her, standing next to the

pool, a pie in her hands. "How are you? My goodness, are you pregnant? Congratulations!"

"Thanks." Sara dredged up a smile. "It's a girl."

"That's wonderful. So what brings you to town? Getting your visiting in before you can't travel anymore?"

"Yep, that's right." The manners her foster mother, Anne, had taught her kicked in. "We're getting down off this deck. Why don't you come on inside and have some lemonade and we can catch up?" They hadn't exactly been friends, but when other girls had mocked Sara for her ill-fitting clothes or for her dirty hair when there had been no running water to wash it when they were in middle school, Amber hadn't participated. In fact, a time or two, she'd even shared her lunch or her makeup with Sara. In high school, she had always offered a smile and a hello.

Amber looked the same, just as cheerful and friendly as she always had, a pretty woman with light brown hair and sparkling blue eyes.

It wasn't until they stepped down off the deck and Amber handed Travis the pie with an extra sparkle in her eye that Sara thought to wonder what the hell she was doing there in the first place. With baked goods, no less.

"Thanks, Amber," he said with a return smile. "You know I have a thing for your pies."

Sara tried not to frown. That sounded like a double entendre to her.

It was starting to occur to her—and really irritate her—that Travis and Amber Wynstock might be dating.

Aware that she was dripping water from her plastered hair, and that Travis's boxers were sagging off her butt, yet clinging to her thighs, Sara tried to maintain her smile. "So what are you up to these days, Amber?" She almost asked her if she was married, but that would only mean Amber would immediately ask her the same question in return, and she didn't really want to explain the single parenthood, lack of definitive father situation.

"I teach English at the high school. Freshmen mostly. I enjoy it."

"That's great. So you and Travis work together then." Maybe this was a co-worker pie delivery.

"Yes. We're weren't sure if dating was such a wise idea, given that very fact, but so far it's managed to work out all right."

Amber smiled and Sara suddenly felt the urge to hate her.

Until she added, "Gosh, you just look fantastic, Sara. You really do have that glow. I think mommyhood agrees with you."

Her voice was so sincere and genuine that there was no way Sara could find it in her to despise Amber. She truly was just a decent person, and frankly, the kind of woman Travis deserved. As they crossed the lawn to the back door and headed into the kitchen, Sara fought a contradictory swirl of emotions. She should be happy for Travis. Instead, she was suddenly feeling depressed. Jealous.

"Thank you, that's really sweet of you to say. I feel good, though I'm constantly bouncing off of my car door and the shower wall. Can't get used to this belly." Sara rested her hand on that bump, to reassure herself, of what, she wasn't sure.

Maybe it was just that in a way, she had always felt like Travis belonged to her. Not romantically but just as Travis and Sara. That he would always be there for her.

That she wouldn't have to share him.

Which was ridiculous. Of course at some point Travis was going to fall in love, get married, have children.

But the thought was like a fist around her windpipe. She couldn't breathe.

The warm kitchen felt even warmer and spots swam in front

of her eyes. Grappling for the back of the chair at the table, Sara tried to suck air in and out, the hot nausea rushing up her throat.

"Are you okay?" Travis asked her.

She tried to nod, but the motion made her dizzy.

"Here, sit down." His hands were on her, guiding her down into a chair. "You need some water."

Sara sank gratefully into the chair, her legs wobbly. She was burning up hot, yet the wet clothes made her shiver.

"Oh, your nose is bleeding," Amber said in concern.

"Huh?" Reaching up, she swiped at her nostrils and her fingers came away covered with a bright smear of blood. "Oh."

"I'll get you a paper towel. Just pinch it."

"It's okay," she said, squeezing her nostrils shut. "I learned about this in nursing school. It's all the extra blood flow during pregnancy, especially during the second trimester. It can cause dizziness and nosebleeds."

"I think I should take you to the ER," Travis said, holding a glass of water up to her lips. "You almost fainted."

"I'm fine," she insisted, wondering in sudden irritation how he thought she was supposed to drink water with her nostrils pinched closed. She took the glass from him and set it down. She still felt a little bit like the room was moving and she wasn't, but she was not going to faint. "I think I'm just tired from the drive."

Amber handed her two paper towels, one damp and one dry. "Did you drive it by yourself? No wonder you're tired. When was the last time you ate?"

"I had some cookies an hour ago." Which wasn't exactly food to fuel her.

Travis clearly realized the same. "That's my fault. I gave her sweets. I can make some dinner, though. Just give me twenty minutes."

Sighing, Sara used the damp towel to wipe the remnants of blood off her nose. She was pretty sure the bleeding had stopped. "Don't go to any trouble." She knew she should eat, but she was actually feeling a little sick to her stomach. She wanted a nap more than anything. "I should probably just get some sleep. I'll be fine after a few hours of rest."

Travis had already pulled tongs out of a drawer and he pointed them at her. "You're eating. End of story. I'm going to grill some chicken."

"I'll make a salad." Amber scooped up the bloody paper towel and pitched it in the trash bin. She washed her hands at the sink, then opened the refrigerator, clearly comfortable in Travis's kitchen.

Sara sat at the table, hot and wet, and not in a good way. "What can I do to help?"

"You can go and change out of those wet clothes, for one. That can't be good for you," Travis said, pulling raw chicken out of the refrigerator. He and Amber bumped into each other and he steadied her with a hand on her waist while she gave a giggle.

Ick. Sara felt nauseous again. She wasn't sure if it was because she hadn't really seen Travis with a girlfriend in a lot of years, or if it was because she didn't have that kind of easiness, intimacy, with a man.

Or maybe it was because when she pictured Travis being comfortable with a woman, it was her.

Disturbed by her own confusing thoughts, Sara stood straight up, knocking the chair backward onto the floor. "Oh, damn, sorry." She bent over and reached for the chair to right it.

Travis beat her to it. "I got it."

Feeling like a moron, she felt heat flooding her cheeks. Feelings of inadequacy flooded her and without responding to him,

Sara just bolted from the kitchen. She needed to get her bag out of the car to change anyway. But Travis followed her.

"Do you need help? Where are you going?"

Sara jogged down the wooden steps from his front porch to the brick walkway. "No, I got it. I'm just getting my bag so I can change."

"Don't be lifting a suitcase." The screen door swung shut as he followed her. "Let me get it."

"I'm not an invalid. I'm just pregnant." Sara opened the back door and reached in for her bag. She'd only tossed a few things in it anyway, her drive here impulsive.

When she stood and turned, she nearly collided with Travis.

"It's okay to accept help," he told her gently, prying the bag from her fingers.

"All I do is accept help from you." And she had nothing to offer him in return. She never had.

Travis didn't understand why Sara was actually fighting him to hold on to her bag. "I'm not going to look in it," he told her. "And I haven't seen you in two years, how can you say you always accept help from me?"

She made a sound of exasperation. "I don't care if you look in it. That's not the point. The point is, how am I going to stay here for the next four months, intruding on your life without a penny to my name?"

Travis studied her face. She was worried again, biting her lips, shoving her damp hair out of her eyes. She had been fine earlier. "We already talked about this. We're friends, family, whatever you want to call us. Damn it, Sara, you're important to me."

More important than he could ever fully express. He wanted that baby growing inside her to be his. He wanted her with him, in this house, building a life and a family together.

"I don't think Amber is going to appreciate this arrangement. She's a very sweet person, but as your girlfriend, I can't imagine having a pregnant woman in residence is going to thrill her."

Travis cleared his throat, not sure how to address the Amber issue. "She's not my girlfriend. We just casually date. And I'm sure she'll understand that I'm helping you out."

The truth was, if he had any sense, he would take things more seriously with Amber. She wanted to. But he could never bring himself to take it deeper. He hadn't even slept with her yet. There was no rational reason to be dragging his feet with Amber. She was one of the kindest women he'd ever met.

But she wasn't Sara.

"I don't want to interfere with your relationship." Sara gave a smile, her teeth still digging into her lip. "And I have to tell you, I really don't want to be in the next room when you two are having your naked fun."

He could just leave it alone. It didn't matter, really. But Travis wanted her to know the truth. "I've never had sex with Amber and I'm not planning to anytime soon."

Her mouth dropped open. Her eyes widened. Then she gave a short laugh. "Geez, now I feel like an even bigger slut."

"What! Why would you say that? For the last time, you're not a slut. I swear, if you say it again, I'll wash your mouth out with soap." It infuriated him to hear her trashing herself.

"It's true!" And she burst into tears again.

Travis didn't know what to do other than to pull her into his arms. Surprisingly, she let him, dropping her bag onto his feet. She burrowed into him, her embrace tight and desperate.

"No, it's not true." Then he just held her, petting her back, her hair.

"Sorry to interrupt," Amber said from behind him. "But I left a salad on the counter, and I'm going to head on home. I think you two need some time to catch up."

Travis shot her a grateful look over Sara's head. Amber didn't look pissed off, like most women would. She just looked like she was well aware Sara hadn't driven all the way to Rabbit Hash just for a visit.

"Thanks, Amber," he told her gratefully.

But Sara pulled back. "No, no, please don't leave. Stay and eat, honestly." She wiped her red eyes and bent over to grab her bag. "If either one of you is any nicer to me, I swear, I'm going to just die of embarrassment."

As she ran into the house, her gait uneven and awkward, her hand on her belly, Travis stared at her back in bewilderment. "What the hell . . ."

"The father ditched out, didn't he?" Amber asked.

"In a manner of speaking." Sara's predicament wasn't something that needed to be broadcast.

"Men who do that should be strung up. It takes two to make a baby, and two should raise it." She shook her head. "No wonder her emotions are running high. Not to mention the fact that she's always been in love with you."

Travis swiveled to face Amber, struck dumb. "What? Are you nuts? She isn't in love with me." He only wished she were.

Her eyebrows went up. "Lord, Travis, don't be so dense. That girl has been in love with you since middle school."

"If she were, wouldn't she say something?" he pointed out, his heart suddenly beating way too fast. "She wouldn't have run off to Charlotte."

"She doesn't tell you because she doesn't feel worthy of you."

Amber's voice softened. "You're an amazing man, and Sara has never felt worthy of any man's love, let alone yours."

Sara was definitely insecure, always had been. She'd been a hangdog of a kid, but she had always raised her chin up defiantly when she had needed to. That didn't mean that she wouldn't feel worthy of him. He wasn't anything special. Just a regular guy, trying to do right in life. "I don't think you can be certain on this one."

"I'd bet your life on it."

"My life?"

She laughed. "Well, I'm damn sure, but I'm not going to risk my own life. Now I'm going to leave and I want you to go into that house and tell Sara how you really feel about her. What she needs is you."

Hope suddenly bloomed in his chest. He wanted Amber to be right so bad his desire was painful. But her intent suddenly registered. "Wait. Are you breaking things off with me?"

"Yes. And I'm wishing y'all the best of luck."

Squeezing her arm in gratitude, Travis told her, "You're a good woman. There's a great guy out there who will be damn lucky to find you."

"Maybe someday."

"You sure you don't want to stay for dinner?" he asked out of pure politeness.

She smiled. "No. But thank you."

With a wave, she left, and Travis turned and stared at his house.

Inside was everything he'd ever wanted.

But did he have the courage to go for it?

four

✳

Sara couldn't sleep. It was hot in Travis's guest room and there was zero breeze. The baby was moving aggressively, Sara had to use the bathroom, and she was dying of thirst. Since it was midnight, she figured she could take care of two out of three of her needs without waking up Travis, though nothing could be done about the heat.

Climbing out of bed, she debated getting dressed, but after wiping sweat off her forehead, her upper lip, and between her bra, she axed that idea. If she was this hot at six months pregnant in mid-May, she was not looking forward to August. Nor did she think her breasts could get any bigger. Always small-chested, she now found it was more comfortable to wear a bra all the time to control the burgeoning balloons that had inflated above her rib cage.

Opening the door, she peeked down the hall to make sure the light was out in Travis's room, then headed for the bathroom.

After stealing all the cherry tomatoes out of Amber's salad, she had headed to the guest room while the couple had talked out in the drive. When Travis had come in, wanting to talk to her, she had told him she didn't feel well and just wanted to sleep. He had pressed her for a minute, but she had stuck to her guns, and he'd gone away.

She just hadn't been able to stomach a dinner with Travis and Amber. They were good people and she was just a screwup. She didn't think she could sit there and not feel bad about herself. And they wouldn't want her to feel bad. Which would just make her feel even worse.

Sitting on the toilet, she gave a sigh. She couldn't stay with Travis, as tempting as it was. She couldn't interfere with his life like that. Nor could she feel particularly good about herself, knowing she had no job, no money, and no baby daddy. It was time to go back to Charlotte and stand on her own two feet. She couldn't expect Travis to fix her problems, any more than she could expect Evan Monroe to.

After flushing and washing her hands, she checked again to make sure she hadn't woken up Travis. There was no sound coming from his room. Heading to the kitchen, she wondered if he had fruit juice. She was craving it, that cold, sweet tanginess, and any flavor would do.

Wiping her dewy forehead again, she lifted her hair up and tried to ignore the dampness at her neck. How could she be this hot when she was only in a bra and panties? Grabbing a glass out of the cabinet, she set it on the counter next to the refrigerator and pulled the door open. The cool air floating across her legs and tummy was a welcome relief. Closing her eyes for a minute, she just sighed and let it cool off her damp skin.

"Are you okay?"

Sara jumped, bumping her belly on the door as she turned toward Travis. He was standing in the doorway in his boxer shorts, looking sleepy and concerned.

"I'm fine." She told herself not to look at his chest. That resolve lasted about three seconds, and then she was taking in the span of his shoulders and the firmness of his biceps in the moonlight streaming in from the kitchen window.

Sadie padded past Travis and licked Sara's hand, forcing her to glance down and remember that she herself was not nearly as dressed as she should be under the circumstances.

"Are you hungry? I can fix something for you. I really wish you'd eaten dinner."

"I'm just thirsty. I was looking for some juice."

"I have grape juice in there somewhere." Travis started toward her.

"I got it," she told him, pulling the door closed a little with her behind it so he couldn't see her sweaty pregnant body.

"I may have to dig for it in the back."

"I can find it!"

Travis's eyebrows shot up. "Stop being so stubborn." He pulled the door open all the way and came around, his hand reaching out, right past her backside, to get the juice. "It's behind the . . .

His voice trailed off and he snatched his hand back. "Sorry, I didn't realize . . ."

Feeling her cheeks go pink as Travis gawked at her nearly nakedness, Sara tried to figure out if there was a way to turn to make her less obvious, but there wasn't. No matter which direction she was facing, he was going to get an eyeful of giant breasts, big belly, and her brand-new booty. All sweaty. Every inch of it.

"I was hot. I didn't think you'd be up this time of night."

"Sorry, I . . ." Travis was just staring at her, his eyes running from her neck to her knees, up and down and back again.

"Will you stop gawking at me?"

"It's just . . ." Finally, his lifted his eyes to her face. "Sara, you look beautiful. Amazing." His hand came out like he wanted to touch her belly. "I've never seen anyone look so . . . beautiful."

Travis wished he had better words to describe her, but that was the best he could do. He couldn't believe how ripe and soft and glowing she was, her skin dewy, her tummy firm and round, her body free of all those sharp bony angles for the first time in the entire length of their friendship.

"I don't look beautiful," she scoffed. "I'm sweaty."

Maybe, but it only added to the exotic quality of the picture she made, standing there in a simple cotton bra and panties, their plain white lace trim bright in the moonlight against her lightly tanned skin. The bra was too small, her newly developed breasts spilling over the cups, and her panties were low in front, and exposing a lot of her firm bottom in back. She did look beautiful, and sensual, and feminine.

Seeing her naked belly without the T-shirt she'd had on earlier when he had touched her and felt the baby move urged him to do what he had been lying in bed all night contemplating. He couldn't stop himself. He had to at least try for the future he wanted.

"Sara, I love you," he told her, reaching out and taking her hand. "Will you marry me?"

A gasp flew out of her mouth and her eyes were like dinner plates. "What? What do you mean?"

"I mean, I want you to do me the honor of becoming my wife. I want to be with you here, in Rabbit Hash, raising this baby together. As a family." Each word he spoke out loud rang stronger and truer as Travis found the nerve to tell Sara what he felt, what he knew. "I want to spend the rest of my life with you."

But she shook her head rapidly. "You don't have to marry me out of pity. I'll be all right, I really will. You deserve something more than being burdened with cleaning up my mess, and this is making me stronger."

"I don't want to marry you out of pity. I want to marry you because I love you." He leaned down and whispered it in her ear. "I love you."

She shivered, her head tilting slightly toward his. "Like a brother?"

Inhaling the scent of her flesh and her shampoo, Travis ran his thumb across her fingers as he held her hand. "No. The way a man loves a woman. The way a husband loves his wife."

"What about Amber?"

Travis dropped a kiss on her earlobe and brushed his lips over her jaw, murmuring, "Amber is wonderful, but she's not the one for me. It's always been you."

"Really?" She sounded doubtful, like what he was saying was incomprehensible.

He hoped that didn't mean her feelings weren't the same. "Really. I love you." He kissed the corner of her mouth. "I love you." He kissed the other corner. "I love you." Looking deep in her eyes, hoping she would believe him, hoping that she could love him even a tenth of the way he did her, Travis kissed her ripe lips.

Sara couldn't believe what was happening. Travis was kissing her. He had told her he loved her. He had asked her to marry him. She didn't know what to think or say or feel, so she poured all of her emotion, her elation, her wonderment, into her kiss.

He felt wonderful, his hands on what was left of her waist, his mouth warm and delicious. She gripped his shoulders and kissed him back, amazed that this was real, that all her girlhood fantasies were coming true. Throwing her arms around his neck, Sara kissed him on and on and on, sighing when his tongue swept over hers.

When she finally pulled back slightly and stared at him in elation, she told him, "I love you, too. I've loved you since I was thirteen years old."

"You have?" Travis grinned and pulled her closer to him. "So that means you'll marry me?"

"Yes." She didn't need to think about it at all. There was no man she'd rather be with than Travis. He had her heart and her back, and he always had.

"So we're getting married then." He hand shifted to her belly. "And we're having a baby. God, Sara, I'm so happy."

Sara felt an absolute peace and happiness descend over her, settling into her bones. "You'll be an awesome father. The best. This baby is so lucky to have you."

"I'm the lucky one." Travis stared into her eyes. "I have you. And a daughter."

Travis's hands had started roaming over her body, up to her sensitive breasts, down past her belly as he kissed her. Sara sighed in delight. If she could give back every sexual experience for just one night with Travis she would, and here he was telling her she was going to be lucky enough to have her whole life to share a bed with him. She wanted him desperately, her heart and hormones on overload. Yet she knew what she needed to do.

Stepping back, she ignored the ache between her thighs and the way her body responded to Travis. "I know this is going to sound weird, but as much as I want to make love to you, I really want to wait until we're married."

Travis just stared at her, a healthy erection visible in his boxers and lust mixed with love in his eyes. Yet he didn't question her. He just swallowed hard and said, "Okay."

Which made her love him even more. Sara rushed to explain. "It's just that, I've had casual sex, and it's like my yes doesn't have any value if I've never said no, do you know what I mean? I want the moment that we take that step together to be special. I want to be your wife when we make love for the first time. All yours, with the past truly the past."

Hoping he didn't think she was nuts, given that she had admitted to two one-night stands just a few months earlier, Sara ran her fingers through his hair, down his cheeks, to his lips. It amazed her that he wanted her. That they were going to be together, forever.

Travis nodded. "I know what you mean. You never have to worry about me judging you or caring about your past, but I'm all for anything that makes you feel good and shows that this is special, something different from the ordinary."

He kissed her fingertips. "I'm so glad you came home, baby."

"Me, too." Sara felt the tears welling up in her eyes. "I'm home and I'm never leaving."

razor's edge

✳

SYLVIA DAY

acknowledgments

My gratitude goes to Cynthia D'Alba, whose early input in this story really helped me pull it together. I send hugs to Shayla Black, whose friendship has brought me much joy and support on my writer's journey, and to Lori Foster, whose Brava Novella contest led to the sale of my first book. What a thrill it is to share a book with you, Lori! (As well as Erin, Kathy, and Kate with whom I've also shared drinks, hotel rooms, and too many laughs to count.)

one

✳

When Jack Killigrew's phone rang, it usually meant someone's life was on the line. Since he was on leave from the U.S. Marshals Service office in Albuquerque, the only calls he would be receiving were in his capacity as a Special Operations Group deputy. As such, he was a last resort and on call twenty-four hours a day. His twelve-man response team was activated only *after* the shit had already hit the fan.

There were a lot of emotions that filtered through Jack when he was called in, but relief wasn't usually one them. Right now, however, he'd give just about anything for an excuse to head in the opposite direction.

His fellow deputies would laugh if they knew how edgy he was getting with every mile that passed. As a SOG deputy marshal—a Shadow Stalker—he squared off with hardened criminals and suicidal terrorists as a matter of course. He hunted and apprehended the country's most-wanted fugitives. He did his job with mechanical precision, never breaking a sweat. The guys called him "Iron Jack," the man who'd do anything. He faced death as if he had nothing to lose or nothing to live for.

Yet the thought of facing Rachel Tse was shredding him.

"Killigrew," he answered via the hands-free Bluetooth control in his steering wheel. He'd already noted the lack of a shoulder on the two-lane road. With agricultural fields on each side of him, turning his long Chevy Silverado around wouldn't be easy.

"Jack."

Christ. The voice on the other end of the line reverberated through him like a gunshot report.

"Rachel," he replied gruffly, slowly recovering from the husky sound of her voice. "Everything all right?"

"Yes." She said the word breathlessly, which made him hard. "I was wondering if you'd be here in time for lunch."

"Lunch?" God, he was screwed. His best friend's widow was winded from pulling together a birthday party for his eight-year-old godson and he was getting a boner.

It had been two years since he'd last seen her, but apparently time didn't matter. He'd put off this reunion as long as he could, but the time had come to deal with it. Steve's last request had eaten into him far enough to become hazardous. Jack couldn't allow his own personal crap to jeopardize his team any more than it already had.

"Jack? Did I lose you?"

"I'm here. I was just calculating the possibility of my arriving in time for lunch. I don't think it's going to happen."

There was a pause, as if she sensed the lie.

He hated bullshitting her, but he couldn't see her today. He needed time to get his head on straight. He hadn't taken a leave of absence in years and without work to occupy him, he found himself thinking too damn much about her. Visions of her blond hair fisted in his hands . . . her taut, sweet nipples tightening against his tongue . . . her long, lithe legs spreading in invitation . . .

Getting that obsession under control was a necessity if he had any hope of convincing her she was off the hook as far as he was concerned. He was still reeling from Steve's request that he look after her if she was ever left alone. Jack realized his friend must have known how he felt. As careful as he'd been to hide his longing, something must have betrayed him.

And that killed him. No man should have to deal with knowing his best friend is in love with his wife.

"Where are you?" she pressed.

"I haven't reached King City yet." Jack had passed King City long ago and was about twenty minutes away from Monterey. He would pick up the keys to his cottage in Carmel from the property managers who rented it out for him, then grab a six-pack of beer and hunker down for the night. He'd get his bearings and be better capable of facing her in the morning.

"Let's make it dinner, then. Riley's spending the night at a friend's house so I can wrap his gifts without him peeking. It'll be just you and me. We can catch up."

Just her and him. At night. With Riley gone until morning? Yeah, right. Jack could imagine the mess running through Rachel's head now. She'd been crazy about Steve. Madly in love. If she thought Steve wanted them together, she'd make it work, even though he scared the shit out of her. Part of his job was reading people, and as focused on her as his instincts were, there wasn't a damn thing about her he didn't register. When he walked into the room, she became skittish—nostrils flaring, eyes widening, body moving restlessly. Her primal reaction aroused every predatory sense in his body, making him edgy and sharpening his hunger for her.

"How about I take you two out to breakfast in the morning?" His voice was rough with desire. "Then I'll help you finish setting up for his party."

"All right. But if you make it into town sooner, call me. And be careful on the road."

It wasn't a casual warning for Rachel. Steve had been killed by a drunk driver on the way home from work one night, changing all of their lives forever.

Jack hung up. Shifting on the seat, he adjusted the fit of his jeans, which was now extremely uncomfortable. Ahead of him, the road to perdition wound its way through the tiny town of Spreckles.

It was going to be a long week.

Two

✳

Jack twisted off the top of his fourth beer and tossed the metal cap in the trash. Then he headed back out the open sliding glass doors to his small fenced-in patio. His bare feet sank into the sand and he drank deeply, absently admiring the streaks of orange and pink flaring across the sky. As the sun dipped below the horizon, the temperature fell along with it. It was much cooler here than Albuquerque, but thoughts of Rachel kept him warm enough to go shirtless.

He was beginning to think drinking had been a bad idea. The alcohol wasn't smoothing the jagged edges of his lust at all. He was acutely aware of the fact that Rachel was home alone right now and he was only a short drive away. If he left now, he could be inside her within thirty minutes. He had no doubt he could seduce her. He also had no doubt that she'd regret it in the morning.

It wasn't her fault he was strung out from wanting her. She'd never led him on or enticed him. Rachel was shy and quiet unless she was surrounded by people she felt comfortable with, an after-effect of being raised by an aunt who reminded her daily what a burden she was. At least in his childhood, when he made himself invisible, he'd been left alone. She had been verbally abused and tormented no matter what she'd done.

His cell phone rang and he cursed as he withdrew it from his pocket. The caller ID told him it was Brian Simmons, a fellow deputy and a guy who'd saved Jack's ass more than once.

"Killigrew," he answered.

"So, have you seen her yet?"

"No."

"Man, that would have been my first stop. She owns a cake shop; she might be huge and your problem would be solved."

"Riley e-mails me pictures. No such luck." And the fact was, Jack doubted it would make a difference to him if she had put on weight. He was attracted to the whole package, not just her looks. Besides, a few weeks sharing his bed would take care of any extra pounds.

"Well, then, you should think about what you're throwing away. First off, there are those cupcakes of hers. If she stops sending them, the guys might have to hurt you. Second, I'd give anything to be with Layla right now. It kills me knowing she's out there somewhere in WitSec—hopefully, still in love with me—and I can't have her. You don't have that problem; you've got permission. And although I haven't seen much evidence of it, I'm sure you must have some charm to you. Lay it on her and see what happens."

Jack knew he wasn't what Rachel needed. He had nothing to offer her. Steve had a large extended family that enfolded her with open arms; Jack had only his job, and her and Riley. Steve was the steady and dependable type, a chiropractor who'd come home for dinner every night and was there for breakfast in the morning; Jack never knew when he'd be leaving or when he could come back. Rachel had lived with enough neglect and abandonment as a child. She didn't need it in her adult life as well.

"She deserves better than me," Jack said.

"Yeah, you're right."

Against his determination to be in a shitty mood, Jack's mouth curved. "Fuck you, too."

"Call me if you need anything."

"Same to you." Jack shoved his phone back in his pocket and was lifting his beer to his lips when he heard a car door shut in what sounded like his driveway.

Pivoting in the sand, he canvassed the public beach just beyond his short picket fence. His attention narrowed on the side of his house just before a lipstick red dress rounded the corner. The slender body it encased caught his eye next and held it.

"I guessed you'd be out here," Rachel said, waving. She headed toward the gate with a square cake pan in one hand.

Jack wanted to do the gentlemanly thing and let her in, but he couldn't move. She'd cut her hair short and wore it in sexy, tousled curls that exposed her slender neck and emphasized her fine-boned features. As she passed by him, he saw the back—or, rather, lack of a back—to her dress. Held up by thin straps, the material dipped down to the upper swell of her buttocks, betraying the lack of a bra.

Jesus. She'd lost her mind coming around him dressed like that.

"What are you doing here?" he asked without finesse, his gut aching from a soul-deep longing. He rubbed at the center of his chest with the bottom edge of his bottle but found no relief.

"You said no to lunch and dinner but didn't decline dessert."

She came through the gate, her long legs on display thanks to the short skirt and two-inch slit at her right thigh. There was no hesitation in her approach, which changed the rules of engagement. She'd never outright avoided him, but she hadn't gone out of her way to be near him either.

Lifting onto her tiptoes, she balanced herself with a hand over his heart and pressed a quick kiss to his cheek. "You look fabulous, Jack," she murmured. "It's really good to see you again."

Jack wondered if she was aware of the soft note of invitation in her words or how it made his heart race beneath her palm. He didn't want her under a sense of obligation. He didn't want to be the tie that bound her to memories of her past with Steve. And he sure as hell didn't want her martyring herself in his bed.

"But," she went on, stepping back, "I'm not so sure you're happy to see me."

He took the opportunity to breathe, sucking in the salt-tinged air in an effort to clear his head. "I'm just surprised but in a good way."

Rachel smiled. Her fingertips slid down his arm to his wrist, then circled the neck of his beer bottle. She tugged it loose and took a long pull, her lips wrapped around the top and her throat working with each swallow.

His mind fell straight into the gutter.

He turned as she skirted him and went into the house. He hadn't bothered to turn the lights on and she didn't, either. Instead, she used the fading sun as a guide to reach the kitchen island. A moment later a flare in the shadows preceded the igniting of a candlewick. The property management company had scattered groupings of seashell-covered candles all over the house, part of the nautical theme they'd utilized throughout.

"I'd forgotten how charming this place is," she called out to him.

Jack debated the wisdom of following her inside, knowing the leash on his hunger was tenuous at best. "I can't take credit for it. It's staged by professionals to appeal to the vacation renters."

"I wish you'd reserve more time here for yourself." She lit another candle. "We'd love to see you more often."

"I'm thinking about it." Knowing it would be ridiculous to keep shouting at her from outside, Jack entered the living room. "I'd like to start spending more time with Riley, now that he's older."

"He'd love that." Turning away from him, she searched the cupboards.

"The plates are to the left of the fridge," he directed. He watched the way the hem of her skirt lifted a couple tantalizing inches as she reached upward. Feeling like a randy dog, he looked away, then couldn't resist looking back again. "What have you got there?"

She looked over her shoulder and her mouth curved. "Better Than Sex cake."

Jack searched for a sign that she was joking. "Whoever came up with that doesn't get out much."

Her laughter hit him like a punch to the gut. He'd always loved that carefree sound. It said so much about her. She made him laugh, too, with her e-mailed stories about hysterical run-ins with customers. He'd startled his fellow deputies more than once by laughing aloud at something she sent him. She brought light into his life, which made him even more aware of the darkness he could bring into hers.

It figured he would fall for the one woman he was the worst possible fit for.

Kicking off her low-heeled sandals by the island, she padded over with a single plate in her hand. "I make a cupcake-sized version of this at the store. It's one of my most popular flavors."

"Everything you make is popular. You're an awesome cook."

"Thank you. I can't grill, though, so I'm relying on you to handle the hot dogs and burgers tomorrow."

"Put me to work. That's one of the reasons I'm here."

One dirty blond brow rose with challenge. "Don't complain later when I take you up on that."

Again, there was a suggestive undertone to her words. He forced his gaze away and down at the cake, noting what looked to be caramel drizzle over the top. He wanted to drizzle caramel all over her body and tongue it off slowly. Endlessly. Licking through it to the sweeter flesh beneath.

"Here." She stabbed at the cake with the fork in her hand and lifted a bite to his lips.

He opened his mouth. The cake was rich but not too rich. "Very good," he praised, happy to see her cheeks flush with pleasure. "But it's not better than sex."

Her blue eyes sparkled with silent laughter. "Prove it."

three

The tension that gripped Jack at her bold statement was so tangible Rachel felt it. She waited with bated breath, her heart skipping at the scorching look he raked her with. That sharply focused intensity had been too much for her when she'd been younger.

Dear God . . . he was gorgeous. Impossibly sexy. Standing there in only button-fly jeans with the top button undone. He was leaner than she remembered, his features more angular. She bet he wasn't taking care of himself. He was likely working too hard and not eating often enough. There wasn't an ounce of extraneous flesh on him. Every muscle was clearly, deliciously defined. His arms, his pectorals, his abdomen.

He could drive a woman crazy, especially with that air of danger clinging to him. It was evident, just by looking at him, that there were very few things he wouldn't do if necessary. There were scars all over him—a puckered bullet hole by his shoulder, slashing scars across his abdomen, an old burn mark on his forearm, just to name a few.

As long as Rachel had known him, he'd always lived life on a razor's edge, first as a U.S. Army Ranger and now as a deputy marshal. Any woman who loved him would have to accept the hazards inherent in the work he did. His job would always be his mistress. It would pull him from his wife's bed at all hours of the night, luring him into deadly situations while the scent of his desire still clung to her skin.

Rachel hadn't believed she could ever take on a man like him, but she'd underestimated her capacity to grow and change. Since she and Jack had first met, she'd had a wonderful eight-year marriage. She had persevered through an ectopic pregnancy, the death of her mother and beloved husband, the launching of her own small business, and the terrifying process of learning how to be a single mother.

She was no longer the woman who'd been married to Steve Tse. She was now the woman who'd survived him, and they were two very different people.

The woman she was today was more than capable of tackling a challenge like Jack Killigrew. And by God, she intended to.

He finally spoke. "What did you just say?"

Rachel wondered if he knew the impact his low, whisky-rough voice had on women. "It's been a long time for me, Jack."

"Hell." He retreated. Shoving his hands through his short dark hair, he turned his back to her. "You shouldn't have drunk that beer."

Lord have mercy. The way he moved and spoke was intensely sensual. Just the flexing of his muscles was totally erotic.

She became even more determined to have all that virility focused on her. "I don't need false courage to hit on you."

He glared at her over his shoulder. "This isn't you."

"It's me now. You've stayed away for two years. A lot has changed."

Pivoting, he faced her again. "I figured you and the Tses would close ranks while you dealt with Steve's death. I stayed out of the way."

Rachel set the plate and fork down on the glass-topped end table. "I'm glad to hear that's why you've been so distant. I thought maybe it was me."

His jaw clenched and she knew she'd struck a cord. The confirmation hurt more than she'd thought it would.

"I would have asked you to be here," she said, "if I could have used you. I feel comfortable doing that. Even before—when Steve was still here—I knew I could count on you."

He snorted. "You never quite got used to me."

"You're larger than life, Jack. I've never met anyone like you before or since." Her arms crossed. The raw magnetism and intense carnality that once overwhelmed her now set her libido on a steady simmer. She hadn't realized until she started dating again that she was comparing her dates to Jack and finding they left her cold. "You are rarely entirely comfortable with me, either," she shot back.

"So why do this? Why ask me this?"

Rachel was confused. He was looking at her like he wanted to nail her to the nearest wall, but he sounded like that was the last thing he was interested in. "Have you looked in a mirror lately? Do you hear the sound of your voice, all gravelly and sexy as hell? Are you completely oblivious to the bad-boy vibe you give off? Because I'm not blind or deaf."

Jack's dark and steady gaze was knife-sharp. His brows were drawn together in a fearsome glower, but she wasn't intimidated.

She was quickly picking up on the fact that he became the most fierce when his equanimity was threatened. Which meant, for better or worse, she got to him.

"You're physically attracted to me," she said, daring him to deny it. "So what's the problem?"

He mimicked her pose, crossing his arms and displaying powerful biceps. "I'm flattered, but we've got too much baggage—and a future with Riley between us—to make casual sex work."

Why would anything casual delve into baggage?

She looked away, hiding the spark of hope she felt. Jack knew damn well there was nothing casual about the sexual tension between them, and that scared him. Of course, he wouldn't be the first drop-dead gorgeous guy to have commitment issues. In all the years she'd known him, he had never once had a steady relationship. If an event required a date, he'd bring one, but Rachel never saw him with the same woman more than once.

Needing to think, she picked up the plate and moved back to the kitchen. She took a bite of the cake and contemplated her next move. This was her first-ever seduction; she had no Plan B to fall back on. Giving up wasn't an option.

"Rachel?" Jack's voice was soft in the semi-darkness.

She ate a little more. "Hmm?"

"You got awfully quiet."

"I'm thinking."

He exhaled harshly, his head falling back until he was staring at the white-washed wooden beam ceiling. "I'm sure if you gave dating a shot, you'd find someone you liked."

"I like *you*." She spoke around another bite. She had long admired his fierce loyalty, but over the last two years since Steve passed on, she'd come to know Jack even better via his role as Riley's godfather. Through the e-mails and phone calls he shared with her son, she discovered Jack possessed a deep capacity to love and nurture, a marked patience while teaching, and the ability to be open-minded and nonjudgmental. And she damn well couldn't discount how just the sound of his voice turned her on. "But I have been dating."

His head snapped upright. "Who? Do I know him?"

"Do you care?"

"Of course I care. I want to make sure you and Riley are all right."

Rachel met his gaze directly. "I would never put Riley in jeopardy over a guy."

"I didn't mean it like that."

She eyed him surreptitiously, noting his edginess while she felt amazingly calm. He made her feel safe enough to be bold. He didn't yet know what that meant to her, but she intended to show him.

Jack moved toward the open sliding glass door. "What you and Steve had was special."

"Once in a lifetime," she agreed. She'd been the right girl to Steve's right guy at the right time. And she felt that way about Jack. She was so sure they were what each other needed; it didn't seem possible that she could be wrong. If he just gave her a shot, maybe he'd see she was the missing ingredient in his life. And if she ended up being the one in their relationship who loved the other one more, that was okay with her.

"You just have to give it some more time. And be a little open-minded."

"Oh my God." She set her fork down. "Are *you* giving *me* dating advice? No offense, but what the hell do you know about having a serious relationship?"

Jack leaned his back into the doorjamb and shoved his hands

in his pockets, giving her a breathtaking silhouette of long legs and firm pectorals. "Nothing at all. I just know Steve is going to be a hard act to follow. You might have to make some compromises, but you can be happy again. You can find a good guy for you."

"You mean I might have to settle." She straightened and pushed the plate away, ignoring the urge to clean up after herself. Damned if she'd fall into mommy role right now. She was dressed to kill and primed. And she was playing to win, even if that meant playing a little dirty. "I've never settled on the wrong guy in my life, and I'm not going to start now."

"Then what the hell are you doing here?" he said coldly.

"Going down in flames, apparently." She reached for both spaghetti straps of her dress. If he needed to believe she could handle a no-strings-attached one-night stand, she could give him that impression. Then she'd work her way into him from the outside. She just had to start somewhere, and standing on opposing sides of the room wasn't cutting it. "But hey, if that's the way this is going to end, I might as well make sure I gave it my best shot."

Flicking the thin straps off her shoulders, Rachel held her breath. Her dress slithered down her body and puddled on the floor.

four

Jack stared, stunned and aching, as Rachel went from dressed to mouthwateringly naked in a split second. He swore. His knees weakened. He was grateful to be leaning against the house. There wasn't a scrap of material on her. No bra, which he'd known, and no panties to cover her waxed pussy, which he was grateful he hadn't known about or she'd have been bent over the couch already.

Sucking in air like he'd just run for miles, he devoured every inch of her pale body with a ravenous gaze. The proud angle of her chin and shoulders, her small but lushly curved breasts, her flat stomach, and her mile-long legs. She turned in a circle with her arms outstretched, showing off her elegantly curved spine and perky little ass.

"Last call," she said, facing him again. "If this doesn't catch your interest, I'll head out. You can keep the cake."

Christ, she was sassy and bold. Jack had no idea who the

woman standing in front of him was. It damn sure wasn't the Rachel he remembered, a woman who'd coped with her vindictive aunt by staying away from home as much as possible. Staying away from home led to her being assaulted when she was sixteen. Steve didn't elaborate and Jack hadn't pried. That one word was more than enough.

The walls started closing in. Sweat misted his skin and the knot in his gut tightened painfully. He could've said no to the old Rachel. With this one, he was a goner.

Her seduction was the worst sort of perdition. He was terrified he was going to fuck this all up and push Rachel and Riley away, the only people he really considered his family. The people he called on holidays and sent gifts to. The people he thought of when the chips were down and he needed a reason to get his ass out alive, if worse for wear. If he lost them, he'd have nothing. He'd forever be worried that they might be in trouble or need something, and his assistance wouldn't be welcomed.

"You're killing me here, Rachel," he said gruffly.

"Well, it's only fair." Her arms lowered to her sides. "I'm dying for you."

He straightened. He was going to ask her why she was here and if she said Steve's name, he was walking out to the beach and not stopping until the sun came up. If she didn't mention Steve, well . . . he couldn't turn her away. He would take her to bed and try to find some closure. He'd say as much as it was possible to say, do all that it was possible to do, and somehow find a way to act in the morning like nothing had changed between them. He prayed that would ease the way for them to move forward without any awkwardness. If there was the added bonus of her feeling like she'd closed the door on her past with Steve and could move forward unencumbered, he could live with that, as long as he didn't have to know about it.

"Why me?" he bit out.

Her arms fell to her sides. She met his gaze head-on and said, "Because I want to be with someone I feel connected to. Someone who isn't going to fumble around and leave me hanging at the end. A man who knows his way around a woman's body and doesn't need me to tell him what I want."

That was it, then. He was a dead man walking.

Jack strode forward in a controlled rush, his focus narrowed on Rachel and his goal of getting inside her as swiftly as possible. He was highly conscious of how short a time he had with her. A lifetime wouldn't be long enough and he'd been given only a handful of hours.

As he zeroed in, he could see her tremble, but her gaze didn't waver. When he caught her waist in his hands and lifted her, she gasped but didn't recoil. Instead, her slender arms wrapped around his neck and she buried her face in his throat. He was damp with perspiration, but she didn't seem to care. She nuzzled against him, her tongue darting out and licking. Impossibly, his cock swelled further. He was so hard it hurt, his dick throbbing in his jeans, demanding relief from his torment.

He headed toward the hallway leading to the bedroom, holding her partly away from him so they actually stood a chance of making it that far.

Rachel had other ideas. Using her arms for leverage, she pulled up enough to sling her legs around his waist. The brush of her satin-soft pussy against his abdomen caused him to stumble. He aimed for the wall to the right of the hallway entrance, one hand reaching out to cushion her back from the impact.

"Oh God," she breathed in his ear. "You make me so hot."

"*Rachel.*" He pressed his temple to hers and closed his eyes, fighting for control. His chest was heaving with gasping breaths, keeping him ever aware of her breasts flattened against him.

Her fingers pushed into his hair, tugging forcefully until his head lifted. She crushed her soft mouth against his, holding him at the angle she wanted. When his lips parted for a sharp inhalation, she took advantage. Her tongue darted inside, licking and stroking in a hot wet kiss.

Jack groaned, abandoning hope of reining himself in. She was going at him full throttle, her thighs flexing around his hips, her torso undulating against him. If he hadn't wanted her so badly, it would have been molestation. Or a mauling. As it was, he was so damn turned on by her enthusiasm he was about to come in his pants. After what she'd been through in her youth, the fact that she trusted him enough to be so open and aggressive roused every possessive and protective instinct he had. As much as he'd loved her before, it was nothing compared to what he felt for her now.

He tore his mouth away. "Rachel . . . sweetheart . . . slow down. Let me get a grip."

"Noooo," she moaned, pressing kisses along his whisker-rough jaw until she reached his ear. "*Hurry up.* If you don't get inside me soon, I'm going to self-combust, I swear. Or go off without you. This caveman thing is sexy as hell."

He would have laughed if he hadn't felt like he was drowning. She had no idea what she was asking for, but she was about to get it.

RACHEL sank her teeth into Jack's earlobe and tugged on his hair. The dark, exotic scent of his heated skin made her feel wild and uninhibited. And the edge to his voice, the strain evident in his tone and the tension in his body, incited her into pushing him as far as he would go.

As far as she would go, and beyond . . .

She was acutely aware of the nearby open sliding glass door and the proximity of the public beach beyond it. Distantly, she heard voices and music. If the lights had been on in the house, she and Jack would have been on full display. As it was, they were shrouded in darkness while the outside was bathed in the faint light of the rising moon. Still, the risk of discovery was thrilling.

Jack steadied their entwined bodies with one knee against the wall. His hand stroked down her back to her buttocks, where he squeezed the firm swell of one cheek, kneading it, making her really damn glad she'd done all those lunges and squats in preparation for this night. She'd trained like she was preparing for a marathon, expecting a night in Jack's bed would be equally strenuous.

God, she couldn't wait, and she felt conflicted about that. It had been twelve years since any other man but Steve had made love to her, and Jack was so very different. There was nothing comfortable or familiar about his touch, yet it was just what she needed. Just want she wanted. His hands felt as if they should be on her, touching her. Not because he was so confident about it, but because it just felt *right*.

When his hand slid lower, she froze, every muscle tensing in anticipation of his touch going just where she ached for it. Everything was happening so fast, yet not fast enough.

"Shh," he soothed, nuzzling beneath her ear with his lips. Spreading his fingers, he reached between her parted legs from behind.

Rachel sensed the change in him. It felt like the calm before a storm, when the temperature increased, the wind stilled, and the air became heavy with expectation. She shivered, so damn worked up she felt as if the slightest touch could set her off. Her skin felt too tight and hot. Her chest too constricted.

Leaning his head back, he looked at her with heavy-lidded eyes. Watching her, as two fingers slipped inside her.

The sound that escaped her was thready with need. Her pussy rippled with greed, sucking at the two thick male fingers sliding in her to the knuckles. The tension bled away, her muscles slackening as pleasure coursed through her veins.

"You're so tight." His voice was rough as sandpaper. His fingers withdrew to the tips, then thrust deep. Her quivering thighs lost their grip on his hips.

Jack pulled free of her clinging pussy and cupped the backs of her legs, bending down to help her feet touch the floor. She fell back against the wall with her eyes closed, her palms pressed flat against the wainscoting, her breathing quick and shallow.

He caught her face in his hands and kissed her, his mouth slanting across hers with a ferocity he hadn't displayed earlier. Whatever resistance he'd felt before was gone, replaced by a sharply focused determination that made her heart race.

She'd had it so wrong. There was no way she could have prepared for this. As his mouth moved along her cheek to her throat, suckling and nibbling the tender skin, she felt herself unraveling. All the stability and structure she'd forged for herself melted away beneath the scorching heat of Jack's single-minded desire. There was no hesitation in his approach, no tentativeness in his touch, no caution in the command he exerted on her body.

His hands moved from her jaw to her shoulders, then down her arms. As the liquid heat of his mouth surrounded a tightly puckered nipple, he gripped her rib cage in his hands and pulled her to him, arching her backward so that her breasts thrust toward him like a gift.

Her eyes flew open, focusing on the shadowed ceiling above her. The feel of Jack's tongue fluttering over her nipple was so exquisite, she thought she might orgasm. Her stomach quivered and her hips writhed. Her clit pulsed with need.

"Suck me," she begged, needing a quick release to take the biting edge off her lust.

He did as she asked but not in the way she needed. Not fast and not gentle. Every slow, hard suck radiated downward, intensifying the hunger gripping her in an iron fist. The hot tugging at her breast was echoed in her womb, with sharp rhythmic contractions spurring her need to climax and driving her insane.

"Faster."

His mouth moved across to the neglected nipple, his teeth scraping over the hardened crest, pausing at the tip to flicker his tongue across it.

"Jack. Please." Her head fell to the side, her flushed cheek pressing against the cool drywall. "More."

"Beautiful," he murmured. "Soft and sweet. Too sweet to rush tasting them."

"They're smaller than you like," she gasped.

His next suck was so strong it brought pleasure bordering on pain. She whimpered and dug her short fingernails into her palms. He drew hard on her again, then soothed the throbbing point with soft licks.

"*You're* what I like." His hands moved in counterpoint to the recent fierceness of his mouth, his thumbs stroking tenderly across the crease beneath each breast, gentling her. Two sides of the same man—one careful and reverent, the other rough and wild. "Every inch of you."

Urging her back against the wall, his hands slid down past her waist to her hips, his knees bending as he moved lower. He kissed the moist spot between her breasts. "This inch."

His tongue followed his downward path, licking along the center of her stomach to dip his tongue in her navel. "And this one."

When he gripped her buttocks in each hand and pulled her hips forward, electricity raced across her skin. He nuzzled against her bare mound. "Definitely this one."

"Jack . . ." She didn't know how she'd survive it if he put his mouth on her. She didn't know how she'd survive if he didn't.

"Hold yourself open for me," he ordered, his voice husky. "Let me see you."

Her gaze locked with his. Although he spoke with command, there was a softness to the way he looked at her that prevented shyness or second guessing. Inhaling deeply, she reached down and exposed her pussy . . . and so much more of herself than he could possibly know.

five

"Very pretty."

The admiration in Jack's voice flowed through Rachel in a warm rush of pleasure. He blew a gentle stream of air over her and she whimpered.

"And so sensitive," he murmured. "Your clit is peeping out at me, greedy thing."

"Tease," she accused.

"Teases don't deliver." Licking his lips, he leaned in. "I'm going to make you come so hard the neighbors will hear you."

He paused for an endless second, making her wait. When she was about to scream, he stroked the flat of his tongue across her. Biting back a cry, Rachel fought to remain standing. Her hands shook as she kept herself spread for him, her knees threatening to buckle.

"You better hold on to me," he warned darkly, then he dove full force for the aching flesh between her thighs.

Wielding the point of his tongue like a lash, Jack caught the tip of her distended clitoris and fluttered over it with lightning quickness. She climaxed with a low moan, the orgasm tearing through her senses with a force she never knew she could withstand. Her body was wracked by violent shudders, her toes curling painfully into the hardwood floor.

And he didn't let up. His grip on her ass tightened and he tongued her like a man possessed, his hungry growls throwing her headlong into a second climax directly on the heels of the first. Incited by his wildness, she caught his head by the sweat-dampened roots of his hair and rode his working mouth. She took what she needed, grinding against his wickedly skilled tongue. Shameless in her pleasure, she didn't care who heard or saw her. The only thing that mattered was Jack and what he was doing to her.

When the rush ebbed, it took all of her energy with it. She sagged into the wall, gasping for air and trembling.

Jack stood and lifted her over his shoulder, then turned back toward the couch. When she regained the ability to speak, she was going to tell him again how hot his caveman tendencies were to her. Or maybe she'd just show him . . .

He sat her down on the armrest of the couch and stepped between her knees. With a hand behind her head, he urged her backward, balancing her so that her torso hung suspended over the cushions.

With no leverage whatsoever, Rachel could only accept what he gave her—the teasing glide of his tongue along the seam of her lips . . . the nip of his teeth at her jaw . . . the questing of his fingers as they parted her again and pushed through oversensitive tissues . . .

"Jack." Rachel caught him by the belt loops, arching helplessly into his grip.

His fingers curved upward inside her, stroking, searching. She writhed, her abdominal muscles so tense they cramped. The anticipation was a torment all its own, as was the illicitness of their location. The couch was set in front of the sliding glass doors to take advantage of the ocean view. The slanting moonlight ended at the base of the sofa, only an inch or two away from the shadows where Jack fucked his fingers into her.

"There." His mouth curved wickedly as he tapped against her G-spot. "Let's see what happens first: I make you come, or you get into my pants."

Rachel really wanted to win. She wanted to see what he looked like, what he felt like. But she was a mess. Emotionally. Physically. And he had a head start. As she fumbled to rip open his button fly, he pressed and rubbed with his roughened fingertips. Fingertips that were strong enough to hold his entire body weight while rock climbing, yet were achingly gentle with her.

She'd barely freed his cock from the restrictive denim when the orgasm hit her. Moaning, she instinctively tried to pull away from the overload of sensation, but he held her immobile and made her take it. He leaned over her as she quaked, pressing his lips to her ear and crooning words she could barely hear over the rushing of blood in her ears. *Let go . . . I have you . . . You're safe with me . . .* His hand thrust and twisted between her legs, the relentlessness so at odds with the gentle tone of his voice. It felt so much like a feral sort of claiming, a branding, a demand that she surrender to him completely.

That man will never accept anything less than one hundred percent of a woman's soul, her much wiser mother-in-law once said. Rachel used to wonder what kind of woman would be strong enough to share so much of herself. Now, she knew. She went slack in his arms, embracing her newfound fortitude and turning herself over to the passionate side of Jack she'd fantasized about.

"Rachel," he murmured, the one word filled with an aching tenderness. His fingers left her.

She exhaled audibly. "I want to feel you. Inside me."

"I don't have any condoms."

"It's okay. I got back on the pill two months ago, the day after you made plans to come out here."

His breath hissed out between his teeth.

Rachel cupped his cheek. "You never stood a chance."

The kiss he gave her was fierce and passionate, relaying so much more than lust and desire. She clung to him, soaking up the flood of emotion from a man known for his reserve and austerity. *This* was why she could blossom for him, why she felt fearless and audacious. They were so much alike in that way, their still waters running deeper than most.

Jack broke the kiss, breathing heavily. He moved her with unsteady hands, turning her so she draped bonelessly over the couch arm, her back to his front.

She'd never felt more emotionally raw or physically vulnerable. When she heard the rustle of his jeans, her hands fisted beside her head. She stared sightlessly out the open patio door, feeling the cool evening air flowing over her damp skin. There was no longer any tension in her, no resistance, no aggression. When Jack cupped her inner thigh, she widened the spread of her legs of her own volition, needing a deeper physical connection to him.

His hand stroked down her spine, then up again. "You okay?"

Rachel gave a jerky nod.

He brushed her sweat-soaked bangs away from her forehead and pressed a kiss to her shoulder blade. "Can you take more?"

She reached behind her to cup the back of his thigh. Feeling the bunching of his jeans, she realized he'd only bothered to push them down just enough to gain the access he needed. The image of how they must look—she, drowsy and naked; he, tautly focused and partially dressed—sparked a renewed flare of desire. "Yes."

Jack straightened and a heartbeat later she felt the broad, plush head of his cock tuck into the clenching opening of her pussy. He was so hot and hard as steel. The feel of him made her bite her lip while the first slow push had her clawing at the white slipcover.

"Easy." He restrained her hips with a firm yet gentle grip. "Just relax. You're nice and soft now. Let it happen."

He couldn't know what he was asking of her. As the wide crown breached the tautly stretched entrance to her body, the intense feeling of possession was overwhelming.

"Oh God . . ." she breathed, every nerve ending electrified by the leisurely thrusts with which he worked his cock into her.

If she hadn't been so languid, Rachel doubted she could have taken him. As it was, the stretching was so acute she swore she could feel every ridge and vein, every beat of his racing pulse. It was like nothing she'd ever experienced. She was grateful to be facing away from him, needing to shield the raw emotion she knew must be visible on her face. She couldn't scare him away now. Not after this.

Bending his knees, Jack pushed the final few inches inside her. She buried her face in the sofa cushion to muffle her plaintive moan. He was so thick and hard. Every shuddering breath she took made her feel how deep he was.

She felt his tongue slide upward along her back, then a sharp possessive bite at her shoulder.

"Rachel," he whispered, reaching beneath her to cup her breasts in his large hands. Clutching her to his heaving chest, he began to move. Withdrawing partway, then gliding home. Being far too careful, as if she was breakable. Although she felt as if she might shatter, she didn't want his restraint. Not when she'd started falling apart the moment he'd touched her.

She threw her hips back at him. "Fuck me. Don't play with me!"

Jack stilled, which allowed her to feel the fine tremors in his hands and thighs. As deliberate as he seemed, his body betrayed him—he was leashed, but only barely.

As much as she was able, she tightened her inner muscles around the rigid cock throbbing within her.

He cursed and gripped her tighter. "Rachel . . . damn it."

"Now!"

Hunching over her, he pulled his hips back, then slammed deep. The weight of his heavy sack smacked against her clit, sending fire racing along her skin in a prickling wave.

"Is that what you want?" He flexed inside her, teasing nerve endings she hadn't known she possessed. "How hard do you want it?"

"Yes—"

He was fucking her before she finished. His hips thrusting and churning, shafting her tender pussy with hard, heavy drives.

She climaxed with his arms wrapped around her, holding her as she sobbed with the pleasure. He groaned as she rippled around him, joining her, jerking violently with every hot thick spurt. His cheek pressed tightly to her temple and the scent of his skin surrounded her, filling her mind along with her name.

As he emptied himself inside her, it was her name he repeated in a jagged litany, spoken in a serrated voice that pushed her over the razor's edge of infatuation into something far more dangerous.

Somehow, she'd managed to get under his skin. She intended to stay there.

six

Jack tucked one arm behind his head and watched as the ceiling lightened incrementally with the rise of the sun. Rachel lay sleeping on the bed beside him, the white cotton sheet tangled around her torso. Her lips were slightly parted, as if in expectation of a kiss, and he fought the urge to wake her and have her again.

He wasn't certain what time she needed to get up to prepare for Riley's party, but it was barely six, so he figured she could sleep for at least another couple hours yet. She needed it. There were dark shadows beneath her eyes. Her breasts were reddened by the scratch of his whiskers. When she'd been curled on her side, he saw the faint indentation of his teeth in her shoulder.

Damn it. She was too tender and soft for him to lose control with her—both emotionally and physically. Jack scrubbed a hand over his face. And he'd made a gross tactical miscalculation. In the light of day, he was no longer willing to be a one-night stand.

She'd been planning on going to bed with him for months . . .

Fuckin' A. Just thinking about it tore him up.

Yes, Rachel deserved better than him, but he could make some adjustments and sacrifices, he could learn what she needed and give his best shot at delivering. He could show her that he could make love to her slowly, sweetly. Take his time. Let her set the pace. He had no option other than to try; he couldn't pretend last night never happened. Maybe she'd come into it because of Steve, but he could give her a reason to stick with it.

Too wired to sleep, Jack slipped carefully from the bed and dressed for a run. He hit the beach and tried to clear his head.

He'd never been good with words.

Now he needed to find the right ones to change the rest of his life.

RACHEL woke to the sound of the shower running. She smelled coffee and smiled, relishing the intimacy of sharing her morning with another adult. Rolling to her side, she searched for a clock and found one on the nightstand on Jack's side of the bed. It was turned away from her, so she crawled over and moved it. Seven forty-five.

Beside the clock was Jack's badge and billfold. She stared at the silver star, feeling a rush of pride and respect. He was a Shadow Stalker, a member of the U.S. Marshals Service's elite Special Operations Group. He'd explained the nickname to her once—the Shadow Stalkers unit hunted dangerous fugitives, or "shadows," and waited in the shadows of federal courthouses during high-profile cases. His job suited him so well that she couldn't imagine him doing anything else. She certainly would never ask him to give it up, even though the thought of losing him terrified her.

Reaching for the badge, she accidentally knocked the wallet to the floor. It landed on its back and flopped open. Her smiling face stared up at her.

She got out of bed. Bending down, she picked the billfold up. It felt wrong to pry, but she couldn't resist. Whose image did he carry with him? Who were the important people in his life?

Rachel turned each plastic photo protector slowly, touched to see pictures of Steve and Riley along with ones of her. But when she reached the end and found only one photo that wasn't of her family—one with several guys in bulletproof vests and sunglasses—she frowned. There were no pictures of parents or siblings, or nieces and nephews. No photos of himself with anyone.

Her heart broke a little. "Jack," she whispered, wondering if he felt as alone as he suddenly seemed to her.

She'd known that Jack grew up in foster care, but she'd assumed he formed some lasting connections with someone. Anyone. Was it possible he hadn't?

If she and Riley were all he had, no wonder he was wary and reluctant. It certainly wasn't from lack of desire.

Standing, she walked to the master bathroom. She gave a cursory knock, then cracked the door open. "Hey."

"Good morning."

His voice was warm and purring. The shower was enclosed with frosted glass, affording her just enough of a glimpse of his perfect body to light her up. She could get used to this.

"Coffee's brewed," he said. "I picked up some of that sugar-free hazelnut creamer you like."

Sweatpants and a sweat-stained T-shirt lay piled on the floor. She couldn't believe he'd exercised after their exertions the night before. She felt like an underachiever. She also felt loved and cared for.

Jack paid attention to her and the things she liked in ways she hadn't fully appreciated until Steve was gone. The flowers he sent weekly were either calla lilies, stargazer lilies, or tulips—her favorites. How did he know that? Perhaps Steve mentioned it. But her favorite Luzianne chicory coffee, which had to be ordered? Or her favorite hand cream, Japanese Cherry Blossom Shea Cashmere, the smell of which was usually hidden by her perfume? Even Steve, the one person who'd known her better than anyone, couldn't remember that.

Maybe Jack's attention to detail was just part of who he was and the job he did. After all, the U.S. Marshals Service was responsible for the Witness Security Program. Maybe the little things he remembered about her were things he'd pick up on anyone, part of the process of wiping a person's identity and erasing identifying habits. But maybe something more personal was involved. She hoped so, because she'd started falling in love with him over those gifts and how they made her feel. After years of having everything she loved denigrated and belittled by her aunt until she didn't enjoy anything at all, Jack had taught her to celebrate the things that made her happy.

Smiling at the thought, she bent down and picked up after him, grabbing his clothes and taking them out to the hamper in the bedroom. It wasn't a task she was particularly fond of usually, but she was beginning to think Jack could use a little looking after. Besides, he'd made the coffee. She was willing to trade quite a bit for the pleasure of waking up to freshly brewed coffee.

"Would you totally gross out," she asked, returning to the bathroom, "if I use your toothbrush?"

"Go for it."

Rachel was rinsing her mouth out when Jack turned off the water in the shower. Straightening, she turned and faced him, determined to catch the view. The door slid open. A dripping wet and gorgeously naked Jack appeared, and she gave an appreciative whistle. He was perfectly sculpted from head to toe. And the package in the middle, impressive even while semi-erect, made her hot and needy. She could *seriously* get used to this.

His mouth twitched with suppressed amusement as he reached for the towel hanging on the wall. He'd shaved and looked less rogue warrior and more *GQ* cover model. She loved both looks on him.

"Wait." She stepped closer, licking her lower lip.

Jack's eyes filled with a heat that made her flush. His arm dropped back to his side. "I'm all yours."

JACK held his position despite the seemingly endless insurgence.

As if Rachel sensed his wariness, she'd brought him a beer earlier, hiding it from the multitude of underage eyes with an insulated bottle cozy. He didn't touch it, knowing from experience that it was best to stay razor sharp when surrounded by unknowns.

From the safety of the grill, he eyed the dozen or so eight-year-olds running around the patio of Rachel's small two-story condominium. It was a madhouse, but he didn't feel as out of place as he'd expected he would. That was certainly because of Rachel, who smiled at him often and made a point of including him.

"Jack."

He turned his head and smiled down at Riley, who looked so much like his dad. Riley had the same smiling sloe eyes and cheerful grin, the same quick laugh and desire to help others. "Hey, sport. Having fun?"

"Totally. I have a question."

"Shoot."

"My Aunt Stella says you like my mom."

He glanced at the picnic table, where most of the Tse family was gathered. "I do."

"Like her like a girlfriend. You know, kissing and stuff."

"Oh?" Jack focused on the burgers and hot dogs grilling in front of him.

"She says guys only pay attention to what kind of coffee creamer a girl likes when she's his girlfriend."

Not knowing how to reply, Jack just nodded slowly and shot another glance at Rachel. She was talking about him to the Tses. He hoped that was working in his favor.

"So it's true?" Riley pressed. "Is my mom your girlfriend?"

"Uh . . ." Jack blew out his breath. "How would you feel about that? Is that bugging you?"

"No. Will you be coming around more? I think you should come around more."

"I'm going to be working on that. I'd like to spend more time with you. There are some things your dad and I used to do together—fishing, golfing, taking some Sea-Doos out to Havasu . . . I think you'll enjoy those same things."

"Sea-Doos?" Riley's dark eyes lit up. "Really? That would be so cool!"

"We'll have to make plans, then."

Riley ran off, shouting at his friends, but skid to a halt a few feet away and came back. "Watch out for Aunt Stella," he said in a stage whisper. "She says if mom doesn't snatch you up, she will. She's cool, but . . . well . . ."

"Got it." Jack somehow managed to keep his face impassive. "Thanks for the tip."

Watching his godson run off, Jack rocked back on his heels and felt hopeful. If the Tses were endorsing him, he had a chance in hell. He'd take it.

His cell phone rang and his light mood sank like a stone. Pulling it out of his pocket, he answered, "Killigrew."

"Hey, Jack." Gary Lancet's grim voice was like a cold shower. "I'm sorry to interrupt you on leave, but I figured you'd kick my ass if you found out after you got back."

Jack set down the tongs he'd been using to turn the hot dogs. "What is it?"

"One of Terry's old collars went to his house. Fucked the place up and killed his dog. Callie's a mess."

"Jesus. Are she and the kids okay?"

"Yeah, they're shaken up but fine. It's a miracle they weren't home at the time. Her damn radiator hose took a shit on the way back from picking them up from school. Otherwise . . . Well, it could have been a lot worse."

Looking at Rachel and the festive scene around him, Jack finally felt the sensation of being the odd man out. He should have felt it earlier. His life, such as it was, didn't fit here. He'd forgotten that for a while. The grisly reminder was a timely one. He hadn't yet laid his heart on the line; retracting it would have been a lot harder than just bailing early. "Am I needed?"

"We've got it covered. I just knew you'd want to know."

"Absolutely. Tell Terry to call me if he needs anything. I still have some things to wrap up here, but nothing that can't wait."

"I'll keep you posted."

Jack hung up and stared at the phone for a long minute. Just imagining what Terry must be going through made his gut knot.

Thinking about a close call like that happening to Rachel and Riley about doubled him over. Sweat beaded his forehead despite the coolness of the northern California weather. He rubbed at the tightness in the center of his chest. "Shit."

Rachel's voice came from behind him. "Is everything all right?"

He turned, grateful for the sunglasses shielding his eyes. "Something's gone down back home."

"Oh." She bit her lower lip. "Do you have to go?"

Facing her disappointment only strengthened his resolve to stop being selfish. He had to think of her first. "Not yet."

Her chin lifted. "I'd understand if you had to go. Riley would, too."

"You shouldn't have to understand."

One of her brows arched. "Really? Says who?"

"Let's not do this now."

"Later, then. Right after this is over."

It was already over. Not that it ever really had a chance to begin.

RACHEL picked up the last bit of torn wrapping paper that had blown beneath the patio table and straightened. Her house was almost back to normal . . . except for the brooding deputy attacking her gas grill with a steel brush.

Jack had grown strangely quiet since taking that phone call a couple hours before. He managed smiles for Riley, who'd loved every one of the too-many gifts Jack had given him. Gifts that were craft sets or science projects or models. Things that were taught or built. Rachel took note of the fact that a man who worked with death and destruction was fostering a love of discovery and creation in her son. But Jack was unable to muster even a ghost of a smile for her. Instead, when their gazes met, he looked . . . ravaged.

She shoved the trash in the garbage bag beside her and yanked on the handles to seal it. Then she approached Jack, coming up behind him and wrapping her arms around his lean waist. Even though he'd seen her coming, he tensed when her arms encircled him. She was grateful her mother-in-law and Stella had taken Riley to Target to spend his gift cards. It gave her the chance to get things straightened out with Jack.

She slid her hands beneath the hem of his shirt and caressed his washboard abs. "Stella tells me I need to keep you around and exploit your mad grilling skills."

He set one hand over hers, stilling her movements. "Flipping burgers isn't enough to fix my faults."

"Oh my God, you have faults? What a relief! I was beginning to think you were perfect."

Jack set the brush down and turned carefully to face her. "Rachel."

She pushed up his sunglasses to reveal his eyes. They were completely shuttered. "What was the phone call about?"

"Nothing you should have to worry over."

"Bullshit. Whatever was said to you has you pulling back. Since I'm the one you're pulling back from, I deserve to know why."

Exhaling harshly, he pulled off his sunglasses and hung them from the collar of his T-shirt. "One of the guys on the team had a scare today."

Rachel listened to his voice as he told her what happened. It was tight and clipped, his jaw taut. Someone he cared about— one of the very few—was hurting now and that was hurting Jack.

"You know you can talk to me about anything, right?" Her

fingers stroked soothingly across his nape. "The good, the bad, and the ugly. It helps to get it out."

"I don't want you involved in stuff like this."

"I'm already involved."

"You don't need this crap in your life," he said harshly. "Riley doesn't need it."

"We need *you*," she retorted, "and you and the job are a package deal."

"You've got me." His dark gaze was stormy. "I'll always be here for you, just as I've always been. We just need to keep things simple."

That was ridiculous. What they had was totally complicated. *He* was complicated, and he was used to keeping his circle of friends small and tight. Letting her in probably scared the shit out of him on a level he didn't even recognize. Because then he could lose her, one way or the other.

He was going to figure out, real quick, that she had absolutely no intention of getting lost.

seven

❖

"Simple, huh?" Rachel backed away from him and headed into the house. She needed a beer. Maybe two. "As simple as living in the same town?"

Jack followed her. "As simple as keeping things the way they have been until last night."

She wondered if he heard how gruff he sounded, how defensive.

Reaching the fridge, she pulled out two beers and set one down in front of him. They faced each other across her kitchen counter with equally wary and examining glances.

"You don't get to make that decision by yourself, Jack." She twisted off the top of her beer and took a swig.

His gaze narrowed. He had his game face on, dangerous and inscrutable. "I'll make the decision if it keeps you safe."

"I think the person you're trying to save is yourself." She pointed at him with the neck of her bottle. "I scare you."

"Thinking of something happening to you scares me." He opened his beer and drank, watching her as he swallowed.

"So, you ride off into the sunset, and I'm here safe and sound . . . until I get carjacked at the gas station. Or robbed at the store."

"Not the same thing," he argued. "The level of inherent risk with me is much higher."

"Shouldn't I be more worried about *you* not coming home than the reverse?"

"I know what I'm getting into when I go to work. You didn't sign up for this." Jack ran his hand through his hair. "The last thing I want to do is bring more traumas to your life. You and Riley need someone who comes home every day. Someone who leaves their work at the office. Someone—"

"Like Steve?" she interjected. "A guy who never had a moving violation in his life. No speeding tickets. A guy who never drove without his seat belt on. Who would have thought he'd die in a car wreck? No one. Terrible things happen to unsuspecting people every day. It's part of living, Jack. There's no way to go through life risk-free."

"I'm not bringing the shit from my job to your doorstep. Period."

Rachel's foot tapped on the tile floor. "You think I didn't know what I was taking on when I seduced you? I'm a grown woman with a child who depends on me. I don't jump without looking. You seem to be forgetting how well and how long I've known you."

"Steve didn't know the gritty details of what I do. If he had, he never would have wanted you anywhere near me on a permanent basis."

Her gaze moved to the photo of Steve and Jack on the mantel in the next room. She could barely make out the details from where she stood, but the image was indelibly etched on her mind;

she could see it with her eyes closed. Both men were dark-haired and brown-eyed. Both were tall and fit. But that was where the similarities ended. Steve's handsome Asian features reflected his fun and easy charm, while Jack's gaze was shadowed and his smile guarded. Steve had been content with the simple things in life—like her. Extroverted and spontaneous, he was known and liked by damn near everyone; Jack was hard to know and harder to understand.

Yet she loved them both madly.

Rachel looked at him. "You were the brother Steve never had. He trusted you with his life. But I don't make my decisions based on conjecture about what my deceased husband would think of them."

"Don't you?" he challenged softly, his eyes so dark they looked black. "Tell me Steve isn't the reason you came over last night."

"Steve isn't the reason I came over last night." She lifted her chin. "I loved my husband. I couldn't have loved him more. He was everything to me and if he were alive right now, what happened last night would never have happened. But he died, and I came to terms with that. I changed. My needs and wants changed. And now, when I look at you, I don't think about him. I don't think about you in relation to him. Half the time, I don't think at all, because I'm too busy appreciating the view. If you gave me some kind of best friend pity fuck last night, that's on you. Don't try and say that's where I was coming from."

Jack was oddly still . . . except for the rapid tempo of his breathing and the fevered brightness of his eyes, both of which betrayed far more volatile emotions.

Rachel frowned, catching on to the fact that she was missing something. She didn't believe he'd made love to her for any other reason than that he'd wanted to, but she was beginning to think he hadn't attributed the same motivation to her. "What's going through your head?"

"It doesn't matter. I was wrong." He looked down at his bottle, which he twisted and turned atop the counter. There was a softness to his features that tightened her chest.

"Most especially in thinking you could put on the breaks and slide into reverse." She bent down and leaned to the side, catching his lowered gaze. "There's only forward, Jack. I stopped looking back a while ago."

JACK stared at the vibrant woman looking at him in a way he'd never allowed himself to even dream about and knew he was done. He was never going to be able to say no to her. Not now. Not in the future. He wanted to give her everything, make her happy, keep her safe.

As if she knew what he was thinking, she said, "The safest place I can be is right next to you."

"Not when I'm the reason you're endangered to begin with."

"So you spend some of your off-duty days teaching me how to shoot a gun until I'm dangerous. You help me pick out an outrageously expensive and comprehensive alarm system for the house."

"Which house?"

"Both. For now." She smiled. "And you wear a bulletproof vest all the time. No crazy heroics."

"All the time?"

"Except when I want you naked."

His mouth twitched. "I was hoping *that* would be all the time."

"After last night, that *is* all the time."

"Then I'll be wearing body armor only rarely."

"If you want me to kick your ass and deny you sexual favors, try it."

Jack lifted his beer to his mouth to hide a smile. It was inappropriate considering the seriousness of the discussion, but Rachel always had that effect on him. She made him happy in spite of himself.

"You can talk to me about anything, Jack," she said softly, all levity gone. "You can ask me anything, and I'll try to come through for you. But you can't tell me to let you walk away. I can't do it, I can't let you go."

He swallowed and looked around the condo she'd bought after Steve died. It was the perfect size for her and Riley. The kitchen boasted new stainless-steel appliances and was big in relation to the overall square footage, which suited someone who baked for a living. The window over the sink had curtains with cupcakes on them—a housewarming gift from Steve's mom.

"You have a good life here," he noted. "You've got family nearby and a new business. Riley has his friends and classmates."

"I do have it good." She set her elbow on the counter, then her chin in her hand. "You do realize, don't you, that I never could have done what I did last night with any other man? I can't even imagine throwing myself at anyone else. Even with Steve, I waited for him to make the first moves. I was always afraid I'd stir up more than I could handle."

Jack forced himself to breath deep and easy, trying to slow the rapid beating of his heart. "I was rough with you. I'm sorry."

"No, you're in love. And I loved every moment with you. I wouldn't change one thing that happened last night. I told myself I was strong enough to take you on, and now I know I can." She smiled gently. "That's not a surprise is it? That you're in love with me?"

"No. I knew." He watched as something hot and tender swept over her face. "I also know loving someone means wanting what's best for them. I'm not good for you."

He held up a hand when she opened her mouth to speak. "Hear me out. Any minute now, my phone could ring and I will have to go. Christmas, your birthday . . . I can't promise I'll be here. Once I leave, I won't always know when I'll be back. One of these days, you're gonna wake up and realize you want someone around full-time."

Rachel straightened. "I've been getting by on my own with Riley for two years. I don't need a man around just because. I don't have any problem going to bed alone. What I want is *you*. Not some interchangeable guy; not someone like Steve. Look at it this way: I already have the cake. You're the icing on top, with sprinkles, candied fruit, and chocolate drizzle."

"And I'm just as bad for your health," he muttered.

"I *want* you going straight to my hips. I want the sugar rush and the toe-curling deliciousness. I've earned it."

She licked her lips and his dick went hard, remembering what that mouth had done to him when he'd stepped out of the shower that morning.

Taking a deep breath, Jack laid it out there. "You're asking me to risk losing you and Riley completely. I can live with what we've got now, but nothing at all . . . I don't think I'd survive it."

Rachel rounded the counter. "I'm deliberately keeping this light, because I don't want to scare you off. I'm saving the heavy stuff for later, when you can't run. I was thinking you should be handcuffed to the bed before I tell you that you're stuck with me for the rest of your life and I'm the last woman you're ever going to bed with."

She walked right into him, hugging him tight. He had to restrain himself from squeezing her too hard. God, he was crazy for even thinking this could work.

"In the meantime," she went on, "we'll start with a race to see who can acquire the most frequent-flier miles by the end of the year, and work from there. Week by week, you'll learn that not being able to live without me means living with me. Eventually, you'll get used to not being alone and we'll both become familiar with this new take-no-prisoners version of myself that you inspire."

"You're making this sound easy," he murmured with his lips to the crown of her head, "but it's not."

She leaned back to look up at him. "No, we're going to have to work on it and make some sacrifices and *take risks*. What I'm saying is it'll be worth it. The difficult part's already over—we both fell hard. It's onward and upward from here."

"Take no prisoners." He shook his head and a small laugh escaped him. God, he was scared shitless. He didn't know how to bring something precious and fragile into his life.

"Except for you." Her hands slid up his back. Her lips whispered across his jaw.

Jack lifted her feet from the floor. "I want to be good for you."

"You have been. You are. You will be." Her teeth scraped lightly over his earlobe, sending a surge of heat and longing through him. "I'm going to show you all the ways I've grown stronger because of you. Because of things you've done for me and said to me. Because of how you look at me. For a long time, I didn't understand why you look at me the way you do, but I knew you saw something in me I wasn't seeing. I can't tell you how many times thoughts of you motivated me when I wasn't sure I could get something done."

He kissed the top of her shoulder, which was bared by the asymmetrical shirt she wore. "You can do anything you set your mind to."

"I'm setting my mind to returning the favor. Together, we can overcome anything—our pasts, your job, a long-distance relationship. I'll send you Better Than Sex cupcakes to tide you over between days off."

"I thought we established that the name is false advertising."

"God, did you ever," she breathed, wrapping her arms around his neck. "But I enjoyed your argument so much, I'd be happy to have you repeat it."

He closed his eyes and pressed his forehead to hers. Right now, he had all he'd ever wanted. They would plan the next steps together. After that . . .

Onward and upward, she'd said.

Jack's arms tightened around her. Onward and upward.

FOR MORE INFORMATION ABOUT
FUTURE SHADOW STALKERS STORIES,
VISIT WWW.SYLVIADAY.COM.

COMING OCTOBER 2011
FROM HEAT . . .

men out of uniform

(WITH MAYA BANKS AND KARIN TABKE)

About the Author

Sylvia Day is the national bestselling author of more than a dozen novels. A wife and mother of two, she is a former Russian linguist for the U.S. Army Military Intelligence. Sylvia's work has been called "wonderful and passionate" by WNBC.com and "wickedly entertaining" by *Booklist*. Her stories have been translated into Russian, Japanese, Portuguese, German, Czech, and Thai. She's been honored with the *Romantic Times* Reviewers' Choice Award, the EPPIE award, the National Readers' Choice Award, the Readers' Crown, and multiple finalist nominations for Romance Writers of America's prestigious RITA® Award of Excellence.

midnight rendezvous

JAMIE DENTON

For Kane, Katelyn, Jadyn, Sam, Cyrus,
Melina, Kinley, Luke, Kaylee, Ariel, Vinnie, Abe, Mya,
Alyssa, Angeleah, and Isaak . . . You are my blessings.

acknowledgments

Erin McCarthy—For steering me in the right direction, and for sharing your beloved New Orleans with me. I can't thank you enough. One of these days, I promise, we'll do the Quarter crawl.

Christy Carlson Esau—For forcing me to look behind the curtain. You were right—it wasn't such a scary place, after all.

Kristine Thompson—For being there every day. My world is right, knowing you're only a phone call away.

Mary Ann Chulick and Rhonda Stapleton—My favorite goddesses of plot. You make my life so much more interesting.

Leslie Crossen—Because you've always been there, my dear friend. I love you.

one

❖

Burnett Dupree snapped his laptop closed, then stretched his arms over his head, satisfied with the evening's progress. The second scene of the first act was shaping up in a way he hadn't anticipated, and that was always a good sign. Two weeks ago he'd been wondering what the hell he'd been thinking in coming to New Orleans. The answer had been simple—New Orleans wasn't New York. Fourteen days later, he had another reason for staying.

Pushing away from the small dinette table pulling double duty as his desk, he stood and snagged the lukewarm bottle of water from the counter. A quick glance at the inexpensive novelty clock above the stove indicated the time was half past midnight. He smiled to himself as he cut the light, then walked to the front window where he leaned against the frame and waited.

Like clockwork, his mysterious landlady appeared. Tonight she wore a short silky robe, but from two stories up, he couldn't be sure if she wore ice blue or white or maybe even silver. Not that it mattered because she'd be bare-ass naked within seconds.

Ten days ago he'd first noticed her. God help him, he hadn't been able to turn away when she'd stripped and dove into the deep end of the built-in swimming pool. The next day, the words he'd feared he'd lost in the bottom of a bottle of scotch had finally returned. From that moment on, he'd labeled her his muse and had been watching her night after night since.

He'd only seen her from a distance, and only after midnight, when much of the world was supposed to be sleeping. She fascinated him, and Burnett couldn't remember the last time he'd been so intrigued by a woman. Especially one he hadn't even met.

With anticipation, he grinned to himself as she shed her robe, letting it fall into a puddle of silk at her feet. Moisture from the heavy Louisiana humidity clung to her sleek curves, making her skin glisten in the moonlight. Once upon a time he'd mistakenly thought the only time a sweaty woman sexy was during a hard and fast ride between the sheets. Yet after the unobstructed nightly view of his very striking, and very naked, muse diving into the crisp, cool water, he'd decided the time had come to alter his opinion.

Cloaked in darkness, he stood to the side of the open window and took a long drink from the water bottle clutched in his hand. Not for the first time he wished he were downing three fingers worth of Glenfiddich, what the serenity-prayer-reciting, Kumbaya-hugging rehabbers would refer to as his drug of choice. His go-to during times of stress, duress, or just plain-ass self-destruction.

He downed another swallow of water.

Sobriety sucked.

He'd been dried out for less than a month, in more ways than one. Was it any surprise the cravings hadn't lessened in degree or quantity? Was it any wonder he'd already become weary of the battle to stay sober?

Just one shot.

He might be a drunk, possibly even brushing up against full-blown alcoholism, but he also understood his personality. He knew better than to tempt himself. A single shot would lead to one drink, which would lead to more booze until he ended up God knew where, with only God knew who, because he'd drank himself into oblivion. One thing Burnett Dupree knew better than anyone, one drink never had been, and never would be, enough for a Dupree.

He scrubbed his free hand down his face, wondering how in the hell he'd come to this place. Not New Orleans, but his current place in the world. A place that had his agent and the executive producers of his last bomb issuing the ultimate of ultimatums. Dry up. Clean up. Get his act together and write a new hit play. Or else.

God, he hated ultimatums. But he could no longer deny the truth. He needed a hit and he sure as hell wasn't going to find it if he was swimming in a bottle of thirty-year-old scotch.

Fortunately, he hadn't pickled his entire brain because he had enough common sense left to recognize that the moneymen were right. Two years since his last hit, he was long overdue for a smash. The few words he had managed to string together in recent months were for an off-Broadway production that had tanked—badly.

He'd been closed down after opening night.

With that abject failure topping his résumé, the next morning he'd packed a bag and hopped a plane for a high-end rehab center located in the swanky, upscale desert of Southern California. He'd lasted a day shy of two weeks.

Since rehab had been his idea and not a court-ordered edict, he'd checked himself out and left Palm Springs in search of his muse. Yeah, he had a drinking problem, but no way was he in as bad of shape as the poor bastards he'd left behind at the Betty Ford Center. For reasons he didn't care to examine too closely, he'd avoided New York and headed straight for New Orleans.

Home. The city of his misspent youth. His soul city. She'd called to him in a way she hadn't in a very long time, and he'd answered.

Determined to remain sober, he'd avoided all of his old haunts and had checked into a five-star hotel on Royal Street. The sort of distraction the French Quarter offered had him lasting all of two days. Before he blew two weeks of sobriety, he found himself a rental agent, who in turn had suggested a small one-bedroom furnished garage apartment that had just become available in the Garden District. He'd offered six months' worth of rent plus agreed to the rather steep security deposit after signing a month-to-month rental agreement that included no pets, no parties, and no use of the swimming pool after 10 P.M. No exceptions. He didn't much care what stipulations were mandatory as long as he was offered a clean place to work far from the lure of Manhattan, Broadway in particular. No interruptions. No distractions.

The way he figured it, two out of three wasn't half bad.

He downed the last of the water as his *distraction* broke the surface of the pool. With efficient strokes, she reached the edge where she turned and braced her back against the side. Resting her elbows on the concrete ledge behind her, she lifted both legs in front of her repeatedly.

He counted her movements in his mind. When he reached fifty, she slid beneath the surface and swam two full lengths of the pool.

Damn, but she was one stunning creature. After several nights of voyeurism, he knew her body intimately—well, at least he did in his imagination. In his mind, he'd touched, tasted, and surveyed every curve and line of her slender shape. He had no idea what color her eyes really were, but in his mind they were a shocking green, large and clear and framed by thick, dusky lashes. Her hair, dark now from the water and plastered to her head, was actually a darkish blond, like the color of melted caramel. Her long, thick tresses looked rich and sun-streaked, falling past her delicate shoulder blades in soft waves.

Tonight, even under the light of the new moon, he still wasn't able to see her clearly. She kept her face averted, shielded from view with her long, wavy hair. But in his lust-filled mind, her lips, full and lush, captured his attention. Her breath hot, her mouth moist, as she covered the head of his dick with her pouty, pink lips.

He blew out a long, unsteady breath and drew back slightly from the open window. Shaking his head to clear the runaway fantasy proved fruitless. All he had was his imagination because he'd never really seen her up close and personal.

She was an obvious recluse, and damn if he didn't want to know why. His curiosity, not to mention his libido, were killing him. Why did she only come out after midnight? What secrets did she need to hide?

As curious as he was about his sexy landlady/muse, he had to admit it was his thoughts of her nude body that had him equally distracted and inspired. And hard.

When at the top of his game, he'd worked in the early mornings at his favorite coffee shop, observing the city coming to life around him. Since his return to New Orleans, his long time habit no longer worked for him. Afternoons were too bloody hot to even think. The one time he'd packed up his laptop and driven his rental car out to the Quarter, the Café du Monde had been brimming with noisy tourists. That's when he realized what he really craved was solitude. As a result, he'd started writing in the evenings.

While he was finally putting words to the page, he admitted he'd spent far too much time fantasizing about the naked neighbor. Yet regardless of how much progress he made on his new project, each night at half past midnight he stopped working and turned off the lights in the apartment. That he chose to shut down when he knew his illusive landlady came out for her nightly ritual was no coincidence. He couldn't decide if he was a glutton for punishment or a voyeuristic fool.

Probably both.

She used the pool for exercise, he knew from his observances, the evidence plain in her long, lean, and fit body. Even in the moonlight, he could tell from the slope of her breasts they were genuine. She was tall, nearing six foot, he estimated. From his perch two stories above, he couldn't help but notice she walked with a fairly pronounced limp and tended to favor her right side more than her left.

With his shoulder propped against the window frame, he continued to watch her as she performed another series of poolside exercises, followed by more laps. Feeling a little too much like a Peeping Tom, he reminded himself he was merely looking *out* of his rented window, not peeking *into* hers. Splitting hairs, the conscience he'd forgotten he had warned, but nothing short of an explosion could've dragged him away from the window now that she'd exited the pool.

She stood facing away from him with her arms stretched over her head. Something about her was hauntingly familiar, the way she carried herself perhaps, or maybe she was just one in the hundreds of beautiful women he'd admired over the years. Supporting actresses wanting leading roles, dancers wanting out of the chorus line, models aching for a small but pivotal role in one of his plays.

Heaven help him, there'd been plenty of women in his life. Seemed the more he drank, the more women he'd gone through, too. Exotic names and beautiful faces that were now nothing but a blur combined with a few snippets of erotic memory. Not exactly the kind of memories he wanted to keep him warm in his old age, but thus far they were all he had managed to accumulate.

Slowly, she bent forward at the waist, reaching down to smooth her hands down the back of her calves, then held the position. His imagination, along with his libido, skyrocketed. He took in the curve of her sweet ass and easily imagined sinking his fingers into her smooth, taut flesh as he ran the flat of his palm up the slope of her back until he reached her shoulder, holding her in place as he ground his cock between her thighs.

He closed his eyes and attempted to blow out a long slow breath, but his mouth was suddenly dry as dust. So dry that his throat tickled, and he coughed.

Shit.

Abruptly, she stood and looked over her shoulder up to his open window. Paralyzed, he stared back at her. She let out a strangled cry, then dove for her robe. She probably thought he was no better than a pervert.

She jammed her arms into her robe as she bolted toward the back door of the main house, her limp even more pronounced. Feeling very much like a garden slug, he moved away from the window. What was he supposed to do now? He'd be willing to bet she was already planning to cancel his rental contract.

He huffed a chuckle. No. Moving was simply unacceptable. For the first time in months, he was writing, and the words were good. Damned good. What harm was there in introducing himself and apologizing for intruding on her nightly ritual? Because if he knew one thing, he wasn't about to leave, not when his muse had finally returned in the form of a beautiful naked woman.

two

❋

Maya Pomeroy pressed her back against the mudroom door as she struggled to catch her breath. Her heart pounded so hard, she feared it would jump right out of her chest. He'd seen her. Worse, he'd been *watching* her.

"Oh God," she whispered.

Twisting the belt of her white silk robe in her hands, she berated herself for her own stupidity. She'd known deep down renting the garage apartment would be a mistake. More important, she'd known taking on a tenant could lead to an invasion of her treasured privacy. Unfortunately, the lousy economy had forced her hand. Not that she was anywhere close to living a hand-to-mouth existence, but she wasn't exactly rolling in disposable income at the moment.

Unlike many in her former line of work, she'd always played it smart with her earnings. Despite the oft times shallowness of the high-fashion world, Maya had lived in the real world most of the time. She'd understood her days on the runway or gracing the covers of *Vogue*, *Cosmopolitan*, and *Vanity Fair* were numbered. The hands of time couldn't be stopped. She could've been replaced by someone younger, thinner, and prettier tomorrow. Except her tomorrow had come a lot sooner than she'd anticipated because of a career-ending accident that had left her broken.

What money she had earned, she'd entrusted to one of the most prestigious accounting firms in her hometown of New Orleans. But even Thompson, McCarthy, and Love had been duped by a Ponzi scheme that had cost many people a great deal of money. That loss, coupled with the abrupt ending of her career and the worst economy the country had seen in decades, had her living on a strict budget. Like so many others, she'd been given a crash course on how to economize. If she cut back any more, she'd be living on bread and water and working on her new clothing line by candlelight.

Her heart rate back to normal, she turned to peer out the crème lace curtain covering the door's window, praying her tenant hadn't followed her. The last thing she wanted was a face-to-freak confrontation. She'd kept to herself for a reason. The same reason she worked out after midnight—so she wouldn't be seen.

Flipping the switch to turn off the overhead light in the mudroom, she still couldn't see much outside her back door window but deep shadows. The pool water was still, not so much as a ripple disturbing the surface. Edging the curtain back in place, she breathed a tentative sigh of relief until a light rap on the back door made her jump and sent her heartbeat racing all over again.

Maya held her breath and waited, hoping, no praying that the tenant hadn't seen her light on and would go away. When he rapped on the door again, she swore under her breath and cursed her rotten luck.

What the hell did he want? She'd escaped into the house. Wasn't that clue enough that she didn't care to speak with him? Since she had been in the nude, he probably thought she was embarrassed, but that was the furthest thing from the truth.

God, he'd *seen* her. And just how much? Her face? The vicious scars?

He knocked again, louder this time. "Hello? Are you there?"

No, she wanted to shout, but that was just ridiculous. She was a grown woman, not a blushing teenager embarrassed because she'd been caught dipping skinny.

"It's late," she said instead. Her hands trembled, so she grabbed hold of the lapels of her robe in hopes of steadying them.

Too bad it didn't work.

"Good night, Mr.—" What was his name again? She couldn't remember, that's how much attention she'd paid to the signed rental agreement. All she'd been interested in was the certified check the rental company had sent, covering the half year of rent that her new tenant had offered in advance. The temptation had been too much, so she'd gone ahead and agreed to let him stay for six months. How could she say no? She'd been given enough money to squirrel some away *and* buy the materials she needed to expand her clothing line.

Sales had been brisk for POE-tential, the workout gear for women that she'd created and sold in a local boutique down in the Quarter. Now she wanted to test the waters by expanding to what she'd termed "sensible lingerie." Items made *for* a woman's comfort, not those scratchy, skimpy patches of lace made to fuel a man's fantasy.

"Dupree," he said. "Burnett Dupree."

She didn't care if George Clooney was knocking on her door, no way was she opening it. She turned and rested her forehead against the door frame. "It's late, Mr. Dupree," she said, hoping he'd take the hint and go away.

"Just a moment of your time. I won't keep you."

She detected the slightest trace of a lazy southern drawl in his voice. An accent he attempted to hide, she wondered, or an affirmation of southern heritage? His voice held an odd but interesting mix of the Deep South and places north. A Louisiana girl born and bred, not even the seven years she'd lived in New York City had she shed her accent completely. Regardless, it made her curious about him, and that bothered her. A lot.

Knowing she was on the verge of racking up yet another error in judgment, she put her hand on the knob and turned it, then cautiously pulled the door open a fraction. Opened it just enough for him to see her good side, the side of her face that wasn't scarred and twisted. The side that hadn't undergone countless surgeries that did little to return her to her former self, but at least allowed her to look in the mirror each morning. The side that wouldn't have him recoiling in horror when he looked at her.

"I'm really sorry about earlier," he said, but she barely heard him.

Goodness, he was one tall drink of cool water. Hardly a slouch herself at five foot ten, he still towered over her by a good five or six inches, which was a rare occurrence for a woman of her height. But it was his smile that had her uselessly wishing she wasn't damaged goods.

He didn't offer her a full-blown high-wattage smile but instead a mildly flirtatious one that registered a level or two above a smirk. That the smile reached his startling blue gaze didn't miss her notice, either. They were blue, like the color of a cloudless summer sky, making her think of sunshine and grape Popsicles.

"Let's just forget about it," she said once she remembered to take a breath. Forgetting him, she wouldn't be doing anytime soon, of that she was certain. Heavens, the man was . . . beautiful. It was the only word she could think of to describe him. Hair, black as a midnight sky, slightly ruffled as if he'd been finger combing it, made her own fingers itch to touch the silky-looking strands. Beneath the dark-colored T-shirt he wore, the fabric stretched taut over wide shoulders and a chest to match. All tucked into a pair of jeans that looked as if they were custom made to fit his perfect body.

A perfect body. How ironic that the first man to actually stir her interest since the accident would be so bloody perfect. Just another of life's little jokes.

She moved to close the door. "Good night, Mr. Dupree."

His hand shot out and stopped her. "It's Burnett," he said. "I feel bad. Why don't you let me make it up to you? Dinner? Tomorrow?"

Was he insane? Had she actually rented the apartment over the garage to a lunatic? He didn't look like the dullest crayon in the box, but looks could be deceiving.

"I'm sorry. I can't."

"You have plans? No problem, how about Friday? I know a place. Best crawfish in Louisiana."

Deep down, down in that place where she wasn't damaged goods, where she didn't have to hide her face or attempt to mask the injuries of her body, she *really* wanted to say yes. She'd been cooped up for so long, she was sick to death of microwave dinners and her own company. For just one moment in time, she'd love nothing more than to share a platter of crawfish and conversation with another human being. To hear more than her own voice or the drone of the television in the background.

"I wish I could," she said, hating the wistfulness that had crept into her voice, "but it just isn't possible. Good night."

This time when she moved to close the door, he didn't stop her. And that saddened her almost as much as turning down his offer.

three

Maya didn't believe in voodoo, hoodoo, or fairy tales. She didn't wish on falling stars. She didn't cross her fingers when she drove over railroad tracks or hold her breath while crossing a bridge, but she knew that on occasion some things just couldn't be explained. Logically she understood that the only reason she'd taken on a tenant had been so she could afford to work on taking POE-tential in a new direction. But what she couldn't explain, and wasn't even sure if she wanted to, was how she looked forward to seeing her sexy tenant again—even if it was only through her kitchen window.

Since their through-the-door conversation two nights ago, she'd only caught a brief glimpse of Burnett Dupree. The apartment had been dark when she'd used the pool, but she didn't know if he was sleeping, hiding in the dark and still watching her, or if he was even home.

What she had done was Google him. The Internet was ever so

useful. And because she now knew her tenant was a womanizing playwright once considered the Prince of Broadway, she'd started wearing a swimsuit during her nightly exercise ritual. She'd had no choice because if she didn't work out, her leg and lower back muscles would cramp and tighten enough to bring her to tears until the muscle relaxers that she'd have to take took effect. Two years after the accident and she still couldn't complete a full cardio workout, the pain was that excruciating.

She hadn't seen him and she really didn't like that she was starting to look for him in the two days since their confrontation. But she couldn't seem to help herself. This morning when she'd been making her breakfast, she'd watched him leave. By 6 P.M., he hadn't returned. Where had he gone?

It's none of your business.

Nearly midnight, his car still wasn't parked in the carport on the left of the garage. She knew because she'd looked.

Twice.

And you care because . . .

Because it was Friday and he'd asked her out for a crawfish supper.

You turned him down, remember?

She sighed. Yes, she had turned him down. It had been for the best, really. Going out in public wasn't particularly enjoyable. For the most part, people were polite, but there were always more than a few stares. More often than not, she detected pity in their gazes, and that bothered her more than the ones who pointed and stared at her outright.

"Oh, get over yourself," she muttered, then slid the straps of her swimsuit in place. Until she could leave the house without frightening small children, she wasn't about to accept a date with a man. Especially a man who had her peeking out her windows at the slightest sound, looking for him after one very brief encounter.

She'd even dreamed of him last night. Could she be any more pathetic?

She let out a disgruntled sigh and promised herself she wouldn't waste another minute thinking about Burnett Dupree. Or dreaming about him. Hot, wild, and sexy dreams, in particular. If the man was half as good in reality as he was in her dream, she'd . . .

What?

She had no answer.

That's what I figured.

She limped to the closet and yanked open the door. She had to stop this nonsense. Really, what good did it do to spend so much time fantasizing about a man she could never have? Okay, so it gave her something else to think about other than the pain that was her constant companion. But she had to stop romanticizing.

Frowning, she dressed in a longer robe than she usually wore, this one of her own design in a robust emerald silk that teased her ankles, then left her first-floor bedroom. The room had originally been a den and still held a trace of the vanilla pipe tobacco her grandfather, then her father, had smoked. The room had always comforted her, but stale pipe tobacco and dusty first editions were a distant second to the comfort of a man's arms around her, holding her close enough that she could feel his heart beating.

Burnett's heart?

She hadn't converted the old den into her bedroom because of some misguided belief she felt closer to her father or grandfather. She hadn't only done it because climbing the stairs to the second floor still caused her far too much pain. She lived on the first floor because she couldn't stand to think of the five unused bedrooms upstairs. Bedrooms that should have belonged to children. The children she'd always dreamed of having but never would unless she went the artificial insemination route. Problem was, she held what some would call an old-fashioned belief that a child needed two parents, not a single mother and a turkey baster.

The formal dining room served as her workroom and the sitting room was now her front room, where she watched the evening news while she ate a boring microwave dinner. Night after night after night. No one but Pat, the woman who came to clean for her once a month, ever ventured upstairs, nor did she comment on Maya's living arrangements.

But damn it, she still held on to those foolish dreams and couldn't let them go. Dreams of her own *someday*. A someday that would probably never come. But she clung to hope. Only she knew better than most how dangerous hope could be.

Frustrated with the limitations of her body and furious with herself for daring to hope that maybe her some day would come, she stalked to the back door. She swung it wide, only to come face-to-face with none other than Burnett Dupree.

four

Poe. In the flash of a nanosecond, Burnett immediately knew the identity of his sexy muse. No wonder she'd been familiar to him as he'd watched her night after night, because he'd seen her before. Plenty of times, in fact. Despite his memory, booze-soaked and fuzzy at best for the past few years, he would swear he'd spoken to her once or twice at some party or another.

She moved to close the door, but he stepped into the threshold and blocked the move with his body before she managed to escape him again. "Poe."

She turned away in an attempt to hide the scars of her accident from him. He couldn't immediately recall the exact details, but seeing her now, he remembered there'd been some scandal linked to her.

"No one has called me that in a long time. I'd appreciate it if you didn't."

"What shall I call you then?"

She peeked at him from behind her curtain of hair shielding the worst of her scars. "Maya," she said, her tone laced with reluctance. "Maya Pomeroy."

"You remember me?" he asked.

She did. He could see it in her clear, green eyes. Large and round and framed by the same dusky lashes in his fantasies.

"I know *of* you," she clarified. "Burnett Dupree, the playboy playwright. Rumor had it you never attended a play that wasn't your own. You only attended opening night, and that was *if* you were sober. Which wasn't all that much, according to various accounts I've read, courtesy of the Internet."

Damn. Why hadn't he thought of doing a Google search of her name? Because he'd had no reason to, until now.

"Don't believe everything you read online," he cautioned.

She smiled coldly. "One critic claimed you had more women than hit plays. So yes, Mr. Dupree. I think I know exactly who, and what, you are."

"Do you now?" He'd detected a hefty dose of distaste in her icy voice, and damn if he didn't resent it, and her, for pointing out his past weaknesses. Annoyed with her for believing more rumor than fact, he almost walked away. But the truth was, he was no longer that guy, rumored or real. No longer the one who'd had little respect for himself and anyone else for that matter. And in some crazy, roundabout way, he had her, his muse, to thank. Although she didn't know it, she had him writing and kept him sober simply by her poolside appearance every night.

"Good night." She attempted to close the door, but with his body in the way, the door remained wide open. She looked at him then, full on, with fiery annoyance burning in her gaze when he didn't move. "What do you want from me?" she demanded.

He didn't flinch at the sight of her scarring, although he suspected that was exactly what she expected of him. Instead, he flashed her one of his best smiles and held up the bag he'd been holding with the orange logo proclaiming Cat's Crawfish was the best in Louisiana. "Dinner," Burnett told her. "I promised you Friday night crawfish. Regardless of what you may have read online, I do keep my promises."

She stared at him for several heartbeats as emotion battled within her gaze. Equal quantities of fear and a wanting that had nothing to do with sex—yet. Eventually the wanting won the skirmish. Despite the wariness still banked in her eyes, she smiled at him, tentatively at first, then as bright as a spotlight, and he forgot to breathe.

"Do you mind if we eat outside?" she asked.

Under the cover of darkness? Not a chance. Besides, they'd be the prime target for every night bug nature had to offer. "How about the kitchen table?" he suggested. "No bugs to fight off that way."

He knew the minute panic set in because her eyes widened and she sucked in a sharp breath. He imagined if he were in her position, he'd feel the bite of panic as well. "I'm not put off by a few scars," he told her.

She made a sound that could've been a huff of caustic laughter, but he wasn't sure. "You and the reconstruction team that put me back together again," she said, her tone most definitely dripping with sarcasm.

"Look, we can stand here and argue about it all night, but I've got a few pounds of food here, and I'm starved." He pushed off the door and strode right past her before she could protest. Through the mudroom and into the kitchen, he hit the switch for the overhead light as he went. "Got any Tabasco?" he called out to her.

A white wicker ceiling fan spun lazily overhead, and Burnett counted the revolutions waiting for Maya to join him. He'd made a bold move but a calculated one. He didn't have to be a rocket scientist to understand her apprehension. She was scarred. Badly. Once stunningly beautiful, tall with sleek curves, the darling of the runway, the good girl who had *bad* written all over her incredible body, had received a hard dose of reality. Whispered accounts he'd overheard, the world as she knew it was forever changed, all because she'd gotten in the car with a friend who'd had too much to drink. He seemed to recall hearing that if Todd Cantrell, one of the fashion industry's celebrity photographers, had survived the crash, he would've blown a 3.6 on the Breathalyzer.

"In the fridge," she said, her tone cautious and resigned. She joined him in the kitchen and limped her way to the overhead cabinet for dishware, the drawer near the sink for cutlery, then moved to the table. Turning to the fridge, she pulled it open and peered inside. "What would you like to drink? I have no alcohol in the house. You have a choice of sweet tea, juice, Coke, or water. Or I could put on some coffee."

He liked the fact that she didn't keep alcohol in the house. After what she'd suffered, he understood and frankly was grateful, considering his own issues with booze. Besides, in his bid for continued sobriety, he figured he could only handle one temptation at a time—and that temptation was none other than Maya Pomeroy, the supermodel formerly known only as Poe.

After snagging the Tabasco and another bottle claiming to be the hottest sauce in Louisiana from the fridge, he went to the cabinet where she'd pulled the plates and found a heavy, round serving platter. "Tea's good," he said as he unloaded the crawfish, corn on the cob, and roasted potatoes onto the platter. While she fixed their drinks, he finished setting the table, then waited for her to be seated before taking the chair opposite her for himself.

He lifted his glass of sweet tea for a toast. "To not eating alone."

Five

Maya wouldn't exactly say she was comfortable being so physically exposed in the presence of Burnett, but so far he hadn't so much as flinched when he looked at her. His seeming indifference made her curious, even though she half expected him to turn away in revulsion at any minute, not sit down to share a meal with her.

She let out a weighty sigh. Maybe she should just shut her inner voice the hell up and enjoy the moment while it lasted. Hadn't she complained that she was sick to death of her own company?

Lifting her glass of juice, she lightly tapped the rim to his. "To not eating alone," she concurred, then took a long swallow. She had enough trouble sleeping at night, and the last thing she needed was the caffeine in a glass of sweet tea at this hour.

Burnett heaped a large helping of food she'd never be able to eat in one sitting onto her plate, then piled his own high. "So, can I ask what you do now that you're . . ."

"No longer on the runway?" she finished for him. Making do with second best, she thought, but that was just her inner self-pity talking. Her clothing line might sell well locally, but Bergdorf's or Macy's certainly weren't knocking on her dining room–turned–studio door. "You mean when I'm not entertaining the Garden Club or volunteering with the Junior League?"

He must've gotten the joke because he chuckled at her sarcasm. She had more where that came from. Not that she was bitter. For the most part, she'd come to terms with her lot in life, but every so often anger would give her a hard shove and every step she'd taken forward, figuratively and literally, was ripped out from under her.

"Yeah, that's what I mean," he said, his gaze brimming with humor.

She liked a man who knew how to laugh. A lot. And she just might learn to like Burnett Dupree a whole lot more than was wise for her continued her self-preservation.

The bad thing about not throwing him out of her house after he'd practically stormed his way into her kitchen was that she could get used to seeing those get-lost-in-me blue eyes across the table from her on a regular basis. Better yet, a few inches above her. While she was flat on her back with her legs wrapped around his hips.

The food on her plate suddenly held a great deal of interest when she realized exactly how long it had been since she'd last had sex. She missed sex. Missed the closeness of a man's body, the touching, the kissing, the lovemaking. She kept her eyes averted and hoped she hadn't had one of those hungry, eat-you-alive looks showing on the good side of her face.

She pushed those thoughts out of her head, almost, and concentrated on slathering a square of butter over her corn on the cob. "I design lingerie and exercise wear for women," she said, finally looking at him and answering his question.

He cocked a single eyebrow upward, making him look even sexier. Damn him.

"You any good?" he asked.

She ignored the rudeness of his question because of the genuine interest in his eyes and that heart-stopping smile. How was she supposed to think straight when he was smiling at her like that? Actually smiling and not shrinking away in horror. Plus he showed honest-to-goodness interest in what she had to say. No way could she ignore *that*.

"Of course I am." Not that she was arrogant, but her designs were selling out more and more quickly each time she supplied the French Quarter boutique with fresh inventory. She had high hopes for her new lingerie line, too.

"So, why New Orleans?" he asked her before pulling the meat from the shell and sprinkling it with hot sauce.

"It's not New York." She held the head, then twisted the tail on a crawfish, exposing the meat. "And it's home." A decision that had come easily once she'd secured the services of one of the best plastic surgeons in the country who specialized in reconstruction and craniofacial surgery with an office right there in New Orleans. "What brings you down south?"

"It's not New York," he mimicked, then popped the meat into his mouth.

New Orleans wasn't just miles away from New York geographically but culturally as well. The city wasn't all about Mardi Gras beads and topless college students hanging from the famed wrought-iron balconies. They didn't call New Orleans the Big Easy for nothing, because there was an ease about the city, a sense of belonging that no other city in the world offered to anyone who graced her presence—if they were smart enough to accept what the grand lady had to offer.

"And it's home," he added as he reached for the salt.

"I had no idea the infamous Burnett Dupree hailed from the Crescent City. Where 'bouts?"

"Not far enough away from the city to stay out of trouble," he said, then added a sheepish grin. "Misspent youth."

"I longed for a misspent youth," she told him.

"Let me guess," he said slowly while eyeing her critically. "Honor student. Probably valedictorian or at least salutatorian. Head cheer-leader. Prom queen."

"You're forgetting head of the yearbook committee and co-captain of the debate team."

"Overachieve much?"

She couldn't help herself. She laughed. The sound came out a little rusty and felt just a tad awkward, but after such a long time of nonuse, what did she expect?

"Maybe a little," she admitted. "My older sister did it all, so I thought I had to as well."

"Competitive?"

"Ruthlessly." She aimed for slyness, but figured her smile was crooked at best on a good day. "So, how misspent was this mis-spent youth of yours?"

"Terribly," he said, his grin turning positively wicked.

Suddenly all she could think about was sex. Not the gentle, tender kind, but the kind of sex that was raw and hot and sensual. The kind of sex that would leave them spent and breathless with their hearts pounding out of their chest.

She let out a long, uneven breath. "How do you do that?" she asked, frowning. Annoyance crept into her voice, and she blamed him. He was the one responsible for making her think of the things that had been missing in her life since the accident.

He ripped apart another crawdad and drizzled it with Tabasco. "Do what?"

Her frown deepened at his totally innocent expression. Maybe she was to blame for going down that very sexy road, not him. Still, mistrust had her narrowing her eyes.

Was he flirting with her? She appreciated the thought, but really? Not likely.

"Never mind," she said, then snagged the little bottle of hot sauce and doused the crawfish she'd just freed from its shell.

His innocent expression turned to one of concern. "Did I do something wrong?"

She regarded him as she popped a crawfish into her mouth, then shook her head. He hadn't. Not really. She was what was wrong. Her. And her broken body.

"Why are you flirting with me?" she asked. Her head and heart couldn't chance another rejection even if he did appear interested in her. The accident had taken away not only her looks but her confidence as well.

"Because I find you attractive."

That was a statement she'd thought she'd never hear again in her lifetime. Nor one that she believed, not because she was scarred but because of the source of the flirtatious compliment.

"Coming from the playboy playwright? Yeah, that's reliable." She forced the laughter, hoping to take the sting out of her cynicism. "Is there a woman you don't find attractive?"

His grin turned sheepish, and she thought he looked adorably embarrassed.

"Actually, yes," he admitted. "There have been a few."

"That many, huh?"

"Several, now that I think about it."

"Oooh," she said before taking a quick sip of juice. "A whole seven or eight? Why, I think I might actually be impressed. Apparently you are more discriminatory than your online critics implied."

"My reputation may precede me, but like I said, don't believe everything you read on the Internet."

Despite her skepticism, she was enjoying herself a whole lot more than she should. In truth, she decided she didn't much care. Although he made a great verbal sparring partner, she was in no danger of falling for her über-sexy tenant. The man was a known womanizer. Yet on the other hand, with a guy like him, a woman always knew where she stood.

Sex. That's what the Burnett Duprees of the world were all about. And if she were being honest, she couldn't deny a certain appeal in such a situation. No strings, no commitments, no drama. Just . . . *sex*.

A half hour later, their meal finished, Maya stood to clear the table. Burnett joined her, and before she knew it the leftovers were tucked in the fridge and the dishwasher loaded. For as much as she hated their midnight rendezvous to end, she did still need to complete her nightly exercise ritual.

She leaned back against the tiled counter and folded her arms in front of her. "Thank you for dinner," she said. "It was nice to share a meal with an actual human."

"The pleasure was all mine." His mouth quirked as he dried his hands on the dish towel hanging from the hook next to the sink. "Perhaps we can do this again."

A statement, not a question. Interesting, she thought. Presumptuous, too, as if he expected her to agree. She was half inclined to turn him down flat, but she was nothing if not a southerner. Manners dictated that she return the favor. Common sense told her to run as far away from him as humanly possible. The man was a lethal combination of good ol' boy Southern charm and New York sophistication. And impossible to resist.

"Are you free for Sunday supper?" she asked, ignoring the satisfied glint in his sexy-as-sin blue eyes. "I can fry a mean chicken."

"I'd be honored," he answered, then took a step in her direction, narrowing the already too short distance between them. Before she could react, he reached toward her and reverently cupped her scarred cheek in his warm palm.

Heaven help her, she wanted to crawl away and hide somewhere safe. She should protect herself from the exact thing she craved—the promise of more.

"Say around four?" Her voice warbled, making her come off nervous and pathetic, not at all like a woman who'd seen a thing or two in her lifetime.

"Four sounds perfect," he said, his own voice a soft, sexy, and velvety caress of sound that ignited her imagination.

With every ounce of strength she possessed, she fought the strong urge to turn her face more fully into the warmth of his palm. The gentleness of his touch overwhelmed her, and she nearly wept. When he bent down and brushed his lips lightly over hers in a feathery kiss, she closed her eyes and for that one second where his lips rested against hers, she pretended she wasn't damaged goods.

He pulled back and when she opened her eyes to look at him, she didn't know what to say. "Thank you" seemed just a tad too sad, so she searched for something a little less needy. "Care to join me for a swim?"

"I'd love to, but I didn't pack any trunks," he said.

He did that on purpose, she thought. Used his deep, lazy drawl to put the image of him naked and wet and hard in her mind for the sole purpose of making her crazy with desire. She knew what this was all about, this impossible wanting she'd been suffering with since the minute she'd laid eyes on him.

Depravity, that's what. Making her crave him. She couldn't help herself, either. Twenty-four months without sex did that to a girl.

"Perhaps another time," she said politely before she did something really desperate, like start rubbing up against him like the cat in heat she was obviously channeling. Because as of right this second, abstinence was a virtue she no longer wished to practice.

six

In the two weeks since that night he'd barged into Maya's kitchen with a bag full of crawfish and a whole lot of attitude, Burnett had learned a lot about his sexy landlady. First and foremost, despite her previous career, Maya Pomeroy was in no way, shape, or form a good-time girl like so many of her former contemporaries. She might scoff at the idea of marriage, but he suspected her stance more of a defense mechanism courtesy of a shallow boyfriend who'd taken one look at her post-accident and disappeared. No doubt the scarring she was so conscious of was the culprit, because now that he knew her better, he didn't need Google to peg her as a white-picket-fence, lots-of-babies, forever kind of girl.

He usually avoided her kind like he avoided bad reviews. But something had changed because he couldn't seem to get enough of being in Maya's company. Sobriety, maybe? Perhaps, he thought.

Or perhaps the change had nothing to do with his previous booze-soaked existence and everything to do with the woman he couldn't stop thinking about for more than a minute.

Not that he needed an excuse to see her. They'd spent practically every night together having supper and talking into the late evening hours before she'd excuse herself shortly before midnight. He'd return to his apartment where he pretended to write but instead would watch her from the window as she worked out in the pool. He thought about joining her. He ached to join her, to slip into the cool water with her and make her his in the most elemental way possible, but after that first night, she hadn't issued him another invitation.

Better that she hadn't, he thought. Why invite trouble? With a capital *T* trouble. The kind that changed ideals and preconceived notions.

Tonight would be no different from the rest of the time they'd spent together, he thought, as he helped her clear the supper dishes while she put the leftovers into a plastic container and tucked them into the fridge. As she bent over, he caught sight of her sweet backside encased in a pair of soft denim capris and his testosterone gave him a hard shove. The urge to smooth his hands over her rump had his fingers tingling.

God help him, he couldn't take it any longer. He'd been a gentleman for two long weeks. Screw chivalry. He wanted Maya. Gallantry be damned.

She said something he couldn't hear over the ringing in his ears. Straightening, she closed the refrigerator and turned to face him. Confusion lit her gaze as he took a determined step, then two, toward her.

"Enough already," he said roughly. He took hold of her hand

and gave a gentle tug, pulling her to him. The space between them evaporated as she easily slid into his embrace. His hand moved to the curve of her throat where he pressed his thumb against the pulse wildly beating there. He waited, and when she didn't protest he lowered his head and kissed her.

Her lips were smooth, yet firm beneath his. She tasted of ripe strawberries from the dessert she'd made. Despite her tentative response, she kissed him back. No, not tentative, he thought, cautious. Protective. From who? Him?

He lifted his head and looked down into her wide eyed gaze. "Relax," he told her, then dipped his head to nuzzle the smooth skin of her neck. "Enjoy."

"Burnett, I don't . . . Oooh . . ." She moaned when he laved the spot right below her ear. Tipping her head to the side, she gave him better access and he took advantage of the invitation to trail hot kisses down her throat, to her chest, to the V of her blouse where the gentle slope of her breasts taunted him.

"This is a bad idea," she whispered when he dipped his tongue between her breasts, then lightly nipped her skin. A tremor passed through her and he smiled against her skin. He couldn't remember the last time a woman actually trembled in his arms.

"The worst," he agreed, but that didn't stop his hands from sliding down her back to cup her bottom. God, how he'd fantasized about touching her, the feel of her skin against his hands, the weight of her body on his as she rode him hard.

"We probably shouldn't," she murmured, shifting her weight so she was pressed against him. "We do have a signed contract."

"I promise not to sue."

She made a sound that bordered on laughter. "You're right," she said. "It's just a kiss."

"Right." He flicked his tongue over the swell of her breast. "A kiss is all this is," he said, seconds before his mouth settled over hers. A kiss was all it ever would be.

Right?

Maya closed her eyes and the room spun when Burnett deepened the kiss. His tongue swept over hers, teasing her, tasting her until she was convinced she'd slid into a whirlpool of pleasure. She clung to his wide shoulders for support, convinced if she let go, she'd drown.

From a kiss.

From a hot, openmouthed kiss that had her toes curling and her insides melting.

In her opinion, it wasn't a matter of *if* she made love with Burnett but *when*. The sooner the better, as far as she was concerned.

Quick! she thought. Get him naked before he comes to his senses and realizes he's making love to a freak.

She'd boarded the Pity Party Express tonight and despite the heat and desire unfurling through her, she couldn't shake off the melancholy. Not only had it been a while since she'd been with a man, in all honesty she hadn't thought any man would ever find her attractive again. She was scarred. The skin on the right side of her face and neck so twisted and marred that Poe, the darling of the runway, was unrecognizable. Then there were the other physical issues she dealt with, like the constant pain from the muscle and nerve damage to her right side. All that was left was Maya, a scarred, unknown clothing designer trying to scratch out a worthwhile existence while living in a rambling old house far too big for one person.

She squeezed her eyes tighter, determined to shove the self-loathing aside and enjoy what time she had with Burnett. He didn't belong in New Orleans, and he sure as hell didn't belong in a furnished apartment over her garage. Burnett Dupree was the Prince of Broadway and his days of slumming would be over soon. Once the play he was working on was finished, he'd be on his way back to where he belonged. Exactly when that would be, she was afraid to even ask.

She shoved her fingers into his thick, black as midnight hair. The low moan deep in his throat emboldened her. She clung to him, pressing her body against his, crushing her breasts to his wide chest, imprinting the feel of him on her memory so she could have this moment forever in her mind where it would never end. His hands slid up her back and settled on her shoulders, and before she could beg him to take her right there on the kitchen table, he abruptly ended the kiss and gently set her away from him. With every ounce of willpower she possessed, she kept her moan of protest silent.

He dragged his hand through his hair, his bluer than sin eyes the color of purple irises in spring and still blazing with desire. For her.

"Was it something I said?" she asked in an attempt at levity she was nowhere near feeling.

"We should say good night."

Stunned, she stared at him. The rejection ripped through her. Like a javelin to her heart, she ached. She hurt so badly she wanted to throw something. Directly at Burnett's head. The first time she decides to make an effort to experience what she'd been missing out on for two long years, and she ends up rejected, her fragile confidence obliterated.

"Good night?" She hadn't meant to ask a question. She'd meant to *tell* him good night, as in good-bye. As in get the hell away from her before she started to cry.

"I'm sorry," he said, then stepped around her, walking away without explanation.

Not that one was necessary, she thought as she gripped the counter for support, catching a glimpse of her own hideous reflection in the darkened window.

seven

❋

Frustrated, uncomfortable, and sweaty, not to mention more than a tad cranky, Maya stripped bare, then dove into the deep end of the pool where she pounded the water for four full lengths. The water, cool against her heated skin, did little to lessen her anger—at Burnett and herself.

Little good a punishing workout would do her tonight after Burnett's hurtful rejection. Swimming away the sexual frustration that had been her constant companion since he'd barged into her life was nothing but an exercise in futility. He'd made her hungry for more than just the company of another human being, for the promise of hope. The hope of more. The hope of normal. In truth, she almost envied him. She wished she were capable of turning off her emotions as easily as he had done.

She didn't know if he was watching her tonight or not, and quite frankly she didn't much care one way or the other. At least that's what she tried to make herself believe. She planned to complete her workout and then escape back into the house where she would go back to microwave dinners in front of the television and only her own sorry self for company. After his cold rejection, there wasn't a chance in hell she'd ever put herself out there like that again and risk having the invitation thrown so cruelly back at her.

Lungs near bursting, she surfaced and took in huge gulps of air. God, what had gone wrong? For the past two weeks she'd come to believe that her scars didn't matter to him. He'd never shrunk away from her, never once looked at her in horror the way Gavin had done that morning in a New York hospital following the accident. She and Burnett had even discussed the accident that had ended her career, how she'd gone with Gavin to a party in the Hamptons and the argument they'd had because Todd Cantrell, a photographer at the party, had come on to her. She'd been furious with Gavin for behaving like a possessive ass and so she'd left the party with Todd when he'd offered to drive her back to the city. She knew he'd been drinking, but she hadn't realized how much, until it was too late.

The accident had been her fault as much as Todd's, but despite her injuries she had survived. Todd hadn't. And that was a truth she'd had to live with every day.

Hanging on to the side of the pool, she did a series of leg exercises and still couldn't come up with a plausible answer for Burnett's abrupt departure. Now that the sting of his rejection wasn't as sharp as it had been a few hours ago, she suspected her physical appearance was not responsible for his about-face. Something had spooked him, but what?

Maybe he just wasn't interested, she thought as she slipped beneath the water and swam the length of the pool again. But that hardly made sense, either, because he'd watched her night after night. She came up for air and frowned. Maybe he was merely being nice to the cripple because he'd been taught not to kick puppies, pull the tails of kittens, or be rude to people with scars. What if the only reason he kept coming for supper night after night was because her cooking skills were better than average and he hadn't had a home-cooked meal in months? Maybe all the appetite he had was for food and not her.

He watched her—from a distance. Because he couldn't stomach her scars?

She let out a frustrated groan and pushed off the side. That made no sense. He'd touched her face and he hadn't so much as blinked. He'd cupped her twisted flesh in his warm palm and kissed her. Like he meant it. How many times had she caught him looking at her, those get-lost-in-me eyes of his simmering with desire? Practically every night they'd been together, that's how many.

She ignored the twinge of pain in her hip, and her heart, and pushed herself harder. So what the hell was his problem? She was no blushing virgin. She knew a thing or two about desire, and damn it, he'd wanted her tonight. Perhaps alcohol wasn't the only vice he'd given up in his bid for sobriety. Just her luck. The moment she realizes her sex drive is alive and well, the one man she decides she wants to take a test drive with is on a sexual sabbatical.

She hit the side, spun, and pushed off for another underwater lap. Maybe she should take matters into her own hands. Shyness had never been one of her failings, so why didn't she just tell him she wanted to have sex with him?

She broke the surface of the water and latched on to the side for another set of leg exercises. Because she was afraid, that's why. Afraid he'd reject her.

Again.

Which was plain stupid, she thought, and lost count of her leg lifts. The first night they'd had dinner together he'd told her he was attracted to her. How had that changed?

She let out a growl of annoyance with a hefty dose of disappointment and a dash of self-pity thrown in for good measure and slipped beneath the water to swim across the pool and back again. When she came up for air, she came nose to toe with a battered pair of brown loafers. Tipping her head back to get a better look, she frowned because her heart did a little flip as it always did whenever she saw Burnett. She was angry at him for hurting her, angry at herself for being hurt. Even if she did want to tear off his clothes, she wasn't sure she wanted to see him right now. She was too vulnerable, too raw.

Too damned thrilled to see him.

She frowned at him. "You're bad news, Dupree, you know that?"

A half smile tipped his mouth. He crouched down and rested his forearm over his knee. "Would it help if I apologized?" he asked, looking contrite.

For a split second she hated him for making her care. "What exactly are you apologizing for?" When he said nothing, she added, "Feel free to jump in and defend yourself at any time."

He reached out to touch her, but she pulled back, afraid if he did her resolve to stay angry with him would crumble like a cheap promise.

"I hurt you tonight, and I'm sorry."

Her heart pounded so hard, she was certain he could hear it. "Care to explain what happened back there? I thought . . ." What? That he was going take her right there on the kitchen table?

A girl can hope.

"I don't want to hurt you."

"I think we've already established that you did."

He shook his head. "You know I can't stay here."

She blew out a stream of breath and pushed off the side of the pool. "No one's asking you to." Irritated, she slipped beneath the water to swim to the other side. She understood. He was a playwright and his work required him to be in New York for months on end. She had no intention of ever going back to the city that had essentially rejected her once she was damaged goods.

But that didn't mean they couldn't enjoy each other for what time they did have together. Did it?

A renewed spark of anger had her surfacing and wiping water from her eyes so she could glare at him from across the pool. "What did you think was going to happen? We'd have sex and I'd beg you to stay in New Orleans? Boy"—she issued a caustic burst of laughter—"you have a very high opinion of yourself, don't you?"

He frowned suddenly. He looked formidable and sexy, and God help her, she wanted him despite the fact that her common sense was practically screaming at her to run as far away in the opposite direction as she could.

"That's not what I meant," he said, "and you know it."

She'd had enough. Of him. Of her own stupidity. Heading to the ladder, she exited the pool and limped unashamedly to the Adirondack chairs where she'd left her robe and a large fluffy towel. After wrapping herself in the towel, she turned to face him. "I don't know any such thing," she said, squeezing the excess water from her hair, "because you didn't bother to stick around long enough to at least explain yourself. What the hell was that?"

He straightened and started toward her. The determination evident in his eyes had her breath hitching. She thought about listening to her common sense and running but stood her ground instead. There wasn't a snowball's chance of survival in New Orleans that she'd run and hide from him. Not anymore. She was pissed off and her pride was hurt, but damn it, she'd survive. She'd survived worse.

He stopped inches in front of her. "I'm here now," he said. "Doesn't that count for something?"

"Not really," she shot back. But yes, he was here now. Was it enough? Could she settle for *now* with no promise of more?

She could smell the intoxicating scent of his cologne, could feel the heat emanating from his body while hers hummed with anticipation. Using every ounce of restraint she possessed, she kept her hands at her sides because God help her, she still wanted him. Wanted to slip her arms around him, to have his arms around her, to feel his body slide into hers as they made love.

She shrugged her shoulders as if she didn't care. A lie. He made her want things she had no business wanting. Like tomorrow. Like a bunch of tomorrows.

"I want you, Maya."

She tried to remember to breathe. He wanted her.

For now.

She let out an unsteady breath. She could be all grown up about it, pretend she was the kind of woman to answer a booty call then walk away. But the truth was something else entirely. She wasn't the type to have sex without at least a hint of something more.

Could sex with Burnett be enough? she wondered. Maybe. Because try as she might, she couldn't find a single thing wrong with wanting to be held, to feel passion, even for one night. Problem was, she did want more. She'd always want more.

She let out a resigned sigh. More just wasn't in the cards for her. Not any longer. That kind of future had been destroyed because of one horrendously bad decision. What she wanted and what she could have were never one and the same. She knew that. But was she strong enough to accept it where Burnett was concerned?

She had to be, she decided, and took a step toward him. "I know," she said, surprised that her voice worked. She moved closer and rested her hand on his chest. Through the thin fabric of his gauzy shirt, his heart beat sure and strong beneath her palm. She drew strength from his nearness. "I want you, too."

He settled his hand over hers and laced their fingers together. "Then what the hell are we doing?"

"Avoiding the truth," she said.

"Which is?"

She smiled, then gave his hand a light tug, pulling him with her toward the house. "Which is better left alone," she answered. She stopped at the door and turned toward him. "No regrets allowed, Burnett." Whether she meant for herself or for him, she wasn't exactly certain. "We walk through this door, and we leave regret outside."

"You sure about that?"

No.

"Absolutely." Her voice came out a whole lot stronger than she was feeling as she reached behind and twisted the doorknob. He followed her inside, through the mudroom, across the kitchen where they'd spent so much of their time together, and finally down the corridor to the study she'd converted into her first-floor bedroom.

She didn't bother with candles or soft music. They both knew what they wanted, and for her it was sex, pure and raw. She'd probably end up broken emotionally in some form or another, but the promise of intimacy was too tempting to resist. No regrets, she reminded herself as she turned to face him.

With the simple flick of his finger, the knot of her towel gave way and she was naked before him. She struggled with the urge to cover herself. Ridiculous, considering he'd seen her naked in the pool so often, but this was different. This time he was up close and personal. This time she was more than just nude, she was vulnerable. In her mind, that made all the difference in the world.

She reached for the buttons on his shirt, but he clasped his hands over hers and moved them so her arms wreathed his neck instead. With her body pressed against his, the filmy material of his shirt rubbed against her naked breasts, making them ache for his touch, for his kisses.

"You have on entirely too many clothes," she told him.

He chuckled. "Indulge me," he whispered, bending to nip at the tender skin on her shoulder as his hands swept down her back to cup her rear.

As his fingers skimmed her bottom, she tried not to think about the scars on her upper thigh, where they'd taken skin to use in the numerous plastic surgeries on her face. "Hmmmm," she murmured as his mouth and hands warmed her skin. "Indulge your fantasy?"

He looked at her, his mouth tipped into a crooked smile. "Something like that," he said, then caught her lips in a hot, openedmouthed kiss, deep-sixing her common sense and emotional survival skills.

Desire ripped through her, making her ache for more intimate contact. The press of his mouth against hers made her dizzy and had her toes curling. Digging her fingers into his shoulders for support, she clung to him.

Suddenly the mattress brushed against the back of her legs. She hadn't even realized he'd moved them toward the bed, but she welcomed the soft warmth of the worn quilt when he carefully eased her down upon the mattress.

She reached again for the buttons on his shirt. "Indulge *me*," she whispered when his mouth left hers to nuzzle her neck.

This time he didn't stop her from unbuttoning his shirt. She slid the lightweight fabric from his wide shoulders, marveling at the lean, hard length of his body, the hills and valleys of his muscular, masculine landscape. Her heart beat heavily in her chest. God, how she wanted this man. Any chance of ever showing him cool indifference evaporated at the feel of his torso rubbing up against her. He was so beautiful, so perfect, she nearly wept at the irony. And for tonight, he was hers.

He rested his weight on his forearms. Her breath caught at the unabashed heat simmering in his eyes when he looked down at her. "Do you have any idea how beautiful you are?" he asked.

Once. Maybe. She'd been told that enough by those who'd photographed her, hired her, filled her head with bullshit praise made of nothing but hot air, all contrived to feed her ego so they could manipulate her into doing whatever they wanted her to do. But that was a lifetime ago and she was no longer that person, inside or out, she realized. She'd changed, not just physically, but emotionally. She'd grown up—a lot—in the past two years. But change was not something she wanted to discuss or even think about tonight. Tonight was supposed to be all about Burnett and passion and orgasms.

"You talk too much," she said. With a light press of her fingers to the back of his head, she brought his mouth down to hers for another kiss that had her body shifting restlessly beneath his.

Taking the hint, he dipped his head and laved the slope of her breast. Palming the weight in his hand, he traced his thumb across her nipple, sending a sharp tug of desire through her. When he took her into his heated mouth, she moaned at the exquisite pleasure.

Burnett skimmed his hand over Maya's bare hip, reveling in the silkiness of her skin beneath his fingertips. The feel of her, her softness, her scent, an intoxicating blend of some exotic flower he couldn't name combined with a seductive hint of musk, filled his senses. She had his dick hard and throbbing beneath his khakis.

She reached for his belt. He didn't stop her eager fingers from working the leather free. When she slid down the zipper of his trousers and slipped her hand beneath the fabric of his boxer briefs to wrap her long fingers around the length of him, he nearly came out of his skin.

Need spiraled and settled in his sex, making him throb for even more intimate contact. With each gentle tug and pull of her hand, his breathing labored. If he didn't stop her, he'd end up coming in her hand. Freeing himself from her questing fingers, he urged her back against the mattress, then moved down her body, using his hands and his mouth. He teased her belly button, pressed open her thighs, and used his fingers to delve between her soft, dewy folds to her heated core. She cried out and arched against his hand when he slowly pumped his fingers in, then out, to cover her with her own moisture.

The scent of her sex drew him, and he tormented them both with quick kisses and teasing lashes of his tongue over her clit. Heaven never tasted so sweet or so powerful. He swept his tongue over her, laving, tasting, teasing, loving. Her body came alive, her desire pooled on his tongue as he pushed her closer to release and then finally over the edge, and she came, his name on her lips.

For a split second, Burnett mourned the loss of heat when he left her to shed the remainder of his clothes before rejoining her on the bed. He swept his tongue into her mouth, teasing, tasting her until she writhed against him. Despite her earlier orgasm, with one single kiss he awakened her body again. Want, desire, and need all clamored inside him. He could barely think straight, but one thing he knew inexplicably—he'd give just about anything if the erotic sensations rippling through his body never ended.

He clasped her face between his palms and angled her head so he could deepen the kiss. There'd been plenty of women in his past, but he couldn't recall ever being so drawn to a woman as he was Maya. In the brief time they'd spent together since his coming home to New Orleans, he suspected what he felt for her went far beyond anything he'd ever experienced in his past. Women came and went, and that had always suited him just fine. But not Maya. With her, he wanted something he didn't have the tools to define.

Forever?

Hardly. More like for as long as it lasted. Except his usual modus operandi didn't feel right. Not with her.

He was screwed and he knew it, because somewhere in the back of his mind he'd known since he first watched her dive naked into the pool that something about her was different. He'd known attraction, sexual attraction, in particular. But with Maya, he wanted something deeper and more profound. He wanted . . .

Forever.

Not a chance. Burnett Dupree didn't do forever. He did for as long as the good times lasted. When things got too heavy or complicated, he was gone. Lower the curtain, end of show. He'd even tried to walk away tonight, but here he was, a few short hours later, making love to her, with no intention of leaving her any time soon. With Maya he wanted complicated. He wanted messy.

He wanted her, and that excited him, yet at the same time it scared the hell out of him.

With his arms braced on either side of her head, he positioned himself between her legs and slowly slid his body into hers. She was exquisite. Perfect, as she arched against him, then met him thrust for thrust as he moved against her. Her fingers dug into the flesh of his backside as he pumped his hips, pushing them both to the limit, to that place where time stopped and only sensation existed.

She came again, and dug her nails into his back. He followed her over the edge, his own release so powerful he lost himself in pure sublime pleasure. Eventually, he slowly came back to earth. Moving to his side, he took her with him, tucking her body close to his. As he drifted off to sleep, he couldn't help wondering how in hell he was ever going to leave her.

eight

One month later and Maya was still waiting for the other shoe to drop. Worse, try as she might, she couldn't anticipate how she was going to react when it finally did. She wanted to be cool about the whole thing, pretend to be nonchalant about his picking up stakes and returning to New York, but she wasn't about to make anyone a promise on that score, especially herself. For all intents and purposes, and as far as she was concerned, they were a couple in every sense of the word.

Although he hadn't specifically said so, she suspected the play Burnett had been working on all summer was finished. She knew because he'd essentially moved into the main house with her. He'd stopped escaping to the small one-bedroom apartment over the garage to write a little over a week ago. That he could be leaving for New York at any moment had her feeling edgy. Who knew how long he'd be gone. A week? A couple of months? Forever? There'd been a few phone calls she'd caught snippets of the past few days and she had a feeling their time together would be ending. Soon.

Tossing her pencil on the design table, she leaned back to study the design for a pale turquoise cotton chemise, one of a half-dozen new sleepwear items she'd been toying with for the past couple of hours. Pleased with what she had so far, she lifted her arms over her head and attempted to stretch the kinks from her shoulders. From what Burnett had told her, once he had a play in production, the work was nearly nonstop until opening night. Not that it mattered. He hadn't exactly asked her to accompany him once he answered the siren's call of the bright lights of Broadway.

Despite her disappointment, she couldn't help but be acutely aware of Burnett's deep sense of achievement, something he'd told her he hadn't experienced in ages. Sober and stronger than ever, the Prince of Broadway was back. She hadn't read the play, but based on what he'd told her about *Shattered Illusions,* the story centered around one woman's discussion with the Devil on the eve of what could end up being her suicide. Since he hadn't been back to the apartment lately, she was dying of curiosity to know how the play ended. Did the heroine take her own life or not?

Burnett wasn't the only one who was "back." So was Poe. Or at least Maya Pomeroy and POE-tential.

Earlier this morning while Burnett was still asleep, she'd toyed with a few design ideas after receiving a phone call from one of the buyers at Macy's for their women's sportswear department. They wanted a two-season exclusive of POE-tential workout-wear products. Whether or not they'd carry the lingerie line as well remained to be seen, but she'd be delivering some samples herself next week. There were no guarantees, but she couldn't help feeling confident that her clothing line would be a success. She made clothes that fit a real woman's body, curves and all, not the emaciated stick figures the high-fashion world embraced. Her sizes ran from 4 to 24, with adjustments made to enhance the figure for women of all sizes, from plus to petite.

She heard the water running and realized Burnett must be getting into the shower. She thought about joining him, to share her good news, but she hesitated. If only she felt the same confidence in her relationship with him, which despite a hesitant start, had been on the fast track ever since. On paper, they made sense. They were both creative, he with words, she with a sewing needle. They laughed at the same jokes, enjoyed much of the same music, and read the same books. They even shared the same political affiliation. What more could a girl ask for? In reality, not so much. The main problem she could see with their relationship was geography—and now that didn't seem to be much of an issue since she'd be spending time in the city with the Macy's people, even if it might only be temporarily.

In truth, she wasn't looking all that forward to returning to New York. She had no choice if she wanted to see her clothing line off the ground, although she was determined to keep her base of operations in New Orleans. This was her home and the least she could do was bring a few jobs to her hometown.

By the time she reached the bathroom, Burnett was stepping from the shower and reaching for a towel. He looked up and smiled when he saw her, giving her a tiny thrill of pleasure. God, she wished the answers were easier about this thing between them. But then, when had life ever been all that easy?

"You know, I've been thinking," she said, resting her shoulder against the doorjamb. She hated the hesitation in her voice, that she was nervous about broaching the subject of going to the city with him, but there wasn't much she could do about that. Better to just get it out and deal with whatever came next.

"About?" he prompted as he dried off, then secured the towel around his waist. The terry cloth rode low on his hips and she considered giving the knot a flick. Procrastination worked for her, especially when she was scared witless.

She pulled in a deep breath. "New York," she blurted.

That caught his attention because he looked up and frowned. "Great city," he said, a note of caution in his voice.

Her insides twisted. "Agreed," she said. A month ago she would have disagreed vehemently. Obviously he caught on as well because his frown deepened.

"Really?" he asked. He pulled a can of shaving cream from the medicine cabinet along with his razor, then squirted shaving cream in his hand. "What's changed?"

She hated that the caution in his voice was now mirrored in his sinful blue eyes. Hated that with every small sign, another piece of her heart broke. "An offer."

His eyes widened in surprise. "To model?"

Her pride took a ding on that one, but she shrugged it off. Folding her arms in front of her, she laughed but the sound lacked humor, even to her own ears. "Yeah, well," she said, "that would be a surprise, wouldn't it? No, it's about my designs. It's about POE-tential."

Slowly, he applied shaving cream to his jaw, his gaze sliding to hers through the reflection in the mirror as she explained the situation. Damn him for looking nervous all of a sudden. Damn him for sounding cautious. Damn him for making her fall for him when she knew all along that he would break her heart.

Damn her for being stupid enough to fall in love with him.

"Apparently a buyer from Macy's was in New Orleans visiting relatives recently and the woman's niece was raving about my workout wear," she added in a rush, jamming all the words together as if speaking them in a hurry would make the rejection she sensed coming that much less painful. "The buyer was impressed with what she saw at the boutique in the Quarter and once the contracts are signed, I have a two-season exclusive with Macy's to carry my workout wear. Quite possibly, my lingerie line as well. I have a meeting scheduled there for next week."

He finished shaving and smiled at her, but the curve of his mouth was strained at best. "That's great news, Maya," he said in the least enthusiastic tone she'd ever heard. "Congratulations."

Anger immediately simmered in her veins, reaching a boiling point before she could stop it. "Congratulations," she mimicked in a droll monotone. She made a sound of disgust, then pushed off the doorjamb. "Congratulations?" she railed, a full octave higher.

Using a hand towel, he wiped away the remnants of shaving cream. Still dressed in only a towel, with all that über-delicious male flesh exposed just to torment her, he turned to face her and regarded her thoughtfully. A full minute must have passed before he calmly asked, "What exactly did you want me say?"

"It's not *what* you said, Burnett. It's *how* you said it." Like he knew what was coming and was dreading the moment when she threw herself at him and begged him to take her to New York with him.

Like hell.

He crossed his arms over his chest and stared at her. Like she'd lost her ever lovin' mind. Like he was waiting for her to stop being nuts before he said a word.

She planted her hands on her hips and glared back. She was *not* crazy. Okay, so maybe she was acting a little crazy. But in her current state of mind, she figured she might as well blame him for it. He made her crazy. With need. With wanting something she couldn't have—forever.

"Maybe we need to calm down a minute," he said in a placating tone that set her teeth on edge.

"Maybe *we* need to kiss my ass," she said, then turned and stormed out of the bathroom as fast as she could limp away. What the hell had she been thinking? She should've known he'd reject her. Again. Hadn't she been waiting for that to happen all along?

She didn't make it to the edge of the bed before he'd grabbed hold of her arm to stop her from escaping. "Maya. Wait."

"Don't," she said, tugging free of his grasp. A lump the size of Lake Pontchartrain lodged in her throat when she turned to face him. The wariness in his eyes broke her already battered heart. She'd known this moment would eventually come, she just hadn't expected it to hurt so damned much.

"I get it, Burnett. I really do. No one ever said this was forever." She'd known all that. He wouldn't be staying in New Orleans, and there was no such thing as her own happily-ever-after. That was her life. Except somewhere along the way she'd naively believed their relationship could continue if she went to New York, even if it only was temporarily.

Apparently she'd misjudged the situation.

He reached for her but she sidestepped him. If he touched her again, she'd shatter into a million tiny pieces. Once again, she needed to be strong to weather the hurt. Once again, she was reminded that she was nothing but damaged goods. And everyone knew damaged goods just weren't good enough.

"No one ever said it wasn't."

He'd spoken so softly, she wasn't sure she'd actually heard him correctly, nearly convincing herself wishful thinking had gotten the best of her hearing capabilities. Still, what if she *had* heard him right? Her pride had already been trampled. What did she have left to lose?

"Say that again?" she asked, hating the hopefulness she'd tried hard to ignore.

He took a step toward her, narrowing the distance between them. "No one ever said it wasn't," he repeated, his voice stronger this time.

Despite her fear of being slapped down, she asked, "What are you saying?"

He settled his hands on her shoulders and pulled her closer. She took in everything, the color of his eyes, the scent of his skin, fresh and clean and all male. The weight of his hands and the tingling sensation that rippled over her skin when he swept them down to grasp her fingers. "I'm saying that I love you, Maya. I don't want to be without you. I don't care where we live. Here. New York. It doesn't matter. I want to be wherever you are. I want to wake up next to you every morning. I want your face to be the last thing I see at night before I close my eyes."

Tears blurred her vision and burned her throat so that she couldn't speak. So she nodded. Enthusiastically. And then she wrapped her arms around him and hung on for dear life to this man who loved her. Who didn't care that her body was scarred and twisted. Who didn't care where they lived just so long as they could be together. Who saw beyond the damaged exterior to the woman inside wanting to love and to be loved.

Once she'd soaked his bare chest with her tears, she leaned back and looked into those bluer than sin eyes and knew without a doubt that she'd follow him anywhere. "I love you, too," she finally said. "So much."

With the tip of his finger, he tipped her head back to look into her eyes, his own brimming with the emotion in his heart. "We'll figure it all out," he said.

"We will," she confirmed, then lifted her mouth to his for a soul-reaching kiss that rocked both of their worlds.

epilogue

❉

EIGHTEEN MONTHS LATER . . .

Burnett hefted the carton onto the kitchen table, then sliced it open to reveal author copies of the hardcover release of *Shattered Illusions*. The book would release in another month, one week before the play's opening night. An opening night Maya had been upset about missing since she was already in her seventh month of pregnancy with their twin daughters. But she'd be two weeks from her due date, and the chance of her going into premature labor was already risky.

"Now maybe I can find out the ending," she said, peering around him and plucking a copy out of the box for herself.

He smiled as she lowered herself into the chair he'd pulled out for her. "I didn't think you'd want me to ruin it for you."

"Hmmmm," she murmured, carefully opening the book. "She probably dies at the end, and you didn't want me to nag you about changing the ending."

"You'll just have to read it to find out."

"Or see the play on opening night," she said hopefully.

"Maya—"

"I know. I know," she said, shifting in the chair. "Don't get my hopes up."

"For all I know, they could've changed the ending," he teased. "It's been known to happen." Especially since he wasn't there to babysit his play every step of the way as he'd done in years past. Not that he hadn't tried, but it hadn't taken him more than a couple of weeks to realize his heart wasn't in the production of his work but more in the actual producing of the work itself. A work that had taken on a whole new meaning when he'd been approached by a publisher asking if he'd be willing to write *Shattered Illusions* as a novel. He'd been intrigued by the idea, and with Maya's encouragement he'd signed a three-book contract.

She'd been with him in New York, and while she hadn't complained about the long hours alone, he knew she'd missed New Orleans. So they'd come home. He to write and she to a career that had taken off in ways she'd never expected. Not only were the POE-tential sportswear and lingerie lines both hugely successful, her new spring line of maternity wear was due to launch soon and had received stunning reviews during Fashion Week. Since she was no longer exclusively at Macy's, other high-end department stores had picked up POE-tential and she had more work than she'd ever expected.

Upon coming back to New Orleans, they'd had a small wedding with family and a few friends and officially moved into the big, rambling house as a married couple. The stairs were still difficult for her to climb, especially as her pregnancy advanced, but she'd insisted on using the upper floors and had returned the rooms on the bottom level to their former use. For a wedding present, he'd had the garage apartment remodeled into a design studio for her. She'd updated the study for his home office, dusty first editions included. He'd told her one of the bedrooms on the second floor would have been fine, but she'd insisted. He had a feeling those bedrooms would be filling up with the next generation of Duprees over the next few years.

She turned the page to the title page. "I could just skip to the end."

He laughed. "That's cheating."

"So is not telling your wife how the story ends." She shifted again in the chair. "In fact, I think it's illegal."

He came up behind her and slipped his arms around her, then bent forward and kissed the side of her neck. "No, it's not. But"— he nipped at the sensitive spot just below her ear—"I do know a few things that are illegal in some states."

"Why, Mr. Dupree, I'm shocked," she said, pouring on the southern belle routine. "You're positively scandalous."

He tipped her head back so he could kiss her. "It's what you love best about me," he said, then captured her lips in a kiss that went from playful to hotter than sin in three seconds flat. When they came up for air, she held out her hand for him to help her from the chair. She was really starting to have a hard time getting around, and he almost hoped she did deliver early just so she could get some relief.

She stood, braced her hand on her lower back, then turned the next page of the book. The dedication page. She read it, then looked up at him with tears brimming in her big green eyes. The dedication read:

To M,

Forever.

dime store cowboy

✳

KATE DOUGLAS

Ages ago, I wrote a romantic comedy titled Cowboy in My Pocket. *For years, one of the secondary characters, Mark Connor, begged me for his own happy ending. My thanks to Lori Foster for inviting me to contribute to this anthology. It was such a relief—finally—to let Mark end up with the love of his life.*

prologue

"Unlock that door, Betsy Mae. I aim to talk to you now. Open up, I said."

Betsy Mae Twigg squinted against the painful glare of the overhead light. The foggy bathroom mirror hid the worst of the damage, but she knew her left eye—already swollen almost completely shut—would be black and blue by morning. Carefully, she wiggled her jaw back and forth.

Good. It worked. Hurt like hell but at least it wasn't broken.

"Come outta there, I said. Now."

She ran the cold water and soaked a washcloth under the flow. The pounding on the door made her head hurt even worse and she slanted a quick glare at the solid oak separating her from the best-looking rodeo clown this side of Durango.

Too bad he was an abusive jerk.

Wringing the cold washcloth until it no longer dripped, she carefully folded it and held it to her throbbing jaw.

Relief wasn't instantaneous, but it definitely dulled the worst of the pain.

"Betsy Mae, you open that door now or I am gone for good this time. Gone and not comin' back. You hear me?"

Hell, she'd have to be deaf not to. She opened her mouth to tell Frank exactly what she thought of him, thought better of it, and flushed the toilet instead.

The pounding stopped. A final loud thunk rattled the door in its frame. Probably owing to contact with the toe of a worn-out cowboy boot.

A loud crash outside sent a crack racing through the steamy bathroom mirror. That had to be the door to the motel room slamming shut. The deep rumble she recognized for sure—Frank's old Chevy truck revving up in the parking lot.

Tires squealed for what seemed like forever. She almost laughed at how much rubber the damned clown left as he spun out of her life—for the second time. Once again, she'd pulled a really stupid move. The fog slowly cleared from the cracked mirror. Betsy Mae stared at her battered face. "You dumb shit. Aren't you ever gonna learn?"

How the hell was she going to convince Will and Annie to let her come back home.

Again.

MARK Connor squinted against the glare of early morning sunlight careening off a high-rise apartment window. He checked his watch and glanced once more at the matched set of Hartmann luggage piled at his feet.

A month's rent for his first apartment had cost less than the carry-on bag alone. How the hell had his life come to this?

"So, you're really leaving, eh Mr. Connor?" The burly doorman added one last suitcase to Mark's stack. "Never thought I'd see the day you'd trade in those fancy loafers of yours." He slapped Mark almost affectionately on the shoulder and then took up his post in the foyer.

Mark sighed. What did it say about a man that the only person seeing him off as he made a life-altering move like this—quitting a longtime job, selling the once-coveted Manhattan apartment, and giving up everything familiar—was the doorman to his apartment building?

Mark glanced down at the scuffed toes of his cowboy boots poking out beneath faded denim jeans. He'd considered showing up dressed like this for his last day as editorial director but figured the publishing world wasn't ready for the shock. He thought of the simplistic excuse he'd given his publisher when he'd handed in his resignation—that sometimes a man just knows when it's time for a change.

He hoped like hell he knew what he was talking about, but damn it all! He was almost forty and his life was a book filled with blank pages. There had to be more.

He let out a long gust of air, then glanced east where sunlight rose through the filtered haze of another Manhattan morning. Then he turned his eyes to the west.

To possibilities. Possibilities he'd never dreamed of until a couple of years ago, when he'd spent two of the most amazing weeks of his life at the Columbine Camp dude ranch in Colorado. Nothing had been the same since. New York suddenly felt monochromatic and quiet while his memories of Colorado were high-def color and surround sound.

The place called to him as nothing had ever called before, and the time was perfect for a change. His favorite author, the one he'd started his career with, was retiring. Michelle Garrison had happily chosen motherhood and life with a cowboy—in Colorado, of all places. An omen? Maybe.

Mark slowly shook his head and flashed a grin at the doorman. "I'm not getting any younger, Lester. There's a lot I still want to do."

"Yeah. I know." The big man laughed. "Places to go, people to see. I understand, Mr. Connor." Lester shrugged one massive shoulder and grinned. "It's just not easy to picture you on a horse, if you catch my drift."

"You might be surprised, Les." Mark glanced up as the deliveryman from the car dealership pulled up in front of the building and carefully parked Mark's brand-new shiny red Jeep Wrangler. Mark grabbed a couple of his suitcases while Lester helped with the rest. "Very, very surprised."

one

❋

"Mark, I feel just terrible about this, especially after promising you a room here at the Double Eagle. Maybe next week, when the babies are over whatever bug they've got?"

New York Times bestselling author Michelle Martin, née Garrison—once Mark's lead author and fashionista extraordinaire—wiped at a nasty stain on her faded cotton T-shirt as she juggled a screaming baby girl on one slim hip. An identical-looking little boy cried steadily from his seat in a high chair, and the odor of diapers in need of changing warred with the foul stench of baby barf.

After two days driving straight through to get here, Mark had to fight the urge to let loose with a little screaming of his own. Instead, he smiled calmly and stepped back a distance he hoped was well beyond projectile vomiting. "I'd offer to stay and help, Michelle, but . . ." He shrugged helplessly.

Michelle laughed so hard she snorted. "Men. You're all alike.

Tag discovered a job up on the summer range he just had to do about the time little MC started tossing his cookies. He was out the door before Niki got sick, but don't you worry your purty blond head about us," she drawled. "I'll manage."

In spite of the mess and the stink, Mark was glad Michelle hadn't lost that familiar twinkle in her eyes.

She juggled the now-silent Niki in her arms. "I called Will Twigg. He said he'd get a room ready for you at Columbine Camp, but once everyone's healthy again, I want you back here." She smiled. "I'm so glad you've left that rat race. I've missed you, Mark. Even Tag's been looking forward to your visit."

"Yeah, right." He laughed, but it was bittersweet, thinking of Michelle and her handsome cowboy husband. Mark hadn't realized what he might have had with his bestselling author until it was too late. Still, in spite of the tangled ponytail and dark circles under her eyes, Michelle looked happier than ever. Colorado had done this for her. Colorado, falling in love, and two beautiful—if stinky—little babies.

As Mark headed out to his dusty red Jeep, he wondered if Colorado could do the same for him. Then he thought of those two screaming babies and shook his head. Maybe not exactly the same.

He was still grinning when he drove through the gates to Columbine Camp. Love? After two failed marriages and numerous halfhearted attempts at relationships, that was the last thing he needed.

Leave the love to men and women like Michelle and Tag— youngsters who still had stars in their eyes. He knew better. It might work for some guys, but not for Mark Connor.

Relaxing, getting back in tune with the man he'd almost lost over the years—that was his goal. And maybe a romp in the hay with a willing cowgirl. He might not want love and marriage, but he certainly wasn't a monk.

With the radio set on a good, loud country-western station, he drove up the front drive of Columbine Camp with the unexpected sense of coming home. Small log cabins for guests were tucked in amid a grove of aspen trees, cows grazed beside the big red barn, and a corral held at least a dozen good-looking stock ponies. Blue skies sparkled overhead, the air was redolent with the scent of newly mown hay, and birds twittered in the trees along the drive. It just felt right.

Mark crawled out of the Jeep and stretched his arms up over his head. This might work even better than staying with Tag and Michelle—and the twins. The cabins were set far enough away from the main house where he was sure to get some quiet time and a chance to reassess his life. Just thinking of sitting out on the front porch with a cold beer in his hand and his feet up on the rail had the stress of the past few months fading away.

Then the front door slammed open and Will Twigg stalked across the big front porch. He had a duffel bag slung over one shoulder and his arm wrapped protectively around a tall, obviously pregnant redhead. Mark recognized Annie—he'd met her slimmer version less than a year ago.

She was crying, Will was cursing, and neither acknowledged Mark. He leaned against the Jeep and watched as Will tossed the bag into the back of a Ford truck parked beside the barn and carefully helped Annie into the passenger's seat.

A loud crash had Mark's head snapping around in time to see a gorgeous cowgirl in skintight jeans and tank top. Her tangled blond curls bounced as she came barreling out the front door.

"Damn you, Will Twigg! Get back here. You can't leave now!"

The big man turned and glared at the blonde. "I can and I will,

Betsy Mae. All your rantin' and ravin' isn't good for Annie. She needs a break and so do I. You, my dear little sis, are on your own."

"A break from what?"

"A break from you, damn it!"

Betsy Mae lurched back as if she'd been kicked. Then she snarled and balled her hands into tight little fists. "All you two do is moon over each other. You're making me sick!"

"Good. Then you won't miss us. We haven't had a honeymoon, so we're taking it now. It's time you got back to pullin' your weight around here. Don't forget to check the heifers. There's calves due and you're gonna be full up with two weeks of payin' guests startin' this weekend."

He glanced at Mark, with a definite twinkle in his eyes. "Hey, Mark. Michelle said you were coming. It's good to see you. Don't take any crap off Betsy Mae, ya hear?" Then, obviously trying not to grin, he climbed into the truck.

Mark waved at Will. Then he turned his head and studied the blonde. So this was the infamous Betsy Mae. She stared at the departing pickup with a look of utter disbelief on her face. Then she glared at him, as if all of this was somehow his fault.

He stepped up to introduce himself as she moved out of the shadows. Whatever Mark had planned to say died in his throat.

Her left eye was swollen shut and a huge, purple bruise fading to yellow covered the right side of her jaw. She glared at Mark, silently daring him to say a word. When he merely nodded in greeting, she jerked her head toward the house. "When you're through staring at the freak show, meet me inside so we can get you registered."

Then, without another word, she turned and stalked back inside. Mark glanced longingly at the little log cabin set farthest from the main house. Sighing softly, he followed Betsy Mae inside.

two

✦

Betsy Mae stomped through the front door, planted herself behind the desk, and grabbed the registration book before that damned drop-dead gorgeous dime store cowboy started asking questions. He had to be wondering what happened to her face.

Well hell, so was she. When her ex had called and apologized and asked if she'd be willing to give it another try, Betsy Mae'd honestly thought he'd turned over a new leaf.

Big mistake. And she'd almost rather eat dirt than have to come crawling back to her brother and best friend now sister-in-law, especially after they'd warned her this was going to happen, but damn it all, she'd had nowhere else to go.

No one else to care. And no matter how pissed Will might be with her for going back to Frank in the first place, her brother had still welcomed her back. Sort of.

A big shadow blocked the light from the front window. She looked up, blinking, and wondered how long tall, blond, and gorgeous had been standing there staring at her. Embarrassed to be caught woolgathering, Betsy shoved the registration book across the counter. "Here. Sign in."

His eyes flashed and she felt just the slightest bit guilty over the attitude she was giving him. It wasn't his fault her life was a train wreck, but he took the pen in one large yet elegant hand and without a word scrawled his name across the register. Mark Connor. Tag's new wife's fancy-pants editor.

"What cabin am I in?"

She shook her head. "You're in the main house. All the cabins are reserved through the next two weeks."

His perfect lips turned down in a brief moue of displeasure, but he kept his mouth shut, nodded, and reached for his wallet.

She shook her head. "No charge."

Raising his head, he quirked one surprisingly dark eyebrow over blue eyes so pale they looked silver. "I don't understand."

She shrugged, taking fiendish glee in setting him straight. "We're full up, Will's gone, and I need help. You're not here for vacation, Mr. Connor. You're here to work. Maria will have dinner ready at six every night and I'll expect you in the barn at six thirty tomorrow morning."

She flashed him a big grin, waiting for the fireworks to start. Instead, he raised his head with a smile that turned that already handsome face into drop-dead, wet-panty gorgeous. "Wonderful," he said, like he actually meant it. "If you'll show me to my room, I'll get settled."

BETSY Mae wandered into the kitchen just before six in the morning, but the coffee was already made, a cereal dish rinsed and sitting in the rack, and the house deadly quiet. Maria wasn't due in the kitchen until this afternoon when the dudes would need a decent meal, so it appeared her dime store cowboy had managed on his own. Betsy Mae poured herself a cup of coffee, checked the sitting room just in case her sexy guest was in front of the TV, and then wandered out to the barn.

All the cow ponies had their flakes of hay, the stalls were already mucked out, and even the damned dog had been fed. Frowning, she sipped her coffee and followed the sound of men's voices. Miguel—Maria's husband and Will's sole ranch hand—was pounding nails in a loose fence rail while tall, blond, and beautiful held the board in place.

She stood in the shadows and watched the two men working— Miguel, small and wiry with coal black hair and dark, weathered skin, and that New York City cowboy in his worn jeans, scuffed boots, and red flannel shirt, looking for all the world like he belonged here.

She knew better. He was just a fancy city boy playing cowboy for the summer. Then he'd be going back to his high-rise office and his hoity-toity women—women like that fancy author Tag Martin had up and married. Betsy Mae still hadn't met Michelle Garrison—uh, Martin—though she couldn't blame Tag's wife for that, much as she'd like to.

The thing was, Betsy wasn't ready to see Tag all settled into connubial bliss with a stranger, not after the two of them had been best friends—with privileges—since they'd first discovered a shared interest in those extracurricular privileges.

"Horses are fed and the fence is fixed. What next?"

Betsy Mae's head jerked up. Mark Connor stood there, invading her space and grinning at her like he was actually enjoying himself. *Jerk.* Their first guests would be arriving in less than three hours, and then Columbine Camp was going to be hopping with wannabe cowboys and screaming kids.

She had a feeling it wasn't going to be hard at all to wipe that damned sexy smile off this particular dude's face.

MARK carried his plate to the sink where Maria was scraping dishes. The exhausted guests were settled in their cabins after a full day of activities, the horses fed and put up for the night, and even Betsy Mae appeared too tired to give him grief.

He glanced over his shoulder and watched her for a moment. She sat at the front desk in what had probably once been part of the main living room and was now decked out like a western version of a hotel lobby, pouring over her laptop with the most adorable frown on her face.

He'd heard about Will's ditzy sister Betsy Mae the rodeo queen for so long, he felt as if he knew her, but obviously he didn't know the whole story—like the one behind those bruises.

All he knew for sure was that Betsy Mae had been a national champion barrel racer a few years back, a true rodeo queen in the tradition of the Old West. She and Tag had been an on-again, off-again item for years.

Then she'd run off with a rodeo clown who'd beat the crap out of her a few months after their wedding, but that was ages ago. He wondered who'd hurt her this time. Wondered why it mattered so damned much.

He'd been trying to tell himself he'd feel the same anger over any woman suffering abuse at the hands of some jerk, but for some reason, the way Betsy Mae's injuries affected him went a lot deeper. Maybe it was just the fact he felt like he knew her because he'd heard so much about her.

Her brother had talked about her with a mixed sense of pride and exasperation—according to Will, she was a smart girl who often made stupid decisions. That was back during Mark's first trip to Columbine Camp when he'd come west without a clue what to expect, and he'd found heaven.

Who'd have thought a kid from Queens would take to the cowboy life like a native? Mark had loved everything about ranching. He'd also discovered an adventurous side to himself he never would have known if he hadn't made that first trip out to Colorado to learn about cowboys.

The fact his favorite author had given up her successful career to marry the owner of the ranch next door to Columbine Camp and raise babies had been all the incentive Mark needed when he realized he was ready for a major change in his life.

So here he was, stiff and sore, with blisters on his hands—and most likely his butt, too—working for one of the orneriest, least sociable, sexiest, most confounding females he'd ever met in his life.

They'd hardly exchanged a dozen words all day—he'd taken his orders from Miguel after Betsy Mae had gotten the guests assigned to their cabins. Mark had saddled horses, adjusted stirrups, chased rotten little kids, and led the whole group on a trail ride up through the hills.

He hadn't had this much fun in years, though thoughts of Betsy Mae had kept him from concentrating entirely on the job at hand. Not that she'd shown a lick of interest in him. Not even a flicker, so there was no way at all Mark was going to let her know just how curious he was about her—about those bruises, those beautiful green eyes, those full, sort of pouty lips, and the amazing way she filled out a set of tight Wrangler jeans.

Just as he wasn't going to admit how sore he was, how exhausted . . . or that, somehow, he fully intended to get to know Betsy Mae Twigg a whole lot better.

three

She sensed him before she heard him—sort of a frisson of awareness that raced along her spine. When Betsy Mae raised her head,
Mark was standing just on the other side of the desk. How the hell
a man as big as he was could move so quietly—almost gracefully—
was beyond her.

Maybe it was something city boys learned. "You want something?" She raised one eyebrow and wished she hadn't. Damn,
that bruise hurt! She hoped Frank hadn't broken anything when
he'd hit her, but the swelling still hadn't gone down.

"I'm headed to bed. A shower sounds really good about now.
Just wanted to make sure there wasn't anything else I could do for
you." He grinned, and she felt it right where she shouldn't.

"I'm good," she said, wishing she didn't have a long list of things
she'd like for him to do to, uh, *for* her. "See ya in the morning."

He actually looked a little disappointed. Wasn't the guy tired?
She'd had Miguel work Mark's ass off today, hoping to wear that

smile off his face, but he hadn't balked at a single thing. He'd curried and saddled horses and adjusted stirrups and helped little kids with the ponies. He'd been so damned good-natured through it all, so good-looking, she'd almost forgotten who he was—a city boy, a twink dressed up to look like a cowboy.

As right as he was, she just wished he wasn't so wrong.

Wrong on the most important level of all. She'd give him maybe a week before he turned tail and headed back to New York. The last thing she needed was getting all hot and bothered over a guy who was nothing more than a damned tourist.

Besides, he probably looked at her beat-up face and thought of her as local color. Or else he thought she was a complete idiot for getting beat up in the first place. Which she was.

"You going to be up much longer?"

Betsy Mae blinked. "You still here?"

He grinned. "That I am. I was going to ask if you had any bandages."

He held his hands out and she just about puked. There were blisters all over his palms, a couple of them deep enough to bleed. "Crap. Why didn't you say something?" She slammed the laptop shut and stood. "You need those cleaned up and bandaged. They get infected, you won't be any good to anyone."

Turning on her heel, she headed for the bathroom at the end of the hall.

"It's nice to know you care."

His dry comment made her snort. Damn, she did not want to like the man. "I do," she said, opening the door for him. "I care that if your hands are screwed up, I'll get stuck mucking out the stalls."

She followed him into the bathroom, put the lid down on the commode, and started rummaging through the medicine cabinet. He just stood there. "Sit." She pointed to the closed toilet seat.

"Yes, ma'am." Chuckling, he sat.

She grabbed the antibiotic ointment and some thick bandages, rinsed a washcloth in warm water and took his right hand. "Hands as soft as these, you should have been wearing gloves."

"You're right. I didn't even think about them."

"Even when the blisters started breakin'?" She glared at him, shaking her head. Stupid man. Carefully, she began washing around the blisters, cleaning away the dried blood.

"I guess I was having too much fun."

She snorted again. Perfect. Ladylike sound like that, he'd think she was a complete hick. Carefully, she patted his hand dry, covered the open blisters with antibiotic cream, and bandaged the worst of them. Then she repeated the process on his left hand. "There," she said, grabbing up the scraps of paper left from the bandages. "Keep them clean. And come with me. I've got some gloves that should fit you."

She led him across the hall to her bedroom, and he followed close behind, waiting patiently while she rummaged around in a box of crap she'd found after Frank left. "Here. These should fit." She held up a pair of beautiful deerskin gloves. She'd planned to send all this stuff back to her ex, but to hell with him. Mark needed them worse than Frank.

Quietly, he took the pair and slipped them on. They appeared to fit just fine. "Perfect," he said, flexing his fingers inside the soft leather. "You sure you don't mind if I use these?"

She grinned. "They're yours now. They belonged to my ex. He's not getting them back." She shoved the box back in her closet. When she turned around and glanced up, Mark was holding the gloves in one hand, staring at her.

"What?"

"Is he the one? Did he do that to you?"

Oh, crap. She nodded. Lord, it was so embarrassing to admit. "Yeah, and you don't need to remind me how stupid I was to go back to him. I've already heard it all, ad nauseam, from Will and Annie." She stood up, prepared to show him out.

He touched her shoulder. "Not stupid, Betsy Mae. I imagine you were just hopeful things really would work, right?"

He looked down at her with those silvery eyes of his, and there was no condemnation, no sense that he meant anything other than what he'd said. Something inside her sort of came undone.

"I was." She stared straight ahead. "But I was wrong."

His hand dropped away from her shoulder and she thought about asking him to put it back. It had been so long since anyone had touched her with kindness. Not because he wanted anything, not because he was trying to make a point or take a swing at her. No. It appeared Mark Connor was a lot nicer guy than she'd been giving him credit for—and here she'd been acting like an absolute bitch.

Damn it all.

four

Mark pulled the saddle off of Blue, the roan gelding Miguel had assigned to him the day after he'd arrived at Columbine Camp. He and Blue had gotten real well acquainted in the past two weeks.

The horse shook from nose to tail like a big dog, and as soon as Mark tugged the bridle off, Blue trotted to the center of the corral and rolled over in the dirt.

Feet high in the air, he rubbed his back, kicking dust in every direction. Then with a loud grunt he rolled on over and slowly stood up, shook off the excess dust, wandered back to Mark, and head-butted his shoulder.

"For an animal that can't talk, you sure manage to get your point across." Laughing softly, Mark filled the trough with a scoop of grain, then grabbed the curry comb and brush. Blue buried his nose in the grain. As Mark started brushing the animal's withers,

Blue groaned and shifted his weight to three legs while he cocked the fourth, prepared to enjoy the process.

Mark certainly enjoyed it. Currying his horse after a full day in the saddle was totally relaxing—as was the life he was leading. After two full weeks working at Columbine Camp, his hands were finally developing a thick set of calluses, his skin had lost that pasty, city-boy look, and his hair had bleached out so much it was almost silver.

Either that or he was going gray. Of course, dealing with Betsy Mae Twigg was enough to give anyone gray hair. He glanced at the house and wondered what she was up to this afternoon. He knew she'd spent the last couple of hours checking out their guests as everyone packed up and went their separate ways.

His fascination with her had grown throughout the last two weeks. He'd learned right away that she wasn't the dumb blonde everyone pegged her as—she might occasionally act like a ditz, but her mind was going a mile a minute. It was more than obvious—to Mark, at least—that she knew a lot more about what was going on than she ever admitted.

She hadn't said much about the job he'd done. Instead, like a good businesswoman, she'd added to his chores until Mark was working harder for free than he'd ever worked for a paycheck.

And he'd never had more fun in his entire life. He'd even enjoyed the dudes, though he'd been really careful about calling them guests or wranglers. Columbine Camp was, after all, every kid's, and grown-up's, fantasy—a chance to live and work like a real cowboy for an entire two weeks.

They'd done trail rides and rounded up cows, fixed fences, and gone swimming in the waterhole Will had dammed up alongside the creek. No one had guessed that the cowboy leading their trail rides, tightening the cinches on their saddles, or teaching them the fine art of wrangling was really a city boy straight from New York—and Mark hadn't enlightened a soul.

He'd talked to Michelle once, when she'd called to tell him everyone was over the bug and wondering when he was moving over to the Double Eagle. When he'd explained how Will and Annie had bailed out the minute he showed up, Michelle had laughed so hard she couldn't talk for way too long.

Then she'd said she hoped he survived Betsy Mae and she'd see him when he needed a break.

He hadn't needed one yet. No. If anything, he wanted a little bit more time with that blond firecracker. She fascinated him—all rough edges and attitude—and yet he felt as if there was a lot about the woman he didn't know at all. A lot he wasn't seeing, as if she'd built a wall against the world.

Why, he wondered, had it become imperative that he scale that wall, climb over the top, and find out just who was hiding on the other side? Now that they had the ranch to themselves, Mark intended to do exactly that.

He finished up with Blue and turned the horse out in the pasture behind the barn. After that, he checked on one of the heifers who looked way past her due date. There'd been a half-dozen calves born during the week without trouble, but Betsy Mae'd been worried about this one in particular because it was her first and she looked like she might be carrying twins.

Right now she was settled down in the stall, chewing her cud with a look of total bovine boredom on her face. Mark threw some extra alfalfa in her feed trough and headed to the house.

He paused at the sight of a beat-up old Chevy pickup parked in the drive. He hadn't heard it pull up, but then he'd been at the back of the barn working on Blue.

He let himself in through the front door, moving more quietly than usual—sneaking in, actually, but something felt wrong, and he wasn't about to ignore a hunch that left the hair standing up on the back of his neck.

He heard a man's voice, just a low rumble from the back of the house, then Betsy Mae's, but she didn't sound happy about her visitor. Mark hung his hat on the rack by the door, but he left his deerskin gloves on as he walked through the entryway and down the hall. His room was two doors down from Betsy Mae's, so he had every right to go this way, didn't he?

The door to Betsy Mae's room was shut. He stood there a moment and then rapped lightly. "Betsy Mae? You there?"

"Mark? Come in."

He opened the door and she glanced up with such obvious relief on her face that he didn't feel at all guilty about snooping. Mark nodded at the tall, good-looking cowboy standing way too close to Betsy Mae. He had his fingers wrapped around her left wrist, and he didn't look at all pleased at the interruption.

"Mark Connor, Frank Williams." Betsy Mae flashed Mark a grin that looked more like a grimace. "Mark's helping me out while Will and Annie are gone." She stepped away from Frank, but he held tightly to her wrist and followed, almost like a cutting horse working a calf.

"Well, isn't that nice." Frank sneered at Mark, and he wasn't nearly as good-looking now that Mark recognized the man and the threat. "I'm here now, sweetheart. You just tell your little friend you don't need his help anymore." Frank moved a step closer to Betsy Mae, crowding her even more. He glared at Mark. "Why don't you just go away?"

"I don't think so, Frank." Anger had Mark gritting his teeth, trying to look calm and unconcerned as he leaned against the doorframe with his thumbs hooked in his front pockets. The last thing he wanted to do was put Betsy Mae in any kind of danger. This jerk looked like a loose cannon if ever he'd seen one. "Betsy Mae and I are doing just fine."

Frank puffed out his chest, reminding Mark of a cocky little rooster. "I said you can leave now. My wife and I were having a private discussion."

"I'm not your wife." Betsy Mae jerked her arm, but she couldn't pull free of Frank's grasp.

"Let go of the lady. Now." Mark straightened up and stepped away from the doorframe.

Frank's laughter definitely lacked humor. "Lady? There's no lady in this room. Nothing but my little whore, right, darlin'?"

Mark had really been thinking about trying diplomacy, but that did it. He didn't say a word. Just balled up his fists in those nice deerskin gloves, hauled off, and punched Frank Williams in the jaw.

The man went down like a ton of bricks, taking Betsy Mae with him. Mark caught her before she fell and pulled her close. It wasn't until she was clinging to him with both arms wrapped tightly around his waist that he realized she was trembling.

"Did he hurt you?" He smoothed the tangled curls away from her face. She shook her head, but her eyes were filled with tears and she was still shaking like a leaf. That alone made Mark want to hit the bastard again.

"Just scared me half to death. I didn't hear his truck pull in. I had a headache earlier, so I came in to rest. I was asleep when he barged in and said I had to come back to him."

Mark shook his head. "You're not going back to that bastard, Betsy Mae. Ever. Understood?"

She nodded. "Oh, yeah." She shuddered, and tears sparkled at the edges of her lashes. "Mark, I was such a fool. I never should have married him, never should have gone back to him after the first time he hit me, but Will and Annie were so much in love, and Tag was married and I thought maybe, just maybe . . ." She sighed. "Damn it." Then she glared at Frank, sprawled unconscious on her bedroom floor. "This time I'm calling the sheriff."

"Good girl. I'll take care of your friend here until the sheriff arrives." He started to pull away but made the mistake of glancing down, right into Betsy Mae's upturned face. The tears still sparkling in her eyes tore him apart.

"This is probably a really big mistake," he said. Then he leaned over and kissed her. And kept kissing her, as she shifted in his embrace, pressed that perfect cowgirl body close to his, and turned Mark Connor's entire carefully planned world upside down and inside out.

five

Oh Lordy . . . He kissed as good as he looked and better than she'd been dreaming for the past two weeks. No, even better than that, if it were at all possible. If Frank weren't beginning to stir on the floor beside them, Betsy Mae might have dragged this damned dime store cowboy across the room and right into her rumpled bed.

But Frank was groaning and mumbling, and she still hadn't called the sheriff, and there was no way she was letting her ex get away with breaking into her house and threatening her.

Mark seemed to reach the same conclusion at the same time she did, because they parted as if they'd planned to.

Except no way in hell would she have planned anything remotely like kissing this man—not when she'd been so careful over the past two weeks to keep him at arm's length. She'd been just fine with the fantasies, hadn't she? Well . . . no. Not really.

But the last thing she wanted was to fall for a guy who was

planning to leave. As far as she knew, Mark was just out here to visit Tag and his new wife for a bit.

She did not need this. Still, when she leaned her forehead against his hard chest, she was more than a little gratified to hear the rapid pounding of his heart.

At least she wasn't the only one affected.

Unless, of course, he was reacting to the fact he'd just punched Frank's lights out.

"Dear God in heaven, kissing you was probably a mistake, but I think it's the best one I've ever made." Mark's soft words, whispered against her temple, made her smile.

"Yeah," she said. "Frank's coming around and I wouldn't put it past him to come after you when you're otherwise occupied."

Mark chuckled softly. "I'll take care of Frank. You go call the sheriff." He dropped his arms and stepped back.

She nodded, even though she really wanted to kiss him again or at least find out if he had any intention of kissing her. Probably a bad idea. With a glance at Frank, she slipped out of the room. She immediately missed those strong arms and that broad chest—even if Mark did smell a little bit like horse.

She was back a few minutes later. Mark had Frank in the straight-back chair by her desk, wrists firmly bound behind his back with a pair of nylon stockings. Frank didn't say a word, but the look he gave Betsy Mae scared the crap out of her.

Mark stepped in front of Frank, blocking her view of the bastard. His eyes were troubled, but he smiled at her. "Sorry about the stockings. They were the only thing I could find to tie him."

"Good idea." She glanced around him and glared at Frank. "What made you think of using my stockings?"

Mark shrugged. "I'm an editor. Romances. You'd be surprised what I've learned from all the books I've read."

Betsy Mae'd read more than a few romances in her time. She wondered if he'd paid attention to some of the other parts of those books, and then she blushed. A few of them went into great detail with the more intimate aspects of relationships. Graphic detail. "I can only imagine," she said drily. Then she cast a sideways glance at Mark and caught him grinning broadly at her.

The dog barked out front. Thank goodness. She was beginning to heat up, just thinking of the things Mark might know about women. "Must be the sheriff's deputy." Betsy Mae spun on her heel and escaped before she—or Mark—said anything else.

AFTER Frank had been hauled off in handcuffs, Betsy Mae poured herself a glass of wine and handed a cold beer to Mark. Together, the two of them walked out to the front porch. Mark waited until Betsy Mae took her seat on the porch swing before sitting down beside her. Not too close . . . not too far. He took a swallow of his beer while she sipped her Chardonnay.

The sun was beginning to set. Golden light spilled across the valley. Birds chirped quietly, settling in for the evening, and cattle grazed in the tall grass. The guests were all gone, and Miguel and Maria were off for the night.

Everything felt just right. Maybe that kiss had cleared the air more than he realized. At least she wasn't giving him grief like she'd done for the past two weeks. Mark chuckled, thinking of Michelle's warning that she hoped he'd survive Betsy Mae. The vote was still out on that one. He wanted her so badly he ached.

"Whatcha laughing about?" Betsy Mae raised her head and gazed at him over the rim of her glass.

She'd pulled her hair into a ponytail and wore a soft cotton T-shirt and cutoff jeans. The bruises on her face had finally faded, though he noticed new ones on her arm where Frank had grabbed her. She looked about twelve years old, and when Mark saw those bruises he was glad he'd broken Frank's jaw.

Holding on to his temper, he shook his head. "Nothing in particular." He sipped his beer. "Did you know Frank had priors on him? That he was wanted for assaults against three women?"

Betsy Mae glanced away and shook her head. "Do you really think I would have married him if I'd known that?"

"No. I don't. You're too smart for that." The corner of his mouth quirked up.

She glanced at him and then stared out across the valley. "Well, then you're the only one who thinks that." She sighed and spun her wineglass between her fingers. "Will was always the smart one. I was just dumb old Betsy Mae. Pretty to look at but not good for much else."

Frowning, Mark reached for her, caught her chin in his fingers, and gently forced her to look at him. "What makes you say that?"

Her short burst of laughter sounded too much like a sob for his peace of mind. "Oh, just about everybody. My parents . . . Will. Of course, I never did anything to make them think differently. They pegged me as a dumb blonde from the beginning, and it was just easier to play the part. Tag was the only one who never talked down to me, but that's because he figured he was just a dumb old cowboy. He's not, though. He's smart as a whip."

Mark smiled, leaned close, and kissed her. It was chaste and quick and made him want a whole lot more. "So're you. Smart. And you're wrong about Will. He told me the dude ranch was your idea after your parents died. He said you're the one who set up the website, took care of the permits, and got the cabins built. He gives you a lot of the credit for Columbine Camp's success."

"He does?" She tilted her head and frowned. "He's never said a word. 'Course, he doesn't talk much about the ranch. He leaves most of it up to me, except when I'm not here." She shook her head. "He was really mad at me for taking off with Frank and leaving him here to handle the ranch on his own."

"Maybe it was more than that." Mark set down his beer and moved closer to Betsy Mae. "Maybe it's because he recognized Frank for the animal he is. Maybe Will was worried about you but didn't want to interfere. Ever think about it that way?"

She stared at him for a long, slow moment in time. "No," she said. "Do you really . . . ?"

He leaned close, then closer still, and the soft puff of her breath, the taste of her lips told him this might not be the best idea—but it was the only one he had.

Until a loud bellow of pain had both of them running for the barn.

six

"Damn. What should we do?" Mark stood outside the stall while Betsy Mae knelt behind the laboring cow with her right arm buried elbow deep where she really had no business going, at least as far as Mark was concerned.

She glanced up and shook her head. "This one's a heifer—it's her first calf and it's coming out butt first. I think he's stuck. I can feel him but I'm not strong enough to turn him. Wash your hands good and see if you can do it."

Oh shit. He really did not want to do this, but he stripped off his shirt and scrubbed up to his armpits with an ugly brown bar of soap that smelled to high heaven. Holding his hands high like the doctors on *ER*, Mark stepped into the stall and knelt down beside Betsy Mae.

"What should I do?"

"Crap, you've got such big hands." Betsy Mae let out a puff of air. "Make your hand as small as you can and slide in through the birth canal. You'll feel a bony little butt, but what you really want is two front legs with the head. This little guy's all folded up in there. You need to try and slowly rotate him, but do it between contractions. Just a sec . . . I'm going to wash her off first so we don't introduce any debris."

"Okay." He nodded like he had a clue what she was talking about. She slopped some warm water over the heifer's butt and then he was kneeling down behind the animal and sliding his hand and then his wrist and then most of his arm deep inside the poor creature. And there it was, just the way Betsy Mae had described it—a bony little butt and what felt like a tail.

He ran his hand along the knobby backbone until he found the calf's head, and very slowly began to tug the baby around.

"Careful with the hooves. You don't want them to tear anything."

"Okay." He felt the calf begin to turn.

"Watch for the umbilical cord."

Mark nodded, concentrating on the slow slide of calf, when all of a sudden muscles clamped down on his arm and the cow let out a loud groan. "Shit! What's that?"

"Contraction. It's normal. Just hold still until it's over."

"Hold still? You mean there's an option? Sorry, babe, but there's no way to move when you're caught like this."

Betsy Mae sort of giggled, but it was a nervous sound. He didn't blame her—he was nervous, too, but at the same time he had the most amazing sense that he was actually helping this poor creature—a sense unlike anything he'd ever experienced.

The contraction ended and he got the calf turned until he felt its little hooves pointed forward and the nose was tucked between the front legs. Then he slipped his arm out of the cow and sat back on his heels to let nature take its course.

The heifer tightened up once more, groaned, and two little hooves poked out. Mark was almost sure he held his breath for the entire time it took before that little calf slid out onto the clean straw just the way he was supposed to. And lay there.

Mark stared at it, waiting for the little guy to breathe, but his sides didn't move, his eyes didn't open, his mouth stayed shut, and mama wasn't paying him any attention at all. Then Betsy Mae was rubbing his little body with a clean towel, clearing mucus from his nose and mouth. Then she leaned real close, put her mouth over his nostrils, and started to blow.

Dumbfounded, Mark watched as she breathed life into the newborn calf. Blowing and pausing, blowing and pausing until the little guy snorted and got snot and mucus all over her face, blew a few bubbles, and took a deep breath.

"Oh, yuck." Wrinkling her nose and grinning like an idiot, Betsy Mae grabbed the tail of her T-shirt and used it to wipe away the mess. "Look. Here comes number two!"

Mark had been so intent on the one he'd helped deliver, he had no idea the cow was still laboring. Another tiny calf slid out— easily this time and still encased in membrane. The cow turned her head and began to vigorously lick her new baby—and eat the afterbirth while she was at it. This calf's head popped up almost immediately once mama cleared the way.

"They're both white, but the mother's brown. How come?"

"Will bought the heifer already bred to a Charolais bull. They're a big, sturdy breed. They'll strengthen our herd."

Mark laughed. "Looks like he got two for the price of one." He had no idea how long he sat there in the hay beside Betsy Mae, his arms and chest covered in blood and mucus and other things he didn't want to consider, but time seemed to stop while he watched the two little calves struggle to stand and the cow finally come to her feet. Before he knew it, both calves were licked creamy white and clean, standing on shaky little legs, suckling and butting at mama's udders.

"Ever see a calf born?"

Mark shook his head. "Kittens once. A long time ago. That's amazing." He rolled his head against his shoulder and glanced at Betsy Mae. "Please tell me it's not the same for humans. The idea of eating the afterbirth is just a bit too gross for me to imagine."

Laughing, Betsy Mae grabbed a handful of straw and threw it at him. It stuck to the gunk on his chest. Mark flicked it off with fingers covered in semidried whatever. He glanced down and slowly shook his head. "As much as I could watch this all night, I think I need a shower."

Betsy Mae—every bit as filthy—stood up. "Ya think?"

They were both laughing as she checked the water trough and filled the feed box with fresh grain. Mark held the stall door open and then shut it carefully behind her. Together they closed up the barn and headed back to the house.

A sliver of moon rode high in the sky, and stars shimmered from one side of the horizon to the other. They walked quietly, but inside Mark was singing. If he'd had any doubts about coming west, tonight had answered all his questions. This was the life he wanted. This was what he'd been searching for.

And maybe, just maybe, the woman walking beside him was the one he'd never once imagined really existed at all.

SHE'D been afraid of this. So keyed up after all that had happened tonight, Betsy Mae was still tossing and turning a good two hours after she'd showered and gone to bed.

And, to be perfectly honest, knowing that Mark slept just two doors down wasn't helping her any. She'd been so good staying away from him for the past two weeks, she figured she deserved a damned medal. Then he'd come in like her knight in shining armor and decked Frank, which was amazing, and then . . . then he'd kissed her. That kiss had changed everything.

She'd only read about kisses like that.

In fact, not once in her thirty-five years had she come close to experiencing anything remotely like Mark Connor's kisses.

So, Betsy Mae, what the hell you going to do about it?

Nothing. Not a damned thing. Will and Annie were due home, and Tag's wife had already called to see when Mark was planning to come visit, the way he'd planned. Then she figured he'd go back to New York. For good.

That wasn't what she wanted. Not anymore. Not after seeing Annie and Will so damned happy together, watching her friend grow bigger every day with their baby. She'd never thought she wanted those things for herself, but after hearing Tag wax eloquent over married life, after seeing the way Annie and Will were together, Betsy Mae knew she needed more than a lonely bedroom in her brother's house.

She needed to be more than somebody's ditzy aunt, more than someone's sister. For the first time in her life, Betsy Mae truly wanted to be loved.

Grumbling at how pathetic that sounded, she threw the covers back and slipped out of bed. Will had a bottle of good sippin' whisky stashed in the office, and if a shot of that wouldn't put her to sleep, she might as well just figure on being up all night.

"Not gonna happen."

seven

❖

Mark kept the lights down low as he poured himself another shot of Will's good whisky. Luckily the bottle had still been in the same hiding place where Will had it stashed the first time Mark was out to stay at Columbine Camp.

The two of them had hit it off really well, which was just weird considering how different their backgrounds were, but he'd sat here many nights, hearing Will's stories of growing up on the ranch, of how he and Betsy Mae had turned it into a dude ranch after their parents were gone.

Probably why he felt as if he knew Betsy Mae as well as he did. Why she fascinated him the way she did—because of Will's stories. That had to be it.

He leaned back on the comfortable leather couch and stared at the shot glass between his fingers, remembering. He certainly hadn't realized how that two-week stay at a dude ranch would change his life, but nothing had been the same since.

He'd been thinking about making a change, getting out of publishing, out of New York, but he hadn't had a clue what he wanted to do. Then he'd come here. He'd loved everything, but more than that, he'd learned to breathe. Really breathe deeply and work hard until he was bone-tired and his muscles ached.

And calluses! He'd never had calluses on his hands in his life until he'd been to Columbine Camp. He looked at the palm of his right hand, at the dark ridges of hard callus and grinned. No more lily white, city-boy hands for him. Never again.

"What are you doing here?"

Mark glanced over his shoulder at Betsy Mae. She stood there with her hair all sleep-mussed, wearing her little cotton shorts and camisole top, probably not even aware the fabric was so sheer he could see the dark circles surrounding her nipples. "Come join me," he said, holding up his glass. "I'm stealing Will's good whisky."

She laughed, grabbed a shot glass off the shelf, and flopped down on the couch beside him. "How'd you know where it was?"

"Your dumb brother's still using the same hiding place he was when I was here a couple of years ago." Mark filled her glass.

"He shared his good whisky with you? You must be something special. Will never shares with the guests. He figures if they can afford to stay here, they can afford their own booze." She sipped her whisky and sighed her pleasure.

Mark had to force his eyes away from the line of her throat and the sexy curve of her collarbone. "Probably true," he said, "but I really like your brother. We hit it off from the start. I ended up helping out because you were gone."

She nodded. "I was probably following the circuit. I was still barrel racing a lot then."

Mark put his arm around her shoulders and tugged. She slipped closer like it was the most natural thing in the world to be sitting out here in the middle of the night, she in her jammies and he wearing nothing but a pair of knit boxer shorts.

He wondered if she'd noticed yet that he wasn't really dressed.

"Those days are over, though." She sighed.

"Do you miss it?" Damn, but he loved the way she felt, soft in all the right places, snuggled up next to him, still warm from her bed.

"Sometimes." She tilted her head and gazed at him out of those beautiful green eyes. "Mostly not. It's a lot of hard work for a few seconds of glory. There's so much backstabbing and bickering behind the scenes. It's a young woman's sport. I was getting too old."

"How old are you?" He laughed. "Guess I'm not supposed to ask that, right?"

She shook her head. "It's okay. I'm thirty-five. Not sure how it got here so fast. Sometimes I feel as if I've wasted the better part of my life, racing from one rodeo to the next, never taking time to enjoy the life I could have had here at home." She rubbed her cheek against his bare shoulder. "What about you? How old are you?"

He laughed. "Well, forty's closer than thirty-five. I hit thirty-eight a couple of months ago. Shocked the hell out of me. I realized I was almost forty years old and still hadn't figured out what I wanted to be when I grew up."

"You, too?" She pushed herself away and stared at him wide-eyed. "I thought I was the only one with that problem."

"Is it really a problem?" He wrapped his fingers around the back of her head, tangled them in her blond curls, and pulled her close.

She didn't fight him a bit. No, she met him, lip to lip, kissing him as if she meant it. As if she really cared about him. Mark set his glass to one side, took hers out of her hand, and set it beside his. Then he wrapped his hands around her waist and lifted her until she straddled him, all without ever breaking their kiss.

The moment she settled down atop him, her eyes went wide. Blinking almost owlishly, she scooted her hips around a bit, settling even closer against the hard length of him.

Mark groaned and shifted beneath her, dying for even more contact. "Maybe this wasn't such a good idea after all."

Betsy Mae leaned close and rubbed noses with him. "Either that, or it was the best idea you've ever had."

This time, Mark was the one to blink. He wrapped his hands around her shoulders and held her still so that he could look into those trusting eyes. "You don't strike me as a tease."

She smiled softly and shook her head. "I'm not. We're both grown-ups. Neither one of us appears all that virginal, and while I'm still not sure it's a very smart move, I'm beginning to think that if I don't make it, I'm going to regret it the rest of my life."

"Oh?" He didn't even try and stop the grin spreading across his face. "And why is that?"

"Well . . ." She drew the word out. "I've been thinking of your profession. You're an editor—Michelle Garrison Martin's editor, in fact—and you said you read romance novels for a living, right? That means you know exactly how the hero is supposed to treat his woman. Now, I've never once been with a man who spends his days learning how to treat a woman right, and I imagine it's got to be quite an experience. One no right-thinking girl would ever want to miss."

"You're right, you know. Those books are better than any instruction manual. Written by women, for women. Lots of details. Kissing, for instance." He pulled her close and feathered his lips lightly over hers. Traced the seam between hers with his tongue until she parted on a sigh and let him in. Kept kissing her gently, thoroughly, until her body was all soft and pliable and both their hearts were beating a mile a minute.

When he ended the kiss, her eyes held a glazed expression, and her slow smile made him want to do it all over again.

"Okay," she said. "Kissing is good. You've paid attention."

"Then there's touching."

She nodded slowly. "I like touching."

He proceeded to show her exactly what he'd learned, beginning with soft strokes along her sides as he slowly peeled her camisole top up, baring her breasts before finally tugging the shirt over her head.

She frowned. "This appears to be more in the undressing category than touching."

"No fun, touching through clothes. Besides, I want to see what I'm touching." He leaned close and suckled one pert nipple between his lips, sucking hard enough to draw it up against the roof of his mouth.

"See? You're doing it again!"

Her voice was growing strained, but he released her nipple and backed away, blinking innocently. "Doing what?"

"Skipping straight to tasting. You've gone from undressing to tasting. I'm still waiting for the touching."

He nodded sagely. "How's this?" Leaning close, he drew the other nipple between his lips, but before she could protest, he slipped his hand over her smooth belly and beneath the soft waistband of her shorts. She moaned and tilted her hips forward.

He trailed his fingertips through her soft curls and found the warm, damp cleft between her legs. Stroking her slowly, he carefully worked his fingers back and forth, pressing deeper on each pass until he'd penetrated her sensitive core.

He felt the sharp scrape of her fingernails across his back and the press of her lips against his shoulder, but he kept suckling and stroking as her body trembled and then slipped into a sharp rhythm of need and desire.

He added another finger between her legs, and used his thumb to caress the sensitive bundle of nerves at the apex, bringing a moan to her lips, a series of whimpers, and then, as her body tightened and clenched around him, his name, shouted between gasps and small cries of pleasure.

He kept stroking, kept kissing and suckling as she trembled and whimpered. So responsive to his touch, so mind-numbingly beautiful she made him ache, made him want . . . made him want to run for the hills.

He hadn't wanted this. Hell, who was he kidding? Two weeks of keeping his distance, of keeping his hands to himself, but it hadn't been enough. He'd gotten to know her, discovered just how much he liked her, and now there was no denying the truth—he'd fallen deeper and harder than he'd ever fallen before.

Slowly, mind spinning and heart thundering in his chest, he brought her down from what appeared to have been a bone-melting climax, one that left Betsy Mae sated and limp in his arms and Mark holding her close, his own body hard as granite.

If only his heart was as tough. Right now, Mark felt as wobbly as those two little newborn calves out in the barn. Wobbly and way too vulnerable for his peace of mind.

eight

It took Betsy Mae a few minutes to catch her breath. Longer to get around to opening her eyes, but it was impossible to ignore the fact Mark was still kissing her breasts and his fingers continued their intimate exploration.

And the evidence was there, right under her butt, that he'd done it all for her without taking pleasure for himself. Now that was a first. Slowly she focused her eyes, blinking owlishly as Mark raised his head, grinned at her, and asked, "Did I miss anything?"

She didn't even try and stop herself from grinning like an idiot. "You're kidding, right? How about yourself? I think you might have missed this." She rolled her hips, pressing close against his erection, and he groaned.

Then he planted his hands under her butt and stood up so fast all she could do was cling to him like a little monkey with her arms and legs wrapped around him, and her breasts pressed to his perfect chest. Without a word, he walked her down the hall and into his bedroom, leaned over, and deposited her on the bed.

She lay there giggling while he grabbed his wallet off the nightstand, pulled out a condom, and ripped off the cover with his teeth. "I didn't miss it a bit," he said, as if she'd just asked the question. "But if you were up on your romance novel reading, you'd know that a true hero always protects his woman."

He slid his shorts down his legs. Betsy Mae sucked in a breath as he sheathed himself and crawled across the bed until he knelt between her legs. She reached out and ran her fingers along his full length. "Then what does the hero do?"

Mark shoved his hair out of his eyes and grinned at her. "Why, he makes certain the heroine is truly ready to accept his burgeoning manhood."

"Burgeoning? Ooh . . . I may need to look that one up." She wriggled her hips in anticipation.

"You do that. Later." He fell forward, planting his hands at either side of her face. "Now hold still."

"Yes sir." She giggled and felt all her inner muscles clench, waiting for him to fill her. Instead, he was sliding down, lower, and lower still until he grinned up at her from between her thighs. And then, before she had time to tell him that no, she didn't do that sort of thing, he was tugging her shorts down and doing it—and changing her entire obviously outdated opinion about oral sex.

By the time Mark moved up her body and filled her with all that burgeoning manhood of his, Betsy Mae was limp as a wet noodle and positive she didn't have another climax left anywhere inside her sated body.

She was dead wrong.

THEIR new group of wannabe cowboys and cowgirls showed up two days later. Mark went out early to check on the twin calves and help Miguel feed the stock while Betsy Mae made sure the cabins were all in good shape and ready to go.

The last two days had been amazing, but this morning Betsy Mae had been unusually quiet. Mark found himself looking for her no matter what he was doing, hoping for a smile, a quiet word, even a teasing insult. A couple of times he managed to catch her in a private enough spot where he could grab a quick kiss—every kiss he got in return felt like a gift.

He still couldn't explain it, but somehow, over the course of the past couple of weeks, he'd gone and fallen in love.

He just wished he could be certain that Betsy Mae felt the same. He knew he'd left her satisfied and smiling every time they'd made love. Knew he'd never connected with a woman the way he'd connected with this one. Her touch was molten fire in his veins, her kisses tied him in knots, and the joy he'd found when they made love was unlike anything he'd experienced in his life.

It scared the ever-lovin' hell out of him. And today, while she had kissed him with enthusiasm, she hadn't seemed to seek him out as often as he'd looked for her. When they did meet, Mark sensed something missing, a sadness about her that made no sense. He'd tried to talk to her, but she was always busy, always rushing off.

Something had taken the luster off their loving and left him wondering if there was an important part of the last couple of nights that he'd missed.

A horn honked. Mark looked up in time to see Will pulling

up the long driveway in his big Ford truck. He leaned out of the window as he drove by. "Hey, Mark. I can't believe you're still here! When I talked to Betsy Mae this morning, she swore she hadn't run you off, but I didn't believe her." He parked in front of the barn. Annie waved from the front seat, and both of them looked relaxed and rested.

Mark walked over and opened Annie's door. "Hey, Annie. I didn't get a proper hello last time I saw you."

She blushed. "I know. I'm sorry." She took his hand, crawled carefully out of the truck, and planted a big kiss on Mark. "How's that? I'm so glad you showed up when you did. Will never would have felt comfortable leaving Betsy Mae alone."

Mark nodded. "It's a big job. She handles it well, but I'm glad I could help."

"I imagine you'll be heading over to the Double Eagle, now that they're over their bug, but I really do appreciate your stepping in." Will held out his hand. Mark took it, wondering how to explain that he really wasn't intending to go anywhere.

"Hey, Will." Betsy Mae stepped out of the house and flashed her brother and sister-in-law a big grin. "I forgot to tell you—we had twins! That new heifer you bought, the one that was bred to the Charolais? She threw a bull calf and a heifer, both Charolais white and both healthy."

"She have any trouble?" Will had reached for his duffel in the back of the truck, but he set it back down and headed for the barn with Annie, Betsy Mae, and Mark following.

Betsy Mae shot a quick glance at Mark. "Yeah. The first one was coming out butt first, but Mark got the calf turned. The second one came right after without any trouble."

Will stopped and grinned at Mark. "Mark turned the calf?

Hey, cowboy. Looks like you've settled into the job better than I expected."

"Gee, thanks." He grabbed for Betsy Mae's hand, but she sort of skipped out of reach. He wasn't sure if she'd done it on purpose or just hadn't noticed him.

They all stopped in front of the stall to admire the new calves. Betsy Mae'd managed to put Annie and Will between her and Mark. On purpose? He wasn't sure, but something was feeling less "right" by the moment. At least the calves were in great shape. Their coats were fluffy and clean and the color of rich cream. Mama didn't seem to mind a bit that her babies were a different color. She munched away on her flake of alfalfa and all was right with her world.

Mark glanced at Betsy Mae, but she turned away. Damn. He wished he could say the same about his world, but right now it felt totally screwed.

nine

Betsy Mae watched Mark head back to his room to pack his bags and she knew her heart was breaking, but it was for the best. He would have been leaving sooner or later, and she didn't think she'd be able to let him go if he dug himself any deeper into her life.

The last couple of nights—and days—had been amazing, from delivering the calves to drinking Will's whisky and making love like there was no tomorrow. Except there was a tomorrow, and it was here, now.

Damn it. Mark had made her feel so wonderful she wanted to cry just thinking about it, but that was the last thing Will and Annie needed to see. Michelle Garrison had called again this morning, wondering when he was coming back to the Double Eagle. Now that Will and Annie were here, there was no reason for him to stay. None at all.

It wasn't like he loved her or anything. What they had was

good old-fashioned lust, and it wouldn't last. Couldn't last. Who'd ever think a New York City fancy-pants editor could be happy with a has-been barrel racer? At first she'd thought that maybe they had a chance, but her dreams felt foolish in the cold light of day. They hadn't known each other long enough or well enough to really talk about the future. Probably for the best.

Still, she'd never had so much fun in her life as she had with Mark Connor—especially when they made love. He'd make her laugh even as her orgasm was ripping her to shreds. He made her body sing in ways she hadn't dreamed possible, and he always put her pleasure before his own. Always.

And damn it all, but he'd made her too frickin' aware of just how different they were—him with his big-city manners and style, and her so dumb and naïve that she'd probably turned him off altogether.

That's probably what was going on. It wasn't that he had such amazing control—she just didn't turn him on all that much.

"Betsy Mae?"

She jerked around and he was right there, standing not three feet away with his expensive suitcase in one hand and the keys to his Jeep in the other. "You leavin' already?"

He shrugged. "I guess there's no reason to stay. Is there?"

She shook her head and stared at her boots. "No. No reason. Will you be coming back at all?"

He frowned. "Well, of course I will. It's not like I'm going to be that far away. The Double Eagle's just over the hill."

She nodded. She really didn't think she could say anything without crying, so a nod was the best he was going to get.

"Well, good-bye, then. Be sure and stop by before you go back to the big city, okay?"

He stood there a moment. Then he just turned away and left.

She didn't get a kiss. Not even a handshake. A couple of amazing nights together, and there was no lookin' back.

CURSING under his breath, Mark threw his suitcase in the back of the Jeep, got in, and stuck the key in the ignition. Then he sat there for a minute, going over Betsy Mae's last words in his head. What the hell did she say?

Be sure and stop by before you go back to the big city . . . Why would she say that? He was never going back to New York. Unless . . . what the hell? She didn't really think he was leaving for good, did she?

Of course she does, you idiot. Why wouldn't she?

He'd been trying to forget New York. He'd never mentioned selling his apartment or quitting his job. Suddenly everything fell into place. Mark slammed his hands down on the steering wheel and called himself a few choice names. Then he got out of the Jeep and stalked across the driveway, up the front steps, and into the house. He didn't knock. Hell, this place was more home to him than his apartment in Manhattan had ever been.

He found her in the kitchen, staring out the window toward the hills separating the Double Eagle and Columbine Camp. Her hands were folded, resting on the granite counter, and tears ran down her cheeks. "Betsy Mae?"

Her back stiffened and Mark fought every impulse he had to just drag her into his arms.

"What are you doing here?" She sniffed. "I thought you were already gone. Did you forget something?"

"Betsy Mae? Turn around, sweetheart. Will you look at me?"

She shook her head and sniffed. "No. My nose is all red."

He stepped up behind her, wrapped his arms around her waist, and rested his chin on top of her head. "I love your nose, even when it's red. I could call you Rudolph."

She shook her head and tried to pull out of his embrace, though Mark noticed she didn't try very hard. "Not funny."

"Where'd you think I was going when you asked me to stop by before I left?"

She lifted one shoulder in a halfhearted shrug. "Back to New York. Back to your job."

"I quit my job, sweetheart. Sold my apartment. Put all my stuff in storage. Everything I've got is in that Jeep out front. I came west for a new life, Betsy Mae. I think, deep down inside, I came west for you. I'm not going anywhere."

Slowly she turned and gazed up at him. Her eyes were red-rimmed and swimming in tears. "You're not?"

He tugged his handkerchief out of his back pocket and dabbed at her eyes. Then he just handed it to her and she blew her nose. "Nope," he said. "I'm not. At least, not without you."

"But . . ." She frowned. "I don't get it. You've got this big important job, you live in New York. What's out here? Nothing but trees and rocks and cows."

"You're out here." He leaned close and kissed her. "I think I've been waiting for you all my life, Betsy Mae Twigg. Maybe it was reading all those western romances." He laughed and hugged her tight. She hesitated, as if she didn't quite believe him. Then her arms slipped around his waist and she lay her head against his chest.

It felt right, holding her like this. Standing here in the kitchen at Columbine Camp with the sound of cows mooing and wannabe cowboys yelling the way they thought cowboys should yell. This felt right . . . Betsy Mae felt right.

So did his world. "I love you, Betsy Mae Twigg. I love you

more than I ever dreamed it possible to love anyone, and if you think I'm giving up on something this special for an empty apartment and an emptier life, you're an idiot."

She raised her head and grinned at him. "I thought you told me I was smart. How can you call me an idiot?"

"If you're smart, you'll marry me. You might even think about having babies with me."

"You sure about that?" She reached up and kissed him. "I've been watching Annie. Her ankles swell. She gets bitchy. She wants ice cream at three in the morning."

"Then I promise to rub your feet. I'll make you laugh, and if you want ice cream at three in the morning, I will bring it to you."

She laughed and kissed him, hard. "Did you learn all that in those romance novels?"

"I did."

"I love you, Mark Connor. And yes, I will marry you. I might even think about those babies. Just one thing."

"One?" He kissed her again.

"One. You have to promise me, even though you're not a fancy-pants New York editor anymore, you'll keep reading those romance novels. Think of them sort of like a refresher course."

"I can do that. But I want one thing from you, too."

"Hmm?" She nuzzled under his chin and licked the pulse point on his throat.

"I want you to promise to love me, for better or for worse, forever."

"I can do that," she said.

And she did.

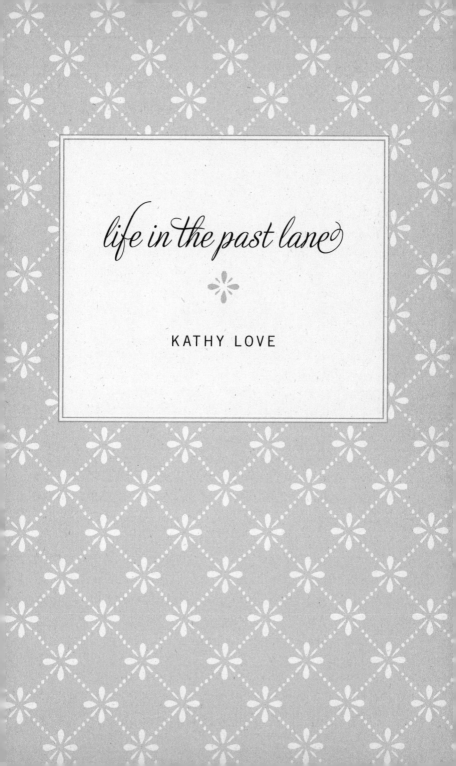

life in the past lane

KATHY LOVE

*

"The Beals Point class reunion."

"Excuse me?" Rocco said, even though he'd heard his managing editor perfectly—he was just hoping he'd misheard.

Daniel tossed a folded newspaper across the desk. It landed on the computer keyboard in front of Rocco, rattling the keys. Rattling him even more as he saw the newspaper's masthead.

Beals Point Preview.

Rocco hadn't seen that paper for years, but nothing about it had changed. Not the font, not the layout. Not the town itself, he was sure.

"I believe this is your hometown, isn't it?"

Rocco stared at it as if the typeset was printed in poisonous ink.

His hometown? As much as anywhere, he supposed.

Finally Rocco nodded, realizing that Daniel expected some sort of a response.

"Well, if my math is right, your high school class is having its fifteen-year reunion," Daniel said.

"Good to know," Rocco said, managing to sound unaffected as he pushed the paper aside. He refocused on the keyboard, trying to remember what he'd been writing before he was interrupted. Ah yes, his date with Charlene, a sweet Georgia peach new to the Big Apple.

"Don't you see where I'm going with this?" Daniel said, obviously ignoring Rocco's attempt to ignore him.

Rocco had hoped nowhere. At most just pointing out something that might interest him. And didn't.

Beals Point. Class reunions. None of that interested him.

"I want you to go," Daniel said.

Rocco's attention shot to his boss. Was he effin' kidding?

"You cannot be serious."

Daniel smiled, his gray eyes sparkling, wheels turning. "It's perfect for your column."

Rocco laughed, although he wasn't amused. "I hardly think a lame small-town reunion is life in the fast lane."

Rocco's wildly successful column, Life in the Fast Lane, followed his misadventures with women, dating, and life as a single male in NYC. A *Sex and the City* for men if you will, although he had just as many female readers as men. Probably more.

"No one is interested in a reunion. I'm not writing Life in the *Past* Lane here."

Daniel chuckled. "Good one."

Rocco forced a smile. Maybe his editor was coming to his senses and realizing how silly his idea was. After all, *People* magazine had recently labeled Rocco "the reigning prince of the hip, fast-paced New York singles scene."

Beals Point was not hip or fast-paced.

"Your readers will love it," Daniel said.

Rocco's smile faded.

"All those woman who still hold a torch for ole Rocco since his high school days. Hearts you broke. The ones who got away. This could be good stuff." Daniel tapped the paper again, then headed back to his office, leaving no room for further debate.

"Good stuff," Rocco muttered, staring down at the paper.

"THIS is so not good," Rocco muttered as he pulled his car onto the two-lane road that led to Beals Point. He'd tried over the past few weeks to convince Daniel his idea was boring, pedestrian, outright awful, but his headstrong editor wouldn't be dissuaded. So here he was, driving back to a place he'd sworn he'd never see again.

He supposed his readers would love this topic for a column, if his past had been anything like Daniel imagined. If the Rocco who'd lived in Beals Point had actually been just a younger version of the man he was now. But the Rocco Vincente, sitting in his new Mercedes, was a total invention. A creation made up to bury the Rocco of the past forever.

He turned again, this road winding through woods, trees rising up and over him like a living cage. Verdant, and utterly suffocating.

Dread and doubt squeezed his chest, a sensation he hadn't experienced in years, a sensation he thought long gone. But it was back just like it had been all those years ago. When he'd first ridden down this twisting road toward an uncertain future. To a place he'd never seen but was supposed to call home.

Then Beals Point rose up in front of him, appearing out of the trees like a picture in a pop-up book. Quaint little houses interspersed with huge old Victorians and classic capes appearing among the craggy hills of the Maine coast. Two church steeples, white against the green trees and blue skies. And beyond the town, the glittering waves of the Atlantic. A perfect little New England town.

Beautiful, really, he could see that now. Idyllic.

Except he'd found nothing idyllic there in his youth. His chest continued to constrict as he turned onto Main Street to drive to the bed-and-breakfast where he'd be spending two nights.

Just two nights, he reminded himself. Not two years, like last time.

He parked his car in the small lot beside the Victorian that had been a bed-and-breakfast even when he'd lived here. The building looked totally the same. Still cheery yellow with green shutters and white trim. Baskets of white petunias hung at even intervals around the huge wraparound porch.

Welcoming, homey. But he didn't feel welcome or any sense of home. Trepidation still sat heavy in this chest. But he forced himself to get out of the car.

He squinted at the sprawling building with its gingerbread trim and cobblestone walk. He'd often walked by the inn and wondered who stayed in a place like that. Honeymooning couples? Vacationing families? Then he'd tried to imagine himself staying there. What that would be like. But even as a kid, he could only imagine himself staying there alone. He couldn't see any family surrounding him. No loved ones.

He popped his trunk and pulled out his suitcase—a small carry-on. No need to pack much.

"Just two days," he repeated to himself, walking up the steps to the front door.

He pushed open the front door and stepped into a foyer. In front of him was a large, curved staircase with a lovely, carved balustrade. The old wood was polished to a warm mellow sheen. He could smell a lemony scent in the air. To one side of the staircase was a short hallway that led to what appeared to be a dining room.

"Hello," a voice called, startling him. "May I help you?"

Rocco turned to his left to see what must have once been a formal living room. Now the room served as a check-in area. A settee and a wingback chair were arranged in front of a marble fireplace. Beyond the sitting area was an ornate desk and behind that a woman rose to greet him.

Rocco had a vague impression he should know the woman, although he couldn't place her. Red hair, the color of polished copper. Pale skin and pale blue eyes. She was not conventionally beautiful but very striking.

A warm smile curved her pink lips. "Hi."

"Hi," he said, walking toward her, offering a smile back, despite his dismay at being here. "I'm checking in for the weekend. I reserved tonight and tomorrow night."

The woman looked down at a log book—no computers for this establishment.

"Well, let's take a look. Are you here for the reunion?" She looked up, her pale eyes scanning over him.

Again he felt that twinge of recognition, but the thought was squeezed aside by the tightness in his chest. "Um, yes."

She smiled again. "Your name?"

"Rocco Vincente."

The woman straightened, tilting her head slightly as she regarded him closely for a moment. "I thought that was you."

Rocco frowned, not sure what to say. He still couldn't place this woman.

"I'm Franny Arsenault."

Rocco studied her for a moment, but still drew a blank. Finally he shook his head, giving her a pained look.

"I'm sorry—" he started, but she stopped him with laugh, no offense in the happy sound.

"Well, I was Franny Mullens. I graduated with you. We had a few classes together. A couple English classes. Algebra, I think. Maybe chemistry."

Rocco studied her, now realizing why she seemed vaguely familiar. Franny—her hair had been redder. And she'd been kind of quiet. Not so—attractive.

Sure, he remembered her.

She was also the one he was supposed to talk to about the reunion. She'd organized the whole event—or debacle as he'd come to think of it. Talk about fortuitous.

"It's good to see you," he said, trying to sound like he meant it.

"Great to see you," she said, and once more he was struck by how sweet and welcoming she appeared. Her smile seemed to envelope him with warmth. But instead of being comforted, he found her friendliness . . . unnerving.

It took him a moment to find his voice, but when he did he managed to stick to his reason for being here. "I actually wanted to talk with you about an interview. You see I'm a—"

She laughed again. "Oh, I know what you are. A writer and the class's star celebrity," she said, then blushed, her cheeks turning a faint, pretty shade of pink.

Ah yes, so that was what was bringing about her sweet reaction. She realized he'd made it big. She was interested in the Rocco Vincente he was now. If he'd returned some average Joe Schmoe, her reaction wouldn't have been nearly so warm. He'd bet on that.

He offered her a smile again. The practiced urbane smile he offered all the ladies who wanted something from him. Usually a date that might result in a column about them. Five minutes of fame, everyone was looking for it.

"Yes. Well, I was hoping to get an interview with you." That should please her. "You know about the reunion—since you organized it," he said, his tone more businesslike. A little cool.

Her warm smile faded, and she busied herself with getting him checked in.

"Sure," she said after she wrote something down in her ledger. "How about later this afternoon? I have a girl who comes in to help at three. I could meet you after that."

"Three is good," he said, wondering why he felt a little sad about the sudden aloofness in her demeanor. Wasn't it better to make it clear he wasn't interested?

"Fine," she said with just a quick, almost indifferent curve of her lips, nothing like her first smiles. "I'll meet you at Freddy's."

Rocco frowned, briefly drawing a blank again before recalling the name. "That's the diner, right?"

She nodded, holding out a key to him. A real key, no key cards here.

"Three it is," he said, accepting it. His fingers brushed hers as he took the silver key, and the brief touch sizzled through him like unbridled electricity.

Suddenly Rocco suspected he understood much what Benjamin Franklin had felt the infamous night he'd flown his kite in a lightning storm. There was a key involved in that event, too, wasn't there?

"Second floor, third door on your right."

Rocco blinked, stunned both by his awareness of her and her dismissal. Did she not feel the spark? Her cool expression certainly didn't reveal that she felt anything.

"See you later," he mumbled, picking up his suitcase and heading back toward the foyer and staircase.

What had just happened? He wasn't sure. And again, he wondered how the hell he ended up back here.

Franny watched Rocco leave the room, then collapsed into her desk chair.

Rocco Vincente.

How many times had she thought about him since high school? How many times had she thought about him during high school for that matter? Hundreds—heck, maybe millions.

She'd had a huge crush on him from the first time she'd ever seen him, sitting on the school steps and smoking a cigarette even though they weren't allowed to smoke on school grounds.

He'd been the quintessential bad boy—all dark, disheveled good looks with brooding, mysterious eyes and a cool attitude. But she'd seen beyond his indifferent mask. She'd realized he was hiding his pain—she understood, because she hid her own. Not behind sullen ennui but by trying to stay quiet, unnoticed. Invisible.

But anyone who'd been paying any attention would have seen he was hiding pain. All they'd had to do was listen to the things he wrote.

So she wasn't surprised in the least that Rocco Vincente had become a writer. She was, however, surprised at the kind of man he'd seem to become. She'd followed his career, read all his columns and his books. And while his subject matter, the adventures of a slick single guy in the city, had surprised her, she had still caught glimpses of the talented, insightful boy she'd once known.

And she was sure Rocco was still the amazing, fascinating person she'd once silently admired across many a classroom.

But now, she wasn't sure.

Disappointment fell heavy in her belly, as if her heart had turned to lead and sunk into the pit of her stomach.

The polished, impeccably groomed man who'd walked into her B&B wasn't at all what she'd imagined he'd be like. Everything about him seemed contrived. Insincere.

Whereas that boy from years ago, he'd been real, raw, and alive in a way she'd appreciated and envied.

Now, well, now she wondered if she'd just imagined who he'd been. Of course, she couldn't claim she imagined her reaction to the fleeting touch of his fingers against hers. She'd felt that touch throughout her entire body. Oh yeah, that had been very real, very raw, and she definitely felt alive. Some parts of her a little more than others.

She groaned. Leave it to her to still long for her high school crush, even when she wasn't really sure she actually liked the man he'd become.

ROCCO dropped his suitcase on the floor and looked around the room. The place was just as he'd imagined when he'd walked past as a kid. Cozy, quaint, homey.

What appeared to be a handmade quilt covered the four-poster bed. A wingback chair and small end table sat near the window. Real watercolor paintings of seascapes—not cheap reproductions— decorated the walls. Lace curtains that looked like they could have been hung by someone's mother covered the windows.

He wandered over to the window, pulling back the lace, noticing the same clean, lemony scent filled this room like it had in the foyer. He looked out to see green lawn, a beautifully kept garden of wildflowers and what appeared to be herbs, and beyond that the ocean.

Most of his New Yorker friends would pay big bucks for a weekend away with a view like this. But he still couldn't enjoy it. Being here was too hard. Too . . . much.

Damn, look at his reaction to Franny. That wasn't normal. His weird, intense awareness of her had to have been triggered by all the emotions of coming back here. And hadn't he spent years trying to leave the past behind him? He didn't need this.

His gaze returned to the garden. Suddenly an image of Franny, working in the flower beds appeared in his mind. Her coppery hair shimmering, lovely against the green of the herbs, the red of the poppies, and the oranges of the marigolds. Her image turned to him, to show him a particularly beautiful blossom. That sweet smile on her lips. Her eyes filled with an emotion he couldn't quite read—something warm and inviting. Something he'd longed for his whole life.

He let the curtain drop, turning away from the window. Okay, clearly he was losing it. Being here was messing with his head. Thoughts and images like that were far too poetic, too romantic for Rocco Vincente. He was practical, snarky, viewing the world as a humorous, yet mostly dysfunctional, place.

He didn't believe in, much less long for, some kind of pretty, pastoral little world with sentiments as pedestrian as home and hearth and simple pleasures. He'd long ago realized the only place to find happiness was in achieving success and obtaining things. He surrounded himself with tangible proof of his ability to survive. A swank loft apartment, an expensive car, designer clothes, five-star restaurants, and beautiful women.

His life made him feel good, in control, important. They made up for a childhood where he'd been none of those things.

He flopped down on the bed, deciding maybe taking a nap until his meeting with Franny was the best way to deal with his strange thoughts.

He rolled on his side, the scent of lavender from the sheets mingling with the clean lemony scent of the floors and furniture. A relaxing mix. Some of the tension in his muscles slipped away.

He bet Franny's scent was just like this. Clean and flowery and calming. There was something about her that was so serene, so enticing. So different from what he usually encountered in his life.

But that touch . . .

He rolled onto his back, staring at the ceiling. Nothing had been calming about her skin against his. But that had still been so enticing. Very, very enticing. In fact, lying here in a bed she'd made, he couldn't help but imagine her there beside him.

Under him. His body deep inside hers. Those pale eyes of hers gazing up at him, filled with tenderness, her smile sweet, her moans sweeter as he made love to her.

He sat up, swinging his legs over the edge of the bed.

Okay, a nap wasn't going to do it, either. Not with the crazy images playing through his brain. He stood, not sure what to do.

Maybe a walk. Maybe some fresh, sea air would clear his head. He doubted it, but lying around fantasizing about a woman who was so not his type wasn't good for his mental health, either.

He grabbed the key and left the room. As he descended the stairs, he heard Franny speaking with someone. Another guest signing in. Her voice reached him like cheery sunshine, heating his skin.

Oh yeah, losing it.

He didn't even look toward them as he passed the living room/

check-in, partially afraid the newest guest was another old class-mate, and he wasn't in the mood for more small talk. But more afraid to see Franny. He couldn't talk to her yet. Not with his thoughts about her going to all kinds of weird places.

He doubled his steps, practically running until he was out to the sidewalk, hoping no one noticed his hasty escape.

"Was that Rocco Vincente?"

Franny's attention snapped back to her newest guests, Jackie Hutchinson and her husband, Bob.

"Yes," Franny said, gathering her scattered thoughts. "Yes, he got in earlier today."

Jackie widened her eyes, surprised. "I didn't know he was coming. He's quite a success, you know."

Franny nodded, focusing on getting the couple signed in. "Yes, I'd heard that."

Jackie turned to her husband. "No one would have believed that guy would make it big. He was a real bad kid. Lived at the boys' home—that place I pointed out to you on Franklin Ave.—all the troubled boys lived there. I don't think anyone in our class ever thought he'd be the big success story."

Before Franny could catch herself, she looked up at Jackie. "I did."

Jackie raised an eyebrow, again surprised or maybe intrigued. "Really? Well, you had more faith than I did, that's for sure."

Franny managed a slight smile and then finished checking them in. Once they were gone, Franny walked to the front door. She stepped out onto the porch and looked around. Rocco wasn't anywhere in sight.

A wave of panic, actual panic, swept over her, stealing her breath like a drowning wave of icy seawater washing over her head. Then she pulled in a slow breath, telling herself to calm down. He wasn't gone. He hadn't taken his suitcase. She walked to the end of the porch and checked the parking lot. She'd be willing to bet the Mercedes was his.

He'd gone for a walk or something. She'd still meet him at three. And if she could actually get up the courage, she would tell him what she thought of the boy she remembered from high school.

Maybe he wouldn't care. Maybe he really had grown into the sarcastic, somewhat shallow man she mostly saw in his columns. But then again, maybe she was right, and there was still some of the boy she remembered inside him. She was sure she saw hints of him amid the glib, urbane, often cynical insights.

She hugged her arms around her. Could she be that brave?

ROCCO roamed the streets, surprised at how much he remembered about the town. The general store where he'd gotten busted for stealing cigarettes. What was the name of the owner back then? He'd been ancient, or at least Rocco had thought so at the time. The old guy had been furious but hadn't turned him in. Rocco wondered if he still ran the place.

Marty's Pizza. The high school kids would hang out there, eating greasy pizza and fries. He'd gone there once in a while. But not a lot. Hanging with the kids who had normal lives, normal families—he hadn't been comfortable with that.

Joey's Garage. The post office. Afternoon Delight, a walk-up ice-cream place with picnic tables and swings. He'd avoided that place at all costs.

Today, the order windows were lined up with parents and kids. Families out for a weekend treat. He watched for a moment but then quickly continued on.

He walked past St. Peter's, the private Catholic school, down the one street he'd never forgotten, no matter how much he tried. His feet moved, one in front of the other as if they were on autopilot, taking him back, both in destination and in time.

Finally he stopped, remaining absolutely still as he looked up at the large white building. The structure didn't have any of the quaintness or hominess of the other homes in the town.

But it was a home nonetheless.

The sign on the front lawn proclaimed it as such.

Chisholm Boys' Home.

Funny, some things in his past were so blurry. Like the memory of his real parents. Or even his grandmother. Even some of the several foster homes he'd been shuttled to and from.

But the day he arrived here. That day was burned into his memory—even after years of not allowing himself to think about it.

Walking up the concrete steps that led from the sidewalk to the front yard. The other boys watching as he'd arrived. He'd been sixteen, and he'd known this was his last stop. All he had to do was bide his time and soon enough he'd be free. Finally.

He'd like to say on his own finally, but the truth was he'd always been on his own. Alone in the world. No family. No one who really loved him. Years of being an outsider.

But he'd moved past that. He had a great life now.

Just walk away. This is your past.

But again his wayward body wouldn't obey his brain. Instead of continuing his tour, he sat down on those concrete steps. The steps that led to his past.

He'd sat there so many times before. Watching the kids at the Catholic school. Watching families, dressed for church, heading farther down the street to St. Ignatius. He'd watched those families every Sunday morning, wondering how it would feel to be part of a loving, caring unit like that.

"Can I help you?"

Rocco shifted on the step to see a woman standing at the top of the steps. Her hair was gray, the color of polished silver. Faint wrinkles fanned out around gray eyes.

She frowned, narrowing her eyes, and then a smile curled her thin lips.

"Rocco? Rocco Vincente?"

Rocco frowned back, then recognition hit him. "Mrs. Martin?" He rose slowly, staring up at the old lady.

"Well, come up here, dear boy."

Rocco felt his feet move up the steps. He was hit with déjà vu, the walk toward Mrs. Martin so surreal.

When he reached the top of the stairs, the old woman hugged him, her arms frail but her embrace somehow all-encompassing despite her size and weight.

"It's so good to see you," she said, standing back to survey him, her eyes actually shimmering with tears.

Rocco shook his head slightly, again the dreamlike quality overwhelming.

"You, too," he managed to say.

"Come in. Come see the place." Mrs. Martin looped an arm through his and led him up the concrete path toward the front door.

She released his arm to turn the knob, then stepped inside. Rocco paused for a moment, uncertain, but then followed her.

The front hallway didn't look much different. Maybe the wallpaper had changed. Pictures, too. But overall, it was like truly walking into the past. The wood floor scuffed and worn. The white woodwork nicked with chips and dents.

"Come to the kitchen," Mrs. Martin said, gesturing for him to come along. "I just made a fresh pot of coffee."

Rocco walked along behind her, taking in the place. The worn but comfortable furniture in the TV room on his left. The stairs that led to the boys' bedrooms. Five bedrooms in all. Two boys to a room. A bathroom at either end of the hallway.

And the big country kitchen. The long table where all the boys sat to eat meals. Meals Mrs. Martin cooked.

He frowned again, thinking about those meals. Hardy home cooking. Lots of food. Lots of chatter.

"Sit," she said, waving to the table. "Sit."

Rocco hesitated, but then slid onto the long bench that lined one side of the table. Again, he was overwhelmed with such a strange feeling of déjà vu. Like it was only yesterday that he sat at this table.

Mrs. Martin poured two cups of coffee, then set them on the table. She returned to the counter to get the sugar bowl and then shuffled to the fridge for some half-and-half.

She placed both items in front of him.

"As I recall, you like your coffee creamy and sweet."

Rocco nodded, bemused. Mrs. Martin remembered how he liked it.

She nodded in return, smiling. "You were my little coffee drinker," she said, a fondness in her voice. "Always sneaking in early to get a cup before the other boys saw you."

He did? Then he paused. He did. He'd forgotten that.

"I'd try to dissuade you," she said as if narrating his returning memories. "I'd tell you over and over that it would—"

"Stunt my growth," Rocco finished for her, suddenly recalling all the mornings she had indeed notified him of that fate.

She chuckled, the sound a little hoarse, but pleasing. "It would appear my concerns did not come to pass. You've turned into a fine strapping man."

It was Rocco's turn to chuckle as he reached for the sugar spoon. *Strapping*. Such a Mrs. Martin word. "Thank you. And thank you for being concerned for my growth."

Mrs. Martin sobered. "You did concern me."

He stopped stirring his coffee and met the woman's eyes. Even now he could see the concern there. Clearly she'd looked at him this way before, but he didn't remember it. Why?

"You were such a closed off kid. Buttoned in on yourself. I knew you'd suffered too much before getting here."

He didn't say anything. He wasn't sure what to say. He had suffered, and this was just the final place to put him before he wasn't the government's problem anymore.

At least that's how he'd always thought of it.

"And coming here your junior year. That's a tough time to move into a new place and new school." She shook her head, and Rocco could see she was still lamenting his hard lot.

"It wasn't easy," he said.

"Well, of course it wasn't. Ernest and I often discussed what we could do to make the adjustment easier for you."

Ernest Martin was Mrs. Martin's husband, a solid, salt of the earth kind of man who'd been there to watch over the boys, too. The janitor, the repairman, the soft-spoken but firm authoritarian. Both of the Martins had expected and demanded respect.

"Ernest? Is he around?" Rocco said, surprised to discover he'd like to see the man.

Mrs. Martin looked down at her coffee mug, curling her gnarled hands around it. She shook her head. "Gone. Passed nearly three years ago now."

Rocco didn't know what to say. No, he knew the right words

to say, but he didn't know how to convey his true sorrow. And oddly he didn't know what to make of the sense of loss that suddenly left his own chest hollow.

"When Ernest passed, my oldest son came to stay with me. I considered retiring, but I had a few boys who really needed routine, and I just couldn't leave. So my oldest son came to work here to help me."

Rocco only had a moment to consider her words, when she continued, "We knew you were one of those kids when you arrived, but you were so resistant to opening up. A real tough nut to crack."

Tough nut to crack. Rocco recognized that as a Mrs. Martin saying, too. Funny he'd remember her sayings but not her generosity. Her concern.

Was she only acting like she'd cared now? And if so, why?

"But Ernest got to see your success before he passed. He was so proud. Me, too."

For a moment skepticism flared.

"You've become a real success," Mrs. Martin said.

Was that what all this was about? Was she impressed that the unwanted, unloved kid somehow grew up to make good? Did she take some credit for that?

"In fact, I'd love for you to talk to one of the boys here now. He reminds me so much of you. Hurt, angry, far too world-weary. But he draws and writes these amazing stories for the other boys. He makes up superheroes. The other boys love them. I'd be thrilled for Billy, that's his name, to see he can succeed—if he just works hard and believes in himself. Like you did."

She wasn't taking credit. If anything, she was giving all the credit to Rocco. And all she wanted from him was to help one of the boys living here now. Boys who were here for the same reason he'd been.

Rocco nodded. "I would be happy to meet him."

Mrs. Martin smiled. "Thank you. Do you mind if I go get him?"

"Sure."

Mrs. Martin rose from the table, her small, frail-looking form moving with the spryness of a much younger woman, as if Rocco's agreement to talk to this boy had given her a new lease on life. Rocco could feel the caring just exuding from his woman.

"Stay here." She paused in the doorway. "Thank you, Rocco, dear boy."

She disappeared and Rocco was alone in the kitchen. How had he never realized, never seen, that the Martins were so concerned with the boys here? With him? In his mind, they'd taken care of him because they had to, not because they really worried about him and wanted him to be okay.

Had he missed an opportunity to have some sort of family? Not a conventional family but people who truly cared? He knew he had resisted any overtures of affection or concern, but he'd always told himself that was because they were given out of duty. Not out of sincerity. Not out of any real emotions.

But seeing Mrs. Martin now, and the genuine joy on her face at seeing him, the very real worry about this other boy, he wondered. Could things have been better while he was here in Beals Point, if he'd just allowed it to be?

A boy appeared in the doorway, his dark eyes sullen, his mouth set in a hard, almost petulant frown. Longish, mussed hair, a baggy T-shirt, and jeans.

Rocco was looking at himself.

"Hey," he said to the boy.

"Hey."

Suddenly, Rocco had a chance. A chance to change things, to finally feel like his life had played out just as it should, and it was okay.

FRANNY sat on the front steps, the sun falling lower in the sky, watching the breeze rustle leaves, feeling like a teenage girl who'd been stood up for the prom.

"Stupid," she muttered, pushing herself up and brushing down her flowered skirt. The bed-and-breakfast was full tonight. She certainly had other things she could be doing besides feeling rejected and sorry for herself.

"Franny!"

She paused, her hand on the doorknob of the front door. She looked back toward the street. Rocco jogged down the sidewalk, waving.

Her heart leapt as he bound up onto the porch, the sea breeze ruffling his dark hair, his dark brown eyes sparkling.

As much as she hated to admit it, he looked far better than any prom date she could have imagined and she was relieved to see him.

"Sorry I missed our meeting at the diner," he said, his deep voice a little breathless as if he'd run from wherever he'd been.

She shrugged, to act more collected than she felt. "That's okay. Although I did wonder if you'd left town or something."

He smiled then, and again her heart did a strange flip in her chest. "Well, I have to admit, I considered it."

For some reason his confession stung a little, even as she told herself it shouldn't. After all, Rocco Vincente hadn't been back to Beals Point in fifteen years. Clearly this wasn't a place he missed.

Stop acting like a damned teenage girl, she silently reprimanded herself again. He hadn't even remembered her—not really. She could hardly take offense that he wasn't thrilled to be back here. Although from his smile and glittering eyes, he didn't look exactly like he was upset either.

"I actually went to the boys' home and saw Mrs. Martin. I also talked for a long time with this boy who lives there now. He's super-talented. Interested in writing and drawing."

Franny smiled, sensing that going back to the place he'd so clearly hated in school had been good for him. Giving him some real peace.

"That's wonderful," she said.

He appeared a bit bemused, but he nodded. "It really was."

For a moment, they just stood there, in the shade of the porch, the ocean air ruffling their hair, grinning at each other.

"So what are you doing now?" he asked.

His sudden question filled her with schoolgirl giddiness. An emotion that could lead to real trouble.

She hesitated, telling herself she should just say she was busy. Yes, it had been years, but for some reason, this man had always done crazy things to her insides and she got the feeling he had the ability to hurt her—badly—if she allowed herself to react to him too much.

But her sensible thoughts about self-preservation didn't stop her from saying, "Nothing."

"Want to go get an ice cream?"

She faltered for a second, but then nodded. "That would be nice."

He grinned again and she was stunned at how amazingly

handsome he was. Tall and muscular in a plain white button down shirt and jeans. His thick hair with a little curl at the ends, still gave him a disheveled look, even though he wore it much shorter than he had in high school. Five o'clock shadow shaded his chin and cheeks, adding to his roguish quality. But his coffee brown eyes were fringed with long, dark lashes and his lips were wide and so beautifully shaped that she'd always found his features a strange paradox of totally masculine and a little pretty. Like some artist's depiction of the perfect man.

That hadn't changed in fifteen years.

He gestured for her to walk down the steps ahead of him, but once they reached the sidewalk he fell into step beside her.

"So did you walk around town, too?" she asked.

He nodded. "Yeah. I haven't been here for so long, I thought I'd look around a bit."

"And? Just as you remembered?" She smiled. "Things don't change much here in Beals Point."

He didn't answer for a moment, his attention focused on the sidewalk in front of them, then he shook his head, that strange, bemused expression back on his handsome face.

"You know, it's actually a lot different than I remember. So how about you?" he asked suddenly. "Have you been happy here?"

Franny considered his words. "Yeah. Yeah, I have."

He nodded, and they walked silently until they reached Afternoon Delight. Both ordered small chocolate soft-serves in a cone and sat on a bench under a large oak tree to enjoy them. The ice-cream shop was still busy even though it was close to dinnertime. Children darted around the play area, laughter and happy voices filling the air. Just a nice summer's evening.

Franny smiled as one girl ran by sporting ice cream around her bow lips like a chocolate goatee.

"You don't have kids?" Rocco asked.

Franny shook her head, swallowing the lick of ice cream she'd just taken. "No. No kids."

She could feel Rocco's eyes on her as she still watched the kids playing by the swings.

"But you want kids, don't you?"

She nodded without hesitation. "Yeah, I do."

Rocco shifted beside her, and she could actually feel a subtle change in the air between them like static electricity. She looked at him and he still regarded her, but she couldn't quite read his expression. Something close to bewilderment, she thought.

From his columns, Franny suspected Rocco wasn't particularly interested in having children. He wasn't particularly interested in marriage, either, by his own accounts. Maybe he couldn't quite fathom why she would want a family, since he was clearly a free spirit with no desire to be tied down.

So she was initially confused when he suddenly asked, "Wait, you aren't married, are you?"

She laughed at his almost dismayed sound. Surely he wasn't so put off by the state of matrimony that her own marriage would disgust him.

"I *was* married. I married Mark Arsenault. I'm not sure if you remember him. He graduated with us."

Unsurprisingly, he shook his head. "Not really."

"Well, we married shortly after high school." After Rocco had left town and all her hopes of her high school crush were gone. "But we only made it four years before we parted ways. He's remarried now, living in Bangor."

A strange sense of relief spread through Rocco, making his muscles almost weak. He shouldn't be so pleased to find out she was single. But he was.

Rocco continued to study Franny. He realized he'd been staring at her since they sat down, but he couldn't seem to stop. For two reasons.

One, she had that serene way about her that he found fascinating. Maybe because it was so different from the intense, harried energy of New York, but whatever the reason, he found her easy tranquillity very . . . well, calming.

Yet exciting, too, he realized. Her movements were languid, graceful—and sexy. She licked the side of her ice-cream cone and he felt his body react.

Which brought him to the second reason he couldn't seem to take his eyes off her. She really was lovely. Her hair fell in loose curls around her pale, elfin face. Freckles, faint and golden, dotted her nose and those pale, pale blue eyes of hers were so unusual, almost hypnotic. Her lips were small but full. The kind of lips made for kissing.

He shifted, forcing himself to think about what they'd been discussing. Her divorce.

Damn, Rocco, don't be a total idiot here.

"I'm sorry," he said, finally managing the appropriate show of remorse. "That must have been hard."

"Not so bad, actually," she said, offering him a reassuring smile. "We were too young to get married. We both realized that eventually, so our breakup was mutual."

"Why did you get married in the first place?" He couldn't imagine doing such a thing. He'd never imagined marriage ever, really.

Again he studied Franny, wondering just for a moment what it would be like to be married. To her.

"I guess"—she quirked her lips as she considered the question—"I wanted stability. A family."

Her words surprised and intrigued him, but before he could ask her more, she continued. "But it didn't work out that way. So once we divorced, I attended college to study business. Then I used the money I'd inherited from my parents and purchased the bed-and-breakfast."

He grew more curious. "Inherited?"

She nodded. "Yes, my parents were killed in a car accident when I was twelve. I moved here to live with my aunt."

Rocco had no idea. Of course, he was quickly realizing he hadn't had a clue about much when he'd lived here. He'd been so wrapped up in his own loss and hurt and anger, he hadn't seen anything else.

Maybe he hadn't really seen anything his whole life.

"I'm sorry. I didn't realize we had so much in common," he said, feeling genuine sorrow. If he'd had a clue, he might have been there for her back in high school. He had no doubt she would have been there for him, if he'd let her.

"It was hard," she admitted. "But I made out fine. I love my bed-and-breakfast. And I have made a home for myself. My aunt is still here. I have lots of friends. I'm really at peace with my life."

He studied her again, realizing what she was saying was true. She was at peace.

"You are a really amazing lady, Franny Mullens."

Franny stared at Rocco, her heart pounding. His dark eyes glittered with admiration and something else that she didn't dare name.

Then to her utter astonishment, Rocco leaned in, pressing his lips to hers.

She'd imagined his kiss hundreds of times before, but they'd been the fantasies of a young girl. This was real, and far more intense than her childish imaginings. Hot and sexy. His lips tasted of chocolate, sweet, but also dark and decadent. And she wanted more.

She moaned, wordlessly begging, and he answered her, his hand on the back of her head, tangling in her hair. He deepened the kiss, his tongue finding hers, sampling her, lost to anything but this moment and their desire. Until the squeal of a child seemed to snap them back to reality at the same time.

They parted, both laughing sheepishly at how easily they'd forgotten where they were. And maybe at their intense reaction to each other and what should have been a simple, first kiss.

"Perhaps we should go," she said, knowing her cheeks had to be scarlet, even in the waning light.

"Okay," he agreed.

He reached for her hand to help her up and neither released the other's as they started back to the bed-and-breakfast, fingers linked.

When they reached the inn and the door of Rocco's room, Franny had a moment of doubt. So they'd kissed. Probably their passionate moment would end right there. Probably it should.

But as she started to tug her fingers from his, he held her fast. His dark eyes searched hers and for a moment, she thought he was experiencing the same uncertainty.

"Good night, Rocco."

He shook his head, offering her what she could only describe as a naughty little smile. A gorgeous, naughty little smile.

He kissed her again and all thoughts of walking away vanished. He stopped only long enough to fumble with the room key, and then they were inside the room, fumbling with each other's clothes.

Soon they both stood naked in the center of the room. Franny would have thought she'd be shy in front of him. Rocco had been her dream, her ideal, for as long as she could remember. But she didn't feel any bashfulness—any doubts. She'd waited so long for this very moment and she was far too busy admiring him to worry about her own nudity.

She'd always found Rocco gorgeous, but the reality of the man was beyond any fantasy. Tall with broad shoulders and lean muscles rippling under golden skin. A smattering of dark hair on his chest that narrowed to bisect his hard, rippled stomach, then thickened again around his very, very impressive erection.

Without any hesitation, she moved forward to touch him there, his penis pulsing at the brush of her fingertips. He gasped and she rose up on her toes to kiss him. Her hand still exploring his delicious body. The hard muscles of his back, his tight little rear end.

When they parted again, his dark eyes were hooded, hungry. His own hands teased over her body, discovering her.

"You are so beautiful," he murmured as his hands moved her breast, his thumbs rubbing and circling her hardened nipples.

She shivered. She felt beautiful.

Then one hand slid lower, skimming over her belly to the apex of her thighs and then deeper still to where she literally ached for his touch.

She dug her fingers into his shoulders, trying to anchor herself, her legs trembling as he stroked her. Driving her mad. His mouth returned to hers, his lips and fingers making love to her until she was moaning, and so, so close to release.

Then both were gone.

She whimpered, the sound one of frustration and despair.

Rocco smiled at her and caught her hand. "I don't want to do this standing. I want you under me, and I want to take my time figuring out exactly what will make your toes curl, make you cry out, and leave you so satisfied you can't think."

She shivered again, her body so aware of him.

"I want that, too," she whispered, following him to the bed. "Very much."

Franny wasn't sure how long he took doing exactly what he'd said, but one thing was for sure by the time he was through, her toes had indeed curled. She had cried out in ecstasy so many times she was sure her voice was hoarse. And her whole body was so sated that she felt like a very happy, very content puddle next to him.

Rocco grinned at her, looking very content, too. He cuddled her close, his large hand idly stroking up and down her back.

She yawned, not wanting to go to sleep, but unable to keep her eyes open.

"Tired?"

She nodded. "Yes, you know how to wear a girl out."

He chuckled, the sound low and rich and wonderful.

"I actually imagined what sex with you would be like," she said, realizing her drowsiness was making it too easy to make admissions.

His hand stilled and she felt him lift his head to look at her, but she didn't open her eyes. Sometimes admissions were easier in the dark.

"I had such a crush on you."

"Really?"

He seemed genuinely surprised, which made her smile.

"Oh yeah."

She felt the pillow dip again as he laid his head back down, then his hand began rubbing her back again.

He didn't say anything more, and at the moment, she didn't care. She was too blissful.

Rocco ran his hand down Franny's back, amazed how delicate

she was, her back narrow, her skin baby smooth. She was pressed against him, both on their sides, their legs tangled.

Her breathing had evened and she slept. But he couldn't. He stroked her skin as if trying to memorize every nuance of her body. Her graceful shoulders, the jut of her collarbone, her pert little breasts with cherry nipples, the slight flare of her hips. The softness of her rounded little derriere. Her sweet lips. Her freckles.

She'd had a crush on him. Damn, the things he'd missed.

The sun rose, shining through the lace curtains, dappling her pale skin in warm light. Her hair gleamed, warm copper. She looked like an angel. Fallen to earth to give him peace. Finally.

She stretched then, her movements languid and sensual.

His body reacted instantly.

She blinked at him, her expression still sleepy but quickly becoming aware.

"Good morning," she whispered, smiling her sweet smile.

He answered her by pressing her back against the mattress and kissing her senseless.

It was a long time before either spoke again.

But this time there was no basking in the afterglow of their lovemaking. Just as Rocco would have fallen asleep, Franny levered herself upright.

"What time is it?"

Rocco glanced to the nightstand. The dials on the windup clock revealed it was a little after seven.

"Early," he murmured. "Come cuddle."

She groaned, swinging her long, shapely legs over the edge of the bed.

"I can't. I'm running late," she said. "I need to get breakfast ready for the guests."

"Want help?" he asked, starting to get up, too, but she returned to the bed, placing her hands on his shoulders and pushing him back against the pillows. She kissed him quickly, slipping out of his reach before he could tug her back into bed.

"You rest. I'm good."

He rolled on his side, enjoying the view as she dressed. She was truly the most stunning women he'd ever seen.

How had he missed all this in high school? Oh the schoolboy fantasies he could conjure about her now.

Once fully clad, she smiled. "Breakfast in twenty minutes. If you are still awake."

"I'd love to come help you."

"Nope." She smiled impishly, then hurried out of the room.

Rocco stared at the closed door for a moment, then fell back against the pillows.

Damn, he had not expected his trip to Beals Point to turn out like this.

*

THE rest of the day flew by for Franny. Between her usual work at the inn and preparing for the reunion, she was on the run.

A few times, she did see Rocco and spoke with him briefly. She couldn't help noticing he seemed distracted, and a little distant, but she refused to let herself worry. She would not overthink last night. She wanted him, and she wouldn't allow herself to regret her actions. No matter the outcome. And she had no illusions about what the outcome would be. He was a successful writer with a life in New York City. She had a life here.

A little pain tugged at her heart, but she pushed it aside.

"No regrets."

By the time the reunion started, her conviction to remain calm about the previous night was wavering.

She kept checking the door of the banquet hall, looking hopefully as every new person entered. But as of yet, Rocco hadn't appeared.

Finally about forty minutes after the reunion had started, he appeared looking utterly dashing in a tailored shirt and pants. He searched the room, seeking her out right away.

"This turned out great," he said as he walked up. He didn't kiss her, but she hadn't expected him to. But he did place a hand on the small of her back, the touch sending tingles right down to the soles of her feet.

But his moment with her was short-lived. After all, he was pretty much their local celebrity and everyone wanted a chance to talk to him.

Franny mingled, too, catching up with classmates she hadn't seen in years. But even as she talked to this person and that, she seemed to sense where Rocco was in the large, crowded room. And he, too, seemed aware of her. Several times, they made eye contact, and the fact he seemed so in tune with her thrilled her.

Just enjoy, she told herself. And she did.

At around midnight, when the crowd had begun to thin and the party was winding down, Rocco finally returned to her side.

"Well, this was a success," he said, handing her a glass of wine.

She accepted it. Both of them watched the room, sipping their drinks.

"Did you have fun?" she asked.

"I actually did," he said, giving her a surprised little smile.

She laughed. "Well, good."

"But I can think of something that would be a lot more fun."

She didn't need him to explain what or ask her twice. She placed her wineglass on the table next to them and said, "Well, let's go, then."

Rocco laughed, clearly pleased by her eagerness.

And her eagerness didn't wane as they fell back into his bed. They spent all night, lost in each other and their passion.

But once the sun rose, Franny woke up to find she was alone. And beside her a simple note in broad masculine handwriting.

Thank you, Franny. Talk to you soon.

Rocco

She stared at the note, fighting the hurt, then pulled in a deep breath. She'd known he wouldn't stay. She had known that.

"IT seems you had quite the trip home."

Rocco stopped what he was doing to turn to his editor. Daniel leaned a hip on his desk, his arms crossed over his chest.

"Yes, I did," Rocco said.

"The column is not what I expected of you, though."

"No. It wasn't what I expected, either."

The men stared at each other for a moment. Then Daniel nodded. "Looks like your column is going to be changing a bit, huh?"

Rocco smiled. "Yeah. I think my column is going to be changing *quite* a bit."

FRANNY straightened, stretching her stiff back, raising her face to the sun. It was a beautiful day, sunny, warm. A nice breeze off the ocean.

She remained that way for a moment, focusing on those

thoughts. She had to do that more often these days. Remember the good things.

There was never any point in focusing on the negative. She'd learned that long ago. She sighed and returned to her weeding. Only the flowers that could survive the cold nights were blooming now. Rudbeckia, phlox, a few hardy geraniums.

She plucked some of the stubborn dandelion greens that didn't seem to notice the changing of the season, and her mind returned to its usual train of thought these days. Rocco.

She understood he had to go, but she couldn't help feeling hurt about how he left and that she'd heard nothing over the past few weeks. She'd considered contracting him but decided that would probably just magnify her sense of loss. Sometimes it was better to just leave things alone.

So she rededicated herself to her life here. But it wasn't easy.

"No regrets," she said aloud to herself. Her personal mantra these days.

"No regrets about what?"

Franny paused, thinking for a moment she must have imagined the voice behind her. She spun, half expecting to find herself alone in her backyard.

But she wasn't.

Rocco stood there, a suitcase beside him. His dark eyes moving over her, unreadable.

"Rocco. What—what are you doing here?" She didn't dare hope it was to see her.

"I need a room," he said as if that would be the obvious reason.

Her heart sank. He wasn't here to see her specifically. She was silly to think he was. Rocco was a good guy, but he was a player, a dedicated bachelor, a city boy—and not the type to return to small-town Maine to date an old high school classmate.

She had to remember that and just enjoy seeing him again.

"Sure," she said with a smile, the gesture feeling forced. She tugged off her gardening gloves and started across the lawn.

Rocco fell into step beside her.

"How many nights?" she asked, trying to sound casual. Like she was just chatting with any old guest.

"Well, I'm not sure."

She stopped on the porch to frown at him. "Not sure?"

He shook his head, giving her an uncertain smile, suddenly reminding of the boy she remembered from school.

"You see, I'm looking for a place to rent, and it might take me a while."

"A place to rent?" She realized she sounded like she was completely addled. But at the moment, well, she was.

He nodded. "So it might take a little time. Can my checkout day be open-ended?"

She nodded, too, not sure what to say. What did this mean? Was he staying here for good? Just for a while? She didn't understand.

Finally she decided just to ask. "Why are you back? Are you staying?"

He shifted, looking down at his feet for a moment. "I was thinking about it."

Her heart jumped, but she wasn't sure if it was out of excitement or fear.

"Why?"

He smiled, seeming to find the question amusing. "Because I realized I wanted to come home. Turns out there is a lot of good stuff here I missed the first time around."

Again her heart did a crazy somersault, but she didn't say anything, afraid she was misreading what he was saying.

He seemed to understand and added, "You see, I have a huge crush on this girl from my high school class, and I was hoping to see if she could have a crush on me."

Franny blinked, then hugged him. "I pretty sure she does."

Rocco kissed Franny, relieved and grateful she wanted to give him a chance. After all, she remembered the hurt, angry kid he'd been and she'd read about the adult he'd become, using his career and column to stay single and cut off from ever having to put himself out there and feel something real.

But he wasn't hiding anymore.

Of course, he would have to admit he'd sort of lied to her just now—he definitely had more than a crush on this girl. He was falling in love with her.

But he'd tell her that later. At this very moment, he was far too busy enjoying being home.

Copyright Notices